The Next Best Thing

Deidre Berry

Dafina Books

KENSINGTON PUBLISHING CORP.
www.kensingtonbooks.com

DAFINA BOOKS are published by

Kensington Publishing Corp.
850 Third Avenue
New York, NY 10022

All Kensington titles, imprints and distributed lines are available at special quantity discounts for bulk purchases for sales promotion, premiums, fund-raising, educational or institutional use.

Special book excerpts or customized printings can also be created to fit specific needs. For details, write or phone the office of the Kensington Special Sales Manager: Kensington Publishing Corp., 850 Third Avenue, New York, NY 10022. Attn. Special Sales Department. Phone: 1-800-221-2647.

Dafina and the Dafina logo Reg. U.S. Pat. & TM Off.

ISBN-13: 978-0-7582-3832-0
ISBN-10: 0-7582-3832-0

First Kensington Trade Paperback Printing: April 2009
10 9 8 7 6 5 4 3 2 1

Printed in the United States of America

To Richard,
my biggest supporter and greatest inspiration

Acknowledgments

First and foremost, I would like to thank God for giving me this opportunity and blessing.

Richard, you already know! It gets greater later, right? Absolutely.

A special thank-you to my Aunt Alberta "Jeannie" Bly. From day one you have been in my corner and stayed there whether I was right, wrong, or somewhere in between. Thanks to you, I am living proof that the prayers of the Saints availeth much.

To all of my relatives in the Berry, Fortner, Reed, Stokes, Jones, and Reid families, I love ya'll!

Lutishia Lovely, your kind words and stamp of approval are greatly appreciated. You are an awesome writer. Keep doin' your thang!

Selena James, you are the best editor a writer could ask for. Thank you for taking a chance on me. I am forever grateful.

Thank you in advance to all the readers, book clubs, distributors, and bookstores across the country. I couldn't do it without you!

You Are Cordially Invited

Together with their families
Tori Lorraine Carter
and
Roland Elijah Davis
request the honor of your presence
at their marriage
on Saturday, the third of April
at one o'clock in the afternoon
Mount Zion Bread of Life
Metropolitan Missionary Baptist Church
of the Living Gospel
338 South Wayne Blvd.
Kansas City, Missouri

Prologue

The Bride Is Coming! The Bride Is Coming!

Finally. After three years of shacking up, Roland and I were jumping the broom—and *baby* we were doing it in style!

The invitations were beautiful. Burgundy suede covers opened to reveal embossed roses and elegant fourteen-karat gold calligraphy. Each one of our three hundred guests received these invites via Federal Express along with a gift basket packed with François Payard praline truffles, a magnum of Laurent-Perrier Rose Champagne, and Cuban stogies from Le Comptoir du Cigar.

Pure Opulence. That was the theme, and "my day, my way" had been my mantra from the minute Roland whispered, *Marry me* in my ear, then collapsed on his side of the bed in a sweaty heap. Two minutes later, he was snoring.

And that was it.

No ring, no loving words of endearment, and nowhere near the romantic marriage proposal that I had been fantasizing about since I was eleven years old.

Afterwards, I pulled the bed sheets up to my chest, shocked, elated, and just a skosh disappointed that Roland had asked for my hand in marriage in such a half-ass manner.

Men were supposed to plan these things out, weren't they?

I mean, seriously—come *onnn*! I can't one day tell my grandbabies that Paw-Paw proposed while he was banging Grandma.

If we could rewind the tape and do it all over again, Roland would have gotten down on both knees and proposed to me on Christmas night in front of my entire family. Of course I would have said *yes!* and the Christmas party would have instantly turned into this big, emotional affair with everyone hugging and crying, happy that Roland was finally going to make an honest woman of me.

Barring that scenario, a hot air balloon ride in the countryside would have been memorable; and atop the Eiffel Tower would have been most impressive. Hell, now that I think about it, the very least Roland could have done was the old ring-in-the-dessert trick.

But, half-ass as it was, it *was* a marriage proposal.

I sprang into action the next morning, giving myself a one-year deadline to plan the wedding of the century.

And to think. This long, crazy journey to the altar began four years ago when the two of us met at a wedding. Courtney Adams, my old roommate from Kansas University, was marrying Aaron Graves, a fraternity brother of Roland's.

Ironically, I hadn't even wanted to go to that wedding.

Not because I disliked Courtney so much, but because I was going through the breakup blues, and just was not feeling very sociable that day.

The source of my doldrums was Joseph.

A wonderful man with whom I had spent eleven wonderful months, only to find out that this fool had umpteen kids by umpteen different women.

Ooh! The breakup was nasty.

It almost got to the point where I had to put a restraining order out on his black ass, because the brother just refused to accept that I was breaking off the relationship.

This is about me and you, Joseph had said with tears in his eyes. *What do my kids have to do with us?*

Hello! Who in their right mind would unnecessarily invite all of that baby mama drama into their life? I'm sure as hell not the one. I don't care how good the sex is.

Besides, if Joseph and I had gotten married his financial obligations would have become my financial obligations, and I just can't see myself handing over my entire paycheck for someone else's child support payments.

Don't get me wrong, Tori loves the kids.

However, when those kids number close to double digits, baby, that's where I have to draw the line. Hasta la vista, baby. See ya next lifetime.

So, there I was at my old college roommate's wedding, single, and cynical as hell.

Roland may have been tall, dark, and Tyrese Gibson–fine, but as he confidently strolled over and introduced himself, I was certain he was just another well-dressed loser who would promise everything, expect everything, and give absolutely nothing in return.

But Roland proved me wrong.

Right off the bat, he struck me as being warm and sincere. By the end of the night, he had won me over enough for me to give him my phone number; and we proceeded to fall for each other fast and hard.

After just a few months of dating, I was already marveling at my good fortune in landing such an outstanding catch. This man was the ultimate romantic. He cooked for me (okay so the meals weren't always that great but the point is, he tried), wrote me poetry (he's no Langston Hughes, but the effort was sweet), and handled his business in the bedroom like no man before him ever had (well, except for Vincent, but that's a whole 'nother story).

As far as I was concerned, I had finally found the one.

In spite of my mother's adamant warnings about giving the milk away for free, I allowed Roland to move into my two-bedroom condo on the Plaza, and all was blissfully right with the world.

Fast-forward four years and here we were, about to become man and wife, with a wedding tab of $202,536.24, and counting. My friend, Simone, jokingly compared the out-of-control budget to one of those telethon tote boards with the numbers rising rapidly by the second, but seeing as how I had an image and a reputation to maintain, I didn't give a damn about the cost. Being a senior event coordinator with over a decade in the business, I'm known for throwing ridiculously extravagant soirees, so naturally, it was expected that my own nuptials be over-the-top *fabu-lous*. It was a lot of work, but it was truly a labor of love, and in the end, the stage that I had so painstakingly set, conveyed over-the-top opulence that had to be seen in order to be believed.

Tori's Big, Beautiful, Fantasy Wedding

ORDER OF EVENTS

The Ceremony

Built in 1873, Mount Zion is the oldest African-American church in the Kansas City area. The massive gothic-style structure boasts a bell tower and magnificent stained-glass windows.

Inside the church, the heavenly scent of seven thousand gardenias fills the sanctuary, which is the size of a football field. Uniformed ushers seat our guests, while an eighteen-piece orchestra plays an assortment of contemporary and classical music.

The wedding party enters to "Ava Maria."

Seven groomsmen escort seven bridesmaids down the aisle. My cousin Cookie is among them, as well as my best girlfriends Simone, Nadia, and Yvette. My bridal court ranges from sizes zero to eighteen, but they are all equally stunning in strapless, burgundy gowns with matching chiffon scarves.

The orchestra segues from "Ava Maria" to the "Wedding March." The chapel doors open and here it is: the big moment I have spent the last year orchestrating, and my whole life waiting for.

Entering on the arm of my father, I am a life-size version of Grand Entrance Barbie in a silk, halter-style Badgley Mischka gown with a hand-beaded bodice, crystal-beaded seventeen-foot train, and satin Manolo Blahnik high-heel sandals. My bridal jewelry includes a gorgeous double strand of Mikimoto pearls and matching pearl earrings encircled with diamonds. I smile at my guests through a nine-foot-long tulle veil, held in place by an antique diamond tiara. Even my bridal bouquet is spectacular, with four-dozen full-bloom red roses interwoven with Swarovski crystals.

Looking up ahead, I see that Roland has tears in his eyes as he waits for me at the altar under an enormous canopy of red roses and sweet-pea blossoms. My man looks so handsome and dapper in his Giorgio Armani Black Label tuxedo that I am already thinking about the honeymoon.

Reverend L. C. Thompson, the man who christened me at birth, leads us all in prayer before Roland and I light a unity candle and exchange traditional vows.

The Wedding Reception

To quote Shug Avery from The Color Purple, *"I's married now!" A Maybach limousine whisks my husband and me to the Roseville Country Club Mansion where we are greeted by our guests, and so many photographers that it looks like an army of paparazzi. (There's no such thing as too many wedding pictures.)*

The reception kicks off with cocktails and hors d'oeuvres out on the veranda, overlooking the rose garden and a twelve-mile long lake.

After an hour of mingling and picture taking, two trumpets sound to signal the beginning of a sumptuous sit-down dinner.

Inside the eight-thousand square foot ballroom, there are so many fresh flowers that it resembles a botanical wonderland. And adding to the elegance are gold and crystal chandeliers that, all together, are worth millions.

In addition to the head table, there are forty round tables that seat eight, each one dressed in gold silk cloths with burgundy overlays, lit by gold four-wick candles, and topped with centerpieces made of lush red orchids and pink peonies in cut-crystal vases.

At each individual place setting, there are gold Tiffany charger plates adorned with gold-rimmed bone china, matching crystal goblets, linen napkins embroidered with our initials, and elegant printed menus that offer:

PISTACHIO SALAD
KOBE FLATIRON STEAK
WITH GREEN PEPPERCORN SAUCE
CHILEAN SEA BASS
ROASTED WHITE ASPARAGUS
LOBSTER MASHED POTATOES
SPICY SAUTÉED SCALLOPS
PASSION FRUIT CRÈME BRÛLÉE
CHOCOLATE FONDUE FOUNTAIN
ROTHSCHILD BORDEAUX 1997
CHASSAGNE-MONTRACHET CHARDONNAY 2002
VEUVE CLICQUOT CHAMPAGNE

Next to each place card is a snow globe containing a black Cinderella holding hands with her prince. The keepsakes are engraved with the words: ROLAND AND TORI—HAPPILY-EVER-AFTER

So cute!

Immediately following dinner, the reception is moved into a separate ballroom where we have a round of champagne toasts, and then cut the seven-tier Grand Marnier chocolate truffle cake with buttercream icing that is adorned with fresh orchids and red rose blossoms made of sugar.

Roland and I dance our first dance as husband and wife while Ms. Patti LaBelle serenades us with her version of "The Best Is Yet to

Come," followed by "You Are My Friend." (Yes, I got Ms. Patti! It cost a queen's ransom, but hey, Mademoiselle LaBelle is worth every penny.)

Once Ms. Labelle wraps up, the DJ takes over, and we party hearty all night long to a mix of everything from Earth Wind & Fire to 50 Cent.

Hours into the festivities, Yvette takes center stage to sing Natalie Cole's classic "Inseparable." I made sure to schedule her performance waaay late into the evening with the hopes that everybody would be too tipsy to notice that the girl can't hold a decent note to save her life. She had begged me to let her sing at some point during the wedding ceremony, which was a definite no-no; but since Yvette is my oldest and dearest friend, whom I love like a sister, I compromised and agreed that she could "sing" one song at the reception.

After partaking in Louis XIII cognac and vanilla-flavored cigars hand-rolled on the spot, we all gather outside for the grand finale, a huge twenty-minute fireworks display. The second that's over, Roland swoops me up into his arms and we head off for a blissful month-long stay at a five-star luxury resort in Aruba.

Sounds like the start of a beautiful life together, right? Well, that was the way I envisioned my wedding day from start to finish. Unfortunately, though, things did not work out as planned. Not even close.

Those beautiful wedding invitations that I loved so much were quickly replaced with announcements that read:

Mr. and Mrs. Cedric Carter announce that the nuptials
of their daughter Tori Lorraine
to Mr. Roland E. Davis
have been canceled and will not take place.
All gifts will be returned. We are sorry for the
inconvenience, and ask that the privacy of this matter
please be respected. Thank you for your support.

1

What happened? Well, before I get to that, let me digress for a moment to say that besides the category-four wind/rainstorm that raged outside the church that day, everything on the inside really was beautiful and fairytale-like. Exactly one hour and thirty-three minutes after the ceremony was to begin, now, that is when things got ugly.

Upstairs in the bridal room overlooking the sanctuary, my bridesmaids and I were all dolled up and ready to go. Counting various relatives, there were almost a dozen people in the room, all of them with big mouths and big personalities to match, but it was so uncharacteristically quiet, that the silence shook me to my core.

No one knew what to say or do, given the circumstances.

"Call him again," I told Nadia, taking deep breaths in an effort to keep from hyperventilating.

"Okay, I'll give it another shot . . ." Nadia sighed, simultaneously exchanging a worried look with Simone.

Nadia had been trying to reach Roland for me for hours, which was inexcusable. The man has two cell phones, and our calls kept going straight to voice mail on both of them.

Since there was nothing else to do but wait, I watched through the one-way glass overlooking the sanctuary, hoping that Roland would come dashing into the church at any minute, apologizing profusely, and anxious to get the show on the road.

Instead, what I saw happening down below were three hundred guests who were all starting to fidget, check their watches, and whisper among themselves.

Daddy paced back and forth in the vestibule with a pissed-off scowl on his face.

Roland's friends, and the rest of his family, were all in attendance, some of them looking just as confused as I felt.

Sophie, my boss, was there, as were a great number of my co-workers and business associates.

Seated on the front pew, my brother Junior kept repeatedly cracking his knuckles, looking as if he were seriously contemplating Roland's homicide. Seated right next to Junior, Aunt Rita was trying her best to comfort my mother while she cried and carried on as if she were at a funeral, instead of what was supposed to be a wedding.

Roland's mother, on the other hand, was obviously thrilled that things were turning out as they were. Mrs. Davis was smiling from ear to ear, looking like she was enjoying herself so much that the only thing missing was the popcorn.

Old, nappy-wig-wearing hussy.

Always up in the middle of our business, giving her opinion whether anyone asked for it or not. I knew going in that Roland was a mama's boy to the tenth power, but I didn't appreciate the fact that this woman knew intimate details about me that no man's mother should ever know. Like how often we had sex versus how many more times a week Roland would prefer to have sex.

You know, stuff he should be discussing with me instead of his mama.

At that point, I was starting to get a clear vision of what the society section in the *Kansas City Tribune* would say the following week:

> You really should have been there. It was all so beautiful and fairytale-like . . . Well, up until the runaway groom texted the anxious bride to say, "Oh, by the way, I won't be showing up for that little shindig you had planned for today. See ya when I see ya, peace!"

Those weren't Roland's exact words, but it was pretty much the gist of it. Actually, his text message read:

> I love you, but I am in love with Veronica. The two of us have been involved off-and-on since long before you even entered the picture. You should also know that Imani is my daughter. Sorry to let you know this way. I'll come over to pack my things once we get back from Aruba. Good luck with everything . . . And Tori, I really am sorry.

Yeah, you're a sorry sonofabitch, all right.

You see, the Veronica that Roland referred to in his text, is his so-called "platonic friend."

The one who was supposedly like a sister to him.

The very same Jiminy Cricket-looking heifer that has had her bony behind up in my home on many occasions. Always smiling in my face, eating my food, and taking full advantage of my kindness and hospitality.

Women who are secure within themselves and their relationship are not intimidated by their man having female friends.

That is the line of bullshit Roland spoon-fed me every time I voiced a concern about the undeniably strong bond he shared with Veronica.

Of course, I was skeptical at first. What woman wouldn't be? But over time, I bought into it. I drank the Kool-Aid. I eventually stopped asking questions and let the issue slide, because I wanted to impress my man by doing the evolved-grownup thing.

What a damned fool. Especially when I think of the numerous double dates and vacations all of us went on together over the years. And on top of all of that, Imani is Roland's daughter?

Wow. How far in the sand did I have my head buried, not to have realized on my own, that that cute little chocolate-drop had Roland's DNA stamped all over her? Same dark eyes, same complexion, and the same lopsided, mischievous smile.

Oh God . . .

My cell phone slipped from my hand and clattered to the floor, as the room suddenly started spinning out of control. I got so nauseous, I just knew I was going to hurl right down the front of my wedding gown.

It didn't help that Yvette had practically taken a bath in Sand & Sable perfume, and with her hovering over me the way she was, the sickeningly sweet smell hit me right in the stomach.

That's when my body went numb; like all the blood was draining right out of me.

I have never fainted before in my life, but I'm here to tell you, there's a first time for everything. When I came to, my head was in Mama's lap, and she was patting my face with a cold, damp handkerchief.

"You okay, baby?" my mother asked softly, concern etched into her usually wrinkle-free face.

My mouth was so dry all I could do was nod dumbly like some kind of shell-shocked mute. Still a little groggy, I managed to stand up, make it over to that little one-way window, and I swear, I almost passed out again when I saw all the destruction down in the sanctuary.

Apparently, there had been the equivalent of a full-blown riot while I was unconscious, because the canopy of red roses and sweet-pea blossoms had been knocked over, and was in complete ruins. Ripped clothing, wigs, torn gardenias, earrings, weave tracks, and even broken musical instruments were scattered all over the place. I was to find out later what that was all about, but in the meantime, Aunt Vera offered me a sip of Crown Royal from her flask, and said, "It's alright, sugar. Better to happen now, than to have to drag his monkey-ass into divorce court later on."

2

By the time I left the church, the storm had passed, and the sun had the nerve to be shining as if a high-voltage storm had never even occurred that day.

The parking lot outside of Mount Zion looked like a ghost town. The only person left was the limo driver, who looked genuinely sympathetic, and nodded solemnly when I told him to take me back to my condo, alone.

"Being alone is the last thing you need right now," Simone, Nadia, Yvette, and my parents insisted all at once.

"Just give me a couple of hours to think, okay?" I said. "After that, I'll be fine, and you guys can come over and whatever—But for right now, I need solitude."

I climbed into the back of the Maybach, which was decorated with gold streamers and had *Just Married* written across the back window. Everyone stepped back and watched the limo take me in the opposite direction of where we all should have been going, which was to the Roseville Country Club Mansion.

"I should have known . . . I should have known . . . I should have fucking known!" I screamed aloud in frustration, not giving a damn that the limo driver was staring at me via the rearview mirror.

The truth is, I did know. Not all the sordid details of who, what, when, and where, but I knew for sure that something, somewhere, was not one-hundred-percent right. I knew, because my woman's intuition pointed out months ago that the closer the wedding date drew near, the more distant Roland became. At the time, I confided in Simone, who suggested that Roland and I attend couples counseling with her life coach, Fatima.

I decided against it. Instead, I chalked Roland's behavior up to pre-wedding jitters, and reminded myself that the wedding express had left the station a long time ago. Honest, open discussions at that point might have led down a road I didn't want to travel.

No. We were fine. Everything was already in place. Dozens of guests were flying in from all over the country, and vast sums of money had already been spent.

Of course, now I realize that it would have saved me a whole lot of time, money, and embarrassment if I had had the courage to dig deeper, ask questions, and call the damn wedding off if I didn't like the answers I was getting.

In retrospect, there were dozens of red flags begging me to notice them, but there were four in particular I really should have paid attention to.

Red Flag #1

Roland took no interest whatsoever in planning the wedding. Whenever I would ask his opinion on anything, his response was always the same: *You're used to making those types of decisions, so you make the call.* Or, *I don't care, baby. Whatever you want. It's your day. Just tell me when and where.*

Red Flag #2

It seemed like Roland was always on-call for Veronica. He would drop everything to rush over and comfort her whenever she was going through some personal crisis. That happened a lot.

Red Flag #3

Marriage is a lifetime commitment, are you sure you're ready? Is this what you really want? That was Veronica. Every time I turned around she was all up in my face trying to talk me out of marrying Roland. Plus, I had asked her to be one of my bridesmaids but she declined, giving me flimsy excuses about her finances, and work schedule, and a bunch of other bullshit.

Red Flag #4

The prenup.

Under the impression that Roland and I were meeting with his attorney in order to create wills and living trusts, I was instead presented by Mr. Mahoney with a meticulously detailed prenuptial agreement that was eighteen pages long. At least.

I was completely baffled. Here we were, less than a month before the big day, and instead of focusing on our wedding Roland was more interested in planning our divorce.

This is not being done to hurt you, Ms. Carter, Mahoney had said, reading my expression and sensing my hesitation. *Mr. Davis only wants to protect his assets.*

My blood was boiling, and the devil kept urging me to step out of my snakeskin Sergio Rossi pumps and kick Roland's *assets* all over the offices of Jackson, Mahoney, and Brown.

But I remained calm, reminding myself once again that too much had been invested and it was too late to back out now. I swallowed my pride, signed by all the Xs, then headed off for an appointment with the florist.

Knowing what I know now, it clearly was all a ploy. Roland was relying on me being so upset about the prenup that I would call everything off, giving him the out that he wanted. When that didn't happen, he took the coward's way out, and just failed to show up. Either way, he never intended to marry me.

Back at home, the first thing I did was remove my veil and

tiara. I took off my wedding dress, placed it back into its garment bag, and hung it in the back of my bedroom closet.

Jackie, my stylist, had put in a lot of time and effort to make sure my wedding hair was beautiful, and that it would last all day, but I went into the bathroom and snatched out every one of those damn bobby pins that had been digging mercilessly into my scalp. I brushed my hair into a neat chignon and changed into a comfortable pair of yellow Baby Phat sweats.

I was removing the pearls from around my neck, when I caught a glimpse of myself in the dresser mirror.

Inwardly I was devastated, but on the outside, it was still the same old Tori. Same dark brown skin as my daddy, same light brown, almond shaped eyes as my mama. Still a size twelve with shoulder-length sandy-brown hair.

However, the smile. Now *that* was different. Some might even call it peculiar, considering the circumstances.

What the mirror reflected back to me was a huge, showing-all-thirty-two-teeth smile that I didn't even realize I was wearing. Try as I might, I could not wipe that thing off to save my life.

Probably because I knew subconsciously that the smile was the coat of armor I needed in order to keep everyone from knowing what I was really feeling.

Company was on its way—lots of it. So even though it felt like my heart had been ripped out and stomped on with cleats, the smile stayed put.

It had to.

I dialed Roland's cell-phone number, and when the call went straight to voice mail yet again, I went ahead and left a message using my most cheerful, upbeat voice.

"Roland, this is Tori. I sincerely hope you and that cock-eyed heifer die in a plane crash and roast in hell, which is where you both belong. There is no need for you to ever come back to the condo, because UPS will be delivering all of your shit to your mother's house, just as soon as I can get them over here to pick it up. Good-bye."

I hung up the phone, rolled my sleeves up and went out into the living room, where I opened up the towering cherry-oak entertainment cabinet filled with all the state-of-the-art electronics that Roland just had to have.

His ass may be getting up out of here, but this bad-boy is definitely staying. Hell, it's the least that I deserve.

I loaded up the fifty-disc CD player with all of the usual suspects, including Aretha, Chaka, India, Anita, Luther, Sade, Maxwell, Mary J., Floetry, and Jill.

Leela James came on first, singing "My Joy," and my smile automatically got even wider because that song suited the situation so perfectly.

"Sing, girl!" I shouted at Leela, feeling a sense of empowerment.

Never again will I blindly put all of my faith and trust in another individual. I believed in everything that man said, and everything he stood for. So much so, that I often found myself deferring to him on even the smallest of decisions. What to eat, what to wear, and how I should feel about myself on any given day. That part is not Roland's fault. I take full responsibility for my stupidity in that area, but from here on out, no man will ever have that much power and input.

Not only that, but there is no man on earth who will ever be able to convince me that his friendship with another female is strictly platonic. Nope. Never again will a man have that much control over "My Joy."

I called Colin, my caterer, and instructed him to shuttle all the food from the reception site, over to my home.

There might not have been a marriage to celebrate, but damn it, nothing could stop me from having a good, old-fashioned packing party! I called my mother and told her to put the word out for everyone to come on over, then I started in the bedroom. It was surprisingly cathartic to rake my arm across the dresser, sending all of Roland's cologne, jewelry, and other miscellaneous bullshit crashing into a cardboard box. What I did not expect to find among the miscellaneous items was the bridal ring set that Roland had bought me. It was still encased in its little black velvet box. And seeing that he had left them here, spoke volumes.

It was all so crystal clear now. The only part I had no answer for was why Roland even asked me to marry him in the first place. After all, he had been doing a good job of having his cake and eating it too for all these years.

I placed the ring box with the rest of my jewelry, and then got down to the business of exorcising Roland's personal belongings out of my condo. Socks, drawers, designer suits, sketches, blueprints, awards, college diplomas—everything had to go.

It was a monumental task, but three hours after leaving the church my place was crammed with family, who had come to help me with the packing; and none of us was being careful with the items that were just as fragile as they were valuable.

"Is this his?" Junior asked me, and then answered his own question by slamming the miniature scale model of a downtown luxury hotel into a box.

The amount of satisfaction I got from that was enormous.

The hotel model was a meticulously detailed architectural project that Roland had been working on for the past eight months, and was very close to being completed.

Now, what he had worked so long and hard to create was in ruins, and he would have to start all over again from scratch.

Pretty ironic, since that is precisely what I have to do with my life. Pick up the pieces, and start all over.

And I'm not moving, either. Even though I will probably be reminded of Roland every time I turn around, I refuse to give up three-thousand square feet filled with all the bells and whistles a girl could ever ask for. An open, gourmet kitchen with granite countertops, oversized fireplace, red-oak hardwood floors, vaulted ceilings, private balcony, and a walk-in closet so spacious that it resembles a mini-boutique.

By 6 o'clock that evening, the packing party was in full swing. There was an overabundance of food, and the booze was flowing like the Nile River.

In fact, there was so much liquid sunshine to go around, that those of us who drank were in very good spirits. Especially Uncle Nate, who always tends to have three drinks too many.

"This belong to that sumbitch?" Uncle Nate slurred, holding up Roland's prized PlayStation3.

I nodded, and BLAM! Into a box it went.

Ditto, for the three-thousand-dollar laptop, the glass bowling trophies, and the expensive photography equipment.

This routine went on late into the night, with a steady stream of folks coming over to offer me their sympathy and support. Even Ms. LaBelle stopped by on her way to the airport to wish me well and to grab a plate of food to go.

Along with condolences, some people felt free to give me advice, as well as their unsolicited opinions.

"Girl, fuck him! He was tired as hell and I for one am not sad to see that sorry motherfucker go," Yvette declared, conveniently forgetting that she had always said Roland was the best thing that ever happened to me.

"I sho' hate what happened to you, baby girl," Uncle Woody said in the same tone that is usually reserved for someone grieving at a funeral. Woody was not a blood relative, but he was Daddy's best friend, and my godfather. He has also been married and divorced more times than even he can remember. "But a man is going to be a man, regardless. Shoot, a woman throws something in my face long enough, and sooner or later I'm gonna give in to the temptation, too!"

"Now don't you believe that, Tori," said Aunt Rita, who is Daddy's sister, and Cookie's mother. "A woman can't force a man to do nothing he doesn't want to do. It's up to *him* to keep his johnson in his pants, and realize that a piece of ass on the other side of the fence ain't worth jeopardizing the good thing he has at home."

"Well, you're a better woman than I am," Cookie told me. "Because if it was me, I'd be on my way to Aruba to kick both of their asses!"

And best believe she's not just bluffing, either.

Cookie is hood to the core, and is one of our family's most renowned scrappers. Growing up, I could always count on my cousin Cookie to have my back whenever I had major beef with other girls.

While she was at it, Cookie filled me in on what transpired down in the sanctuary while I was up in the bridal room passed out cold.

Apparently, Roland's mother had said something to my mother along the lines of *I sure am glad my son didn't marry into your sorry family.*

To which my mother had replied *You sure got your nerve, running around here with your nose in the air, when everybody in town knows that the Davises ain't none but a bunch of fucking crooks and con-artists!*

Mrs. Davis had retorted *You Carters are nothing but common trash, and not one of you are fit to wipe my shoes!*

Poor Mrs. Davis. What did she fix her mouth to say that for? If that witch had done her homework, she would have known that uttering those words in a church full of *my* family members was the wrong move to make—something equivalent to a lamb walking boldly into a lion's den, and expecting to make it out unharmed.

My mother snatched Mrs. Davis's wig off, and the fight was on between members of both families until Rev. Thompson announced that the police had been called and were on their way.

The church and the parking lot both cleared out in about three minutes flat.

Umph! My people, my people . . . Just buckwhylin' all up and through the church.

After hearing Cookie's report, I shook my head and winced

at what my co-workers must have been saying: *Oh my God! Who knew that Tori's relatives were so . . . ghetto?*

I did, that's who. However, I was hoping that my family could at least hold it together in honor of the occasion. Obviously not.

Even at that moment, Junior and some of our wayward cousins were on one side of the room discussing what they were going to do to Roland upon catching his ass out in the streets.

Uncle Blue was taking folks' money at the three-card monte table he had set up in the middle of the living room; and I'll be damned if I didn't smell marijuana smoke drifting out from under the bathroom door. No telling who the culprit was. Probably Aunt Vera.

"Come here, Tori, and let me pray for you," said my cousin Janice, who I noticed had been sneaking sips of champagne all evening, even though she claims to have not had a drink since she got saved two years ago.

With booze on her breath, Janice laid hands on me and prayed with all seriousness. "Father God, I pray that you bless and comfort my baby cousin Tori during her hour of need. May she not rely upon her own understanding, but be assured that your hand is upon her, Lord, and your goodness and mercy will follow her all the days of her life. Father, I pray that you just keep Tori strong, Lord! In Jesus' name we pray . . . Amen!"

I thanked Janice for the prayer, and quickly stepped away from her in order to dodge the bolt of lightning I was sure would strike her backsliding behind at any second.

Daddy sat at my island counter muttering and cursing up under his breath, while also nursing a split lip, and a tall glass of cognac.

Just as cantankerous as ever.

I wouldn't say that my father was completely unsympathetic towards my plight, but he admittedly was not one of Roland's biggest fans, and made it clear before we even left the church that his primary concern at that point was recouping the money he had given me towards the wedding.

How's that for family support?

Then again, that's my Daddy. An ass-kicking, name-taking, Army veteran, who has never been known to sugarcoat, or bite his tongue, on any issue, which is why Mama is always dragging him by the ear and making him apologize to somebody that he has offended.

And speaking of Mama. She was damn near inconsolable.

Three years' worth of free milk and Roland has walked away without buying the cow; just as she had feared from the day Roland moved in with me.

Though it was hard to tell if Mama felt sorrier for me, or for herself.

The prospect of having a successful architect for a son-in-law had become a badge of honor that my mother had rubbed into the faces of the women down at her social club every chance she got.

Now, she was going to have to eat humble pie at the next meeting of the Kansas City Ladies League and answer questions as to why her daughter had been left at the altar looking like a jackass.

I am proud of myself for holding up so well under the circumstances, though. Thanks to that old Carter pride, I did not shed a single tear, all day.

I may have fainted, but I didn't cry.

During the packing party, I laughed and joked with my guests so much, I could tell by their puzzled looks that most of them didn't know what to make of me. There I was, fluttering around the place, offering salmon caviar hors d'oeuvres and refilling champagne glasses, as if I wasn't bothered one bit by being told on my wedding day that the last three years of my life were a complete lie.

However, you can fake the funk for only so long.

After all my guests but Simone had left, loaded down with platters of food and bottles of booze, all that strong-woman bravado went straight out the window. Right along with the ridiculous smile that had been pasted on my face all day.

I was shoving what was left of the wedding cake into a garbage bag, when the first teardrop fell. Followed by a thousand more.

Thank God for Simone! That girl is the most sane, well-adjusted person in my life. She stayed by my side, offering Kleenex and comforting hugs well into the wee hours of the morning.

As I ranted and raved until my voice became hoarse, Simone listened patiently and had the compassion not to utter *I told you so*, which she certainly could have done since she was skeptical of Roland from the very beginning.

"He looks good on paper," Simone had said after first meeting Roland. "But there is just something about his aura that doesn't sit quite right with me."

Being the spiritual, mother-earth type person that she is, I wasn't at all surprised when Simone gave me a beautiful leather-bound journal filled with inspirational quotes for every day of the week.

"You might as well try it," she said, responding to the skeptical look on my face. "It will help you process some of this shit you're going through, and at the same time, bring about a whole new level of clarity to your life that you've never had before."

Simone is a personal-growth junkie, who, through a life coach and a ton of self-help books, has finally been able to get past her bourgeois, overprivileged childhood, which for some reason she previously viewed as tragic.

I, on the other hand, am cynical when it comes to all that holistic, new-age mumbo jumbo crap.

I mean, really. How can something as simple as putting thoughts and feelings down on paper help people who "trust the process," obtain self-awareness to the point where their lives are healed and their souls are transformed?

Give me a break.

If it were that easy, then even sickos like R. Kelly and O. J. Simpson would be sane.

However, the months to come would probably be the toughest of my life, so if there was even an ounce of benefit to be gained from journaling, then damn it, sign me up.

It's a helluva lot cheaper than Valium, that's for sure.

Dawn was just starting to break when Simone left.

I opened the journal and read the inscription she had written on the inside cover:

> *Use these pages to cry, vent, mourn, laugh, dream, and forgive. It's not going to be easy, but if you have the courage to confront and deal with all of your "stuff," (and lets face it, Tori, you do have a lot of stuff, girl!) then you will come through on the other side healthier, happier, and whole. And who knows? That special man that you were really meant to be with could be right there waiting for you, too.*
>
> *Peace, Love & Blessings,*
> *Your sister-friend, Simone*

I chuckled despite myself, then read the quote, picked up a pen and wrote the first entry.

Life is what happens to you when you're busy making other plans. —*John Lennon*

SUNDAY

Lisa, my third cousin twice removed, cornered me at the packing party, and asked, "So, what are you going to do now?"

That annoyed the hell out of me.

I was all set to give Lisa a piece of my mind when I realized that was actually a damn good question.

One of the top ten rules of event planning is to always have a plan A-Z. And while I do that all day every day professionally, I was negligent in doing the same in my personal life.

What am I gonna do now?

At this point, the only thing I know for sure is that I have to do away with that twenty-year plan that included Roland and a bunch of his little chocolate babies. I have to create a brand-new future for myself. Where to start and what the details are? Hell if I know.

That is something I guess I'll figure out, one day at a time.

3

Of all the skyscrapers that make up the downtown area, the Price Morgan Pavilion is the most impressive, with its eighty-six stories and ultra high-tech exterior. The Pavilion is also home to Sophie Wilkerson Events, the most successful event management firm in Kansas City, which is where I work.

Located up on the sixty-eighth floor, I walked through the glass and chrome doors of SWE this morning, and my co-workers were as wide-eyed and startled as if they were seeing a ghost.

After all, most of them were there to witness the fiasco that was supposed to be my wedding, and it was evident in their faces that the last thing any of them expected was to see me bounce back so quickly from such an extreme public humiliation. Half of them were giving me sympathetic looks, while the other half were looking me over for signs of weakness.

The questions of the day were *Tori, what are you doing here?* and *Shouldn't you be taking this time off?*

The phony concern was so transparent it made me laugh. Because the truth is, most of them were probably hoping that I was at home slitting my wrist, so that one of them could move in and take my spot.

At SWE, the title of Senior Event Coordinator comes with

a bull's-eye on your back, so you can't sleep. It is imperative to bring your A-game all day, every day, or it could be a wrap for you in an instant.

We may throw parties for a living, but SWE is just as cutthroat a workplace as any brokerage firm on Wall Street.

Picture fifty anal personalities under one roof amped up on Red Bull, espresso, and Krispy Kreme doughnuts; all backstabbing, tattle telling, and jockeying for better positions, and you got some idea of what our office is like on a daily basis.

That is because Sophie Wilkerson happens to be a shrewd, fiercely competitive businesswoman who breeds these same qualities in the office among her employees; says it inspires greatness, and keeps everybody on their toes.

By the time I made it to my corner office, there were so many people following me that it felt like I was leading a parade.

I turned on my computer and checked my inbox, feeling like I was on display. My co-workers were crowded in my office and around the doorway, staring at me as if I were some rare piece of artwork they were trying to figure out the intricacies of.

I met their gazes head on, with what I hoped was a look of strength and resilience. "Listen, people," I said. "I'm here, I'm fine, so let's get to work. Okay?"

As they were all filing out, I overheard someone in the crowd utter, "Wow, what a champ!"

Hah! *Suckers*!

I laughed and congratulated myself on my stellar acting abilities. If they knew the enormous amount of inner strength and determination it took for me to even get out of bed this morning, they wouldn't be nearly as impressed.

Sophie would be the real test, though. She hired me right out of college, and no one in the company knows me better than she does.

Sure enough, I was faxing an invoice to a client when Sophie got the news that I was back to work. She made a beeline to my office, her green eyes shining with maternal pride that her protégée and heir apparent took such a lickin' but was still standing tall.

If they had a definition for bad bitch in the dictionary, Sophie's picture would be right there. Back in the '70s, her first husband left her with eleven dollars and four babies. She threw rent parties for herself, put on fashion shows—anything to make money. Now, over thirty years later, Sophie Wilkerson Events is a multimillion-dollar-a-year business.

Sophie believes that true ladies do not reveal their ages, so her exact age is unknown. But looking at her even with all the Botox, Thermage, and weekly facials, I would have to put her around sixty. At least.

Either way, she's still fierce with her perpetually bronze skin tone and short pixie haircut.

And talk about a sense of style! Old girl never fails to impress in something chic and free-flowing like the white, Chanel pantsuit she wore today, which made her look like she was floating on a breeze. Immediately, Sophie pulled me into a warm hug and said, "I have taught you well," in her husky, Eastern European accent, which has always puzzled me since she was born and raised in Scottsdale, Arizona.

"It's good to be back," I said, meaning it sincerely.

Over the years, I have learned priceless pearls of wisdom from Sophie, such as *If you're having a bad day, the only person who should know that is you, True professionals never let personal problems interfere with business,* and her favorite, *Crying is for the weak. If you must do it, please let it be on your own time.*

Little did Sophie know that I have been doing just that; crying on my own time.

In the days following my ordeal, I fell into a mini-depression, which I tend to do after every breakup.

This time around, I didn't leave the house for three days straight. During that time, the UPS delivery guy who came to pick up Roland's stuff was the only person I had face-to-face contact with. I did not comb my hair, or go down to the lobby to pick up a newspaper or check the mail.

What I did do, though, was throw myself one helluva pity party. I baked my favorite lemonade cake with the intention of eating every last bit of it by myself. I pigged out on what was left of the spicy scallops, and lobster mashed potatoes, drank way too much champagne, and cried a river's worth of tears. I felt like Sybil, with all these different moods and emotions that would change what seemed like every few seconds. One minute I thought I had a grip on things, and the next minute, I would burst into tears and have a "Damn, damn, damn!" moment like Florida Evans.

Meanwhile, the phone was ringing off the hook with folks calling to check on me and treating me all fragile and shit, the way you would a mental patient on suicide watch.

Mama was so worried about my frame of mind that she suggested I come spend some time with her and Daddy, which is something that really *would* send me over the edge.

As much as I love my parents, eighteen years under their roof was long enough. And I really didn't care to relive the childhood trauma of hearing the two of them making love in the middle of the night.

Anyway, after about the hundredth call, I just stopped answering the phone and let the answering machine pick up.

"Tori, this is your Aunt Vera. I'm just calling to check on you, and make sure you haven't done anything stupid. I love you . . . give me a call."

"Hey, sis, this is Junior. Don't even worry about that Roland stuff, best believe he's gonna get handled! Anyway, I'm a little short on my child support payment this month, think you can let me borrow like, two-hundred dollars? Peace."

"Tori, this is Yvette. Pick up the damn phone!"

"Hey cuz, this is Cookie . . . I know you're goin' through it, but you can at least call me back, shit. Bye!"

I knew they meant well, but I just could not stand to hear any more of that clichéd bullshit that people like to toss around when trying to comfort someone through a devastating crisis. Things such as doors closing, windows opening, and loving something enough to let it go and seeing if it will come back and if it doesn't then take heart because that which does not kill you makes you stronger.

It felt good to completely shut down, and shut the world out, with no cell phone, e-mail, or text messages.

By late Tuesday evening, I was over it, honey. I had one of those lightbulb moments, and suddenly realized that going completely crazy is a luxury that I simply cannot afford. Especially since I now have a three-thousand-dollar-a-month mortgage to pay by myself.

Plus, Mama called at six o'clock this morning and gave me added incentive and encouragement. "This is the day that the Lord has made, rejoice and be glad in it!" she said with the enthusiasm of a cheerleader. "Your Daddy and I raised you to be a *victor*, Tori. Not a victim."

So, using Jennifer Aniston as my role model, I literally drug myself out of bed and put my game face on.

I am far from being over Roland and this whole sordid situation, but I don't see why the rest of the world has to know that. Celine Dion is right. The heart does go on, and so will I—eventually.

In the meantime, my first day back to work was a classic display of faking it till you make it. I shamelessly took all those accolades and pats on the back as if I truly deserved them.

They say a certain percentage of success is just showing up, and I found that to be true today. I showed up. And for that, I am pretty sure I gained some respect back.

"Way to show some of these weak-kneed cowards around here how to take a lickin', and not even miss a step!" Sophie said, still cheering me on.

"You can't keep a good woman down!" I said with a wink.

"Right on, sister!" she said, giving me a fist bump. "So seeing as how you were supposed to be out of the office for a month, and there's nothing concrete on your schedule for today, how about representing the SWE vendor booth at the Bridal Expo this afternoon?"

Ugh. Maybe I should have kept my ass at home.

I planned weddings when I first started out, but I am glad to say that I don't do them anymore. Mainly because you have to deal with the unreasonable demands of bridezillas who think they know what they want but really don't, and everything is your fault and you have to do a tremendous amount of handholding and micromanaging and the migraines that come along with the territory are just not worth it. Besides, after what I had just been through, I was in no mood to deal with anything even slightly associated with weddings.

"What about Margo?" I asked, trying not to sound as unenthusiastic as I felt. "Weddings are her area of expertise."

"True, but Margo went into labor last night and is now officially on maternity leave," Sophie said, peering at me closely. "Now, if it's something you can't handle—"

"What's not to handle?" I asked, with a laugh.

I knew that Sophie was testing me to ensure that I really was as over my personal tragedy as I claimed to be. I wasn't, of course, but handing out brochures and answering questions about the specialties we had to offer was not a big deal. Besides, I wasn't going to have to actually work with any of these people later on down the line, so I could put up with the hoopla for a few hours.

"Looks like it's gonna be a long day," I told Erin, my assistant, the second we stepped into the Overland Park Convention Center.

"Tell me about it," she replied, looking overwhelmed by

the humongous state-of-the-art facility, which really should have its own zip code.

It wasn't even noon yet, and the place was jam-packed with thousands of women running around with goodie bags full of free promotional merchandise, and excitement shining in their beady little eyes.

Erin is fresh from the cornfields of Nebraska, and has only been with SWE for a few months. The girl has no special talent or area of expertise, except for making blankets made entirely out of the hair her cat has shed.

Even so, Erin's rise from intern to assistant had been meteoric, and unprecedented. It's not fair, and it sucks for those who actually deserve to be promoted, but what can you do? She is Sophie's niece, and nepotism will always be alive and well.

Erin and I schlepped our way through the crowd until we found a booth with signage that read: *SOPHIE WILKERSON EVENTS—WE MAKE DREAMS COME TRUE!*

The two of us got to work decorating the booth with white silk fabric, a fresh assorted floral arrangement, and pink and silver balloons. Next, company brochures were set out, along with refrigerator magnets, key chains, coffee mugs, and pink T-shirts that said "Bride" across the front of them. Two seconds after setting up, Erin and I were descended upon by two expensive-looking women who looked like "before" and "after" versions of the same person. Clearly, they were related.

"Oh look, Sophie Wilkerson Events!" exclaimed the older, "before" version. "I forget your name," she said, pointing at me. "But you did my son's bar mitzvah four years ago—Do you remember me?"

Not off the top of my head, I didn't.

I kept a friendly smile on my face while I took in her physical characteristics: guppy-like, collagen-injected lips, heirloom diamonds on every finger, definitely old money.

It took mere seconds for the name to pop up in my mental Rolodex.

"Of course I remember you, Mrs. Swartz!" I said. "How is Bradley, by the way?"

"Well, I don't like to talk about it," Mrs. Swartz said, lowering her voice. "But Bradley's in juvenile detention right now. It's all a big misunderstanding."

The "after" version of Mrs. Swartz rolled her eyes and said, "Yeah, it's a big misunderstanding, alright. He didn't *mean* to nearly beat that homeless guy to death with a baseball bat."

Mrs. Swartz shot a withering look to the "after" version of herself, then said tightly, "This is my daughter, Cynthia. She's the bride-to-be."

"Congratulations!" I said, shaking Cynthia's hand. "When is the big day?"

"Next Valentine's Day," Cynthia snipped haughtily, which instantly let me know that Margo, or whichever planner she ended up with, would have their hands full.

"Valentine's Day, how romantic!" I gushed, as if it were the most original idea in the world. "And you know, that gives us plenty of time to create the fantasy wedding of your dreams—"

"Oh believe me, I know!" Mrs. Swartz interjected. "You did a wonderful job the last time, and exceeded each and every one of our expectations."

"Well, we certainly aim to please," I said. "Now, what's a good day and time for you two to come in for a consultation meeting?"

The Swartz's set an appointment, and Cynthia happily walked away with two coffee mugs and an armload of "Bride" T-shirts. I don't know why, but rich people love to get free stuff even more than the less fortunate do.

"Very smooth!" Erin said, reaching into our stash and setting out more T-shirts. "You're just as good as Aunt Sophie—probably even better."

"I wouldn't go that far . . ." I said modestly, even though it was the absolute truth.

"I can't believe how fortunate I am to be paired up with you," Erin continued, brown-nosing. "And I've learned so much already—you inspire me so much, Tori."

"Well, you just keep learning and growing," I said. "And one of these days you just might head up a department within the company yourself."

"Gee, you really think so?" she asked with wide-eyed wonder.

"Anything is possible," I said, then turned on the charm to greet more visitors.

Throughout the afternoon, I talked with countless prospective brides, all of them annoyingly optimistic, and giddy from sampling too much champagne and wedding cake.

I'm not sure what came over me, but my attitude towards weddings and the institution of marriage became extremely cynical and nasty.

Inside, I was dying to tell everyone who stopped at the SWE booth, the truth as I saw it. *Save your money, girl. He's just gonna end up screwing you over and taking you for granted, anyway,* and *Does your man have any female friends? Watch your back!*

It may have been a case of too much, too soon, because after just two hours of talking to prospective brides, I cut out early and left Erin in charge for the rest of the day. Why not? She may be the boss's idiot niece, but she is still fully capable of handing out brochures and business cards, as well as answering questions about SWE specialties and the laundry list of services we have to offer.

I grabbed my Fendi bag and practically ran out of the convention center, wishing I could find a place nearby that sold Xanax smoothies.

Now *that's* an idea for a franchise!

Nothing is permanent but change. —Heraclitus, 500 B.C.

WEDNESDAY

This journal Simone gave me is really going to come in handy, because every day I discover some loose end that still needs tying.

1) Deactivate the following bridal registries: Williams-Sonoma, Pottery Barn, and Tiffany's.

2) Sell wedding dress through consignment shop.

3) Go shopping for a new king-sized bedroom set, ASAP.

4) Give old bedroom set to the charity I donate to most often, which is Junior.

I also discovered today that being left for another woman is harder for me to accept than if Roland had come out and said that he was gay. He's not, of course, but that, people can understand: Okay, that's him, that's his issue and something he needs to work out.

But if another woman comes in and takes your man, then it becomes all about you and your shortcomings, and what you didn't do right. Now I have to go around convincing people that I'm not the one to blame in this situation, which is no small feat because I'm not 100% sure about that myself.

I mean, let's face it; being left at the altar isn't exactly a confidence booster. And the fact that Roland didn't even upgrade when he left me, makes it even worse. With Veronica, he went from sugar to shit, and I will never know what he sees in her.

I do know that putting up a front is hard work. Exhausting, really. I was supposed to attend an art gallery showing with Simone tonight, followed by a poetry slam, but after a long day of pretending to be alright, every ounce of my energy has been drained. All I feel up to doing is taking a long luxurious bubble bath, putting on my pajamas, and finishing off the last of that lemonade cake.

4

Thirty days after the fact, and the advice and unsolicited comments about my personal business just kept rolling in. My girl Yvette called me this evening, and seemed excited to drop this little gem on me:

"Men are just like the faces on a dollar bill; if one won't do, another one will!" she told me.

That is the philosophy that Yvette has been living by since her divorce, and obviously is the reason she felt compelled to pass my phone number along to a Sean Somebody-or-other, who left a message on my voice mail to get back with him if I wanted to "hook up or something."

Now, Sean and I have never met, so technically, Yvette was trying to set me up on a blind date. I don't do those. Everyone knows blind dates are the equivalent to playing Russian roulette with a loaded pistol. There is a very high probability that things aren't going to turn out well.

"You should be embracing the situation instead of being so pissed off about it," Yvette said when I called her to complain. "Sean happens to be a very eligible bachelor."

"Then why aren't you dating him?"

"Because he's more your type than he is mine," Yvette said.

"So in other words, this guy is not good enough for you, but he's perfect for me, right?"

"No, Tori, and stop putting words in my mouth!" Yvette barked at me over the phone. "I just happen to know what kind of guys you like, and Sean happens to fit that to a tee."

Knowing Yvette as I do, I had to double-check to make sure we were on the same page. "And what is my type, again?" I asked.

"Over six feet, good-looking, and he has to earn a decent living," she said in a *duh* tone of voice.

Well, that is my type. Then again, that's everybody's type, isn't it? I personally don't know too many women who would say that they want a short, broke, ugly man.

But, tall and fine, with a steady income is just the beginning. Maturity is a must, reliability is key, and honesty is non-negotiable.

Yvette, on the other hand, does not have a definite type. This po' chile is forever betting on the long shots, and is what you would call a fixer-upper when it comes to men.

No matter how broke, broken, or unattractive a man is, Yvette will give him a chance just as long as he treats her right. That is the *only* prerequisite. Not too long ago, Yvette introduced me to a guy who I had to literally bite my tongue to keep from asking if he had baboon in his family.

Then there was Corey, the younger by several years male nurse, who we all strongly suspected had quite a bit of sugar in his tank. Okay? The license plates on his yellow Volkswagen Beetle read: **DIVO**, which in case you didn't know, means male diva. And if that's not enough proof, Yvette told me herself that Corey couldn't go more than a week without getting a pedicure, which she reasoned was because he worked on his feet ten hours a day.

"But a French pedicure, Yvette?" I asked.

"My man just likes to pamper himself, that's all," she declared. "He's a metrosexual."

"No, baby, he's a *homo*sexual," I said. "Straight men don't drink pink cosmos."

Yvette didn't have an answer for that. A few weeks after that conversation, Corey admitted that he was, indeed, playing for both teams.

Yvette was taking all comers and going hard at the whole dating thing, because Andre left her two years ago after thirteen years of marriage.

She moped around for a few months, refusing to date, but after reading *What's Good for the Goose . . . The Smart Woman's Guide to Dating the Way Men Do,* Yvette snapped out of the rut she was in and became this ruthless man-eater. These days, she was dating a minimum of four times a week—usually with a different guy each time.

"It's a numbers game," Yvette had said. Which may be true, but it was scary to watch because girlfriend was becoming so consumed with her quest for husband-number-two that her search was taking her into some weird and scary places.

You name it, and Yvette has tried it. Speed dating, the Internet, matchmaking services, singles groups, and even a nightclub called Club Heifers, which caters exclusively to plus-sized women and the men who love them.

As for this Sean person, I was holding my breath waiting for the other shoe to drop. Yvette had the habit of leaving out significant details. Like, maybe the guy has a third eye, a nervous twitch, and stinks all-to-be-damned.

"Give up the dirt, Yvette. What's really wrong with this dude?" I asked.

"Damn! If I thought something was seriously wrong with the man, I wouldn't be trying to hook you up with him," Yvette huffed. "Now, he may not turn out to be soul-mate material, but at least it will get you out of the house and out of that routine you've fallen into lately."

"Oh, so that's what this is all about?" I asked. "Even with my busy schedule, you think I need something to do?"

"Not some*thing*, honey, some*one*," she chided. "It's time for you to permanently erase Roland from your memory bank, and get back out there and start mixing it up."

I sighed, because truthfully I haven't had much of a life lately. My career is my social life, and what little free time I do have has been spent devouring Topsy's cheese and caramel popcorn while watching *Cheaters* and reruns of *Martin*.

While I appreciate what Yvette was trying to do, I was skeptical because I know from previous experience that *out there* is like trying to tread water with only one arm, and *out there* is also a cold, dark, and sometimes scary place where it is possible to be lonely, even in a crowd.

But at the same time, becoming a social recluse is not the answer. I am going to have to get back out there at some point.

I gave in a little. "And exactly how is it that you know this guy, again?" I asked Yvette.

"Okay . . ." Yvette said, sounding excited that I was finally showing some interest. "Sean is an old friend of my brother, Chuck. Girl, he was so fine back in the day . . . Umph! All the girls on my block wanted them some Sean."

"And how did you two become reacquainted?" I asked.

Yvette paused and took a deep breath before answering my question. "Well, see, what had happened was . . . I came across his profile on KCsingles.com—"

"Oh, *hell* no!" I exploded. "So all you really know about this guy is that he *used* to be fine back when he was a teenager?"

"Oh no, don't get it twisted; he's still fine," said Yvette. "Check out his profile if you don't believe me."

When I think of Internet dating all that comes to mind are the horror stories. The most recent being about the woman in New York whose body parts were found strewn across the city in several different garbage bags. They're still searching for her head.

"Internet dating is a waste of time, Yvette," I said. "Nobody does that shit anymore, besides you."

"See, that's where you're wrong," Yvette said. "If you hadn't had your head stuck up Roland's ass for all these years, you'd know that the Internet is the best way to meet men these days."

I didn't want to hurt Yvette's feelings, so I bit my tongue and did not say what I was thinking, which was that looking for love on the Internet is for desperate, defective people who have no other options.

Not that I think she's defective. Desperate? Totally.

"Tell Sean I said thanks, but no thanks," I said. "I have a hard enough time weeding out all the scammers and liars that I meet face-to-face."

Yvette sighed and sucked her teeth. "You know, Tori, you are never going to find a new man being so goddamn cynical about everything," she snapped. "I personally know of several great romances that have blossomed online."

"Name one," I challenged.

"My Uncle James," she said.

"No offense, Yvette, but your Uncle James is weird as hell."

"And I'm not even gonna deny that," Yvette said matter-of-factly. "But the point is he is on his *third* Internet bride, which proves that it can be done. You know? Now, Sean probably won't be your next fiancé, but you owe it to yourself to put down the remote, meet the man for coffee or something, and see how it goes from there."

"Naw, it's just not for me," I said, unapologetic.

"Fine, Tori, have it your way!" Yvette said, then the hussy hung up without even saying good-bye.

I shrugged, and traded the cordless phone for the remote. Monday night. *Top Chef* was coming on.

All I ask of . . . anyone is that they be courageous. —*Maya Angelou*

WEDNESDAY

It's been a couple of days since I talked to Yvette about possibly going out with her old friend, Sean, and I must admit that cu-

riosity has gotten the best of me. Earlier this evening I went into my home office, signed on to AOL, and browsed KCsingles.com. You know, just to get a feel for how this whole thing works, and already, I can totally see what a time-saver this could be. There are hundreds of good-looking men with great-sounding profiles, and it is similar to flipping through a catalog going: I want this one . . . this one . . . and oooh! That one!

> *39-year-old SBM looking for a serious, long-term relationship with one special lady. I consider myself to be a generous, romantic gentleman with a big heart.*
>
> *My interests are working out, customizing cars and motorcycles, investing, eating out, and golfing. Hopefully, you just may be the one I can settle down with and cherish like a queen.*

This is what Sean's dating profile reads. His picture proves that he is not the troll I had envisioned him to be. Definitely not Terance Howard, but not quite Flavor Flav, either.

I stared at Sean's online picture for a few minutes, trying to get some vibe or inkling as to whether or not he is all that he claims to be. The way I see it, the man could potentially be the next Jeffrey Dahmer, or he could be Prince Charming—you never know. The truth is, you are taking a chance on any man that you meet, Internet or otherwise. That guy you met at a dinner party the other night could be misrepresenting himself, too.

The fact of the matter is that you never really know if you are compatible with someone until you spend some one-on-one time with that person. That being said, now is as good a time to start dating again, as any. However, since dating is serious business, I am going to approach it, this time around, like a ruthless, self-serving, man-eating bitch.

If I have to be back out there, then damn it, I am at least going with some set ground rules and a zero-tolerance mindset.

1) One strike and he is out. I will give a guy enough of my time to determine what he's about, and whether the two of us click. If not, I'm yelling next! and we're just gonna keep the line moving.

2) No drama. That means con artists, drug users, men with deranged baby mamas, and close "platonic" female friends need not apply.

3) I will not settle for anything with a penis, just to avoid being alone on the weekends.

4) I am not playing anybody's games or jumping through anybody's hoops.

5) No compromising. Take me as I am, or get the hell out of my face.

With the ground rules out of the way, I threw caution to the wind and called Sean.

We talked for only a few brief minutes, but I must say, he came across as someone I wouldn't mind spending time with.

We're meeting Friday evening at Pierpont's at Union Station.

5

Summertime in Kansas City is a beast. It was so hot today, that the combination of the heat and humidity caused my hair to frizz up something terrible.

My date with Sean was set for seven o'clock, and because I refused to go out looking like Little Orphan Annie, I took off from work a couple of hours early to get my hair blown out; and to have these unruly eyebrows waxed and tamed.

Turning Heads Beauty Salon, located in Midtown, is an ultra-upscale salon that is legendary in Kansas City for being *the* number one spot for trend-setting fashionistas to get their hair laid. Outside the salon, I parked my white Lincoln Navigator among so many other high-end vehicles that the parking lot looked like a luxury-car dealership.

Inside the salon it was like having a front row seat at a fashion show. From Baby Phat and Apple Bottoms, to Prada and Christian Lacroix, the latest collections of every top-notch fashion designer are always well represented up in Turning Heads.

As is typical of most beauty shops across America, there are always lengthy discussions on who among us has the hottest (i.e., most expensive) handbag, the latest Jimmy Choos, whose significant other is on the fast track to mogul-dom, and, of course, who has the biggest diamond. Today, Leah Guthrie was the clear winner, with a six-karat, princess-cut yellow diamond that she said was "Just a little something-something" her husband Kenneth picked up on a business trip to New York.

"I'll bet that's not all he picked up in New York," Jackie muttered to me under her breath, referring to the sad truth that Leah is the only person in town who doesn't know that marriage has not stopped Kenneth from pursuing other women.

An hour in to my salon visit, it became obvious that Jackie's promise to have me in and out in less than two hours was an overly ambitious estimate. I would probably be late meeting Sean for our date.

It didn't help that, as usual, Jackie was running her mouth a lot faster than she was working her hands.

The topic? Men. What else?

"I'm so sick of these women out here hollering about they want 'a good, quality man' when half of 'em ain't about shit their damn selves," Jackie said, setting my hair on huge rollers. "If you want top-shelf, you have to *be* top-shelf. That's how that works."

I threw my hand up to testify on that one. "You can't ask more from a man than you're capable of bringing to the table yourself," I said.

"Nothing from nothing leaves nothing," Pam cosigned, while combing out her client's hair.

Mrs. Odell came from under the hairdryer to throw in her two cents. "You young women want to know what the key is to getting and keeping a man?"

Being that Mrs. Odell was well into her sixties, all talking immediately ceased. The only sounds were the drone of hair dryers and the sizzling of curling irons.

Satisfied that she had everyone's undivided attention, Mrs. Odell continued. "First, you give that man all the good sex he can stand. I mean, wear his ass out!"

"Hey now," said Stephanie, the shampoo girl. "I *know* I can handle that!"

Whoops of loud laughter erupted, and high fives were given all around.

"Second, make your man feel like a king," Mrs. Odell said. "Just spoil him to death! Cook his favorite meals, keep the house clean if you live together, and if you don't live together, keep his place spotless. You have to make yourself indispensable, see? Run errands for him. Give massages without him having to ask—and be sure to rub his feet. Men love to have their feet rubbed after working hard all day."

I could have sworn I heard crickets chirping.

That bit of advice went over like a fart in church. Instantly, the faces of the women in the shop turned sour.

"Nah, see, uh-uh!" said Tyeisha, barely out of her teens. "I wouldn't do all that for love *or* money."

"Yeah, no disrespect, Miss Odell, but that's some old-school mess right there," Jackie said. "Ain't nobody spoiling these knuckleheads by baking cakes and pies and shit. The minute you bow down to a man and start being subservient, is the same minute they start taking your ass for granted."

"And you wonder why you can't keep a man!" Mrs. Odell quipped before dipping her head full of rollers back under the dryer.

In what I assumed was an effort to keep my mind off the time, Jackie asked me what my plans were for the evening.

"My first date in over three years," I said. "A *blind* date, at that."

Oh, boy! I shouldn't have put that out there, because it became a whole new topic of conversation. By the time my hair and eyebrows were done, I had been given so much advice that I felt like a boxer who had been prepped by my corner man for a fight.

Overall, the consensus in the salon was that I should:

1) Keep my expectations low. That way I won't be disappointed.

2) Make lots of flirty eye contact. Smile, and laugh a lot.
3) Do NOT go back to his place.
4) Do NOT let him come to mine.
5) Keep my body language open.
6) Do NOT make out with him.
7) Do NOT give up the coochie before the seventh date.

I went through my closet last night and realized for the first time that I don't own even one outfit with any real *va-va-va-voom.*

In my line of business, it is imperative to look pulled together and in charge, so my closet is full of well-tailored power suits, but nothing accentuating or revealing. Nothing that would make a man say *whoa!*

So after leaving the salon, I made a mad last-minute dash to the mall. Nordstrom was having their half-yearly sale, so I stopped in there to search for the perfect outfit.

Next to eating, sex, and my career, there is nothing I love to do more than shop. But the one thing I hate about the whole experience is those damned three-way mirrors. No matter what you think you look like naked, it is always ten times worse when you stand in front of one of those things.

You get the up-close-and-personal, unvarnished truth, which in my case is 38C's that aren't as perky as they used to be, a not-so-flat tummy, and cellulite for days.

Even so, I still look damn good in my clothes. And I was sure that when Sean saw me, he was going to think so too.

After paying the cashier, I walked out of the department store wearing the outfit I selected. It was simple, but cute, and very chic: a chocolate, formfitting halter dress designed by Tracy Reese, matching peep-toe pumps, and gold accessories.

I was going down the escalator when my cell phone rang.

It was Sean. I sent the call to voice mail, because I was already a nervous wreck. I did not need the added pressure of him reminding me that we were supposed to be face-to-face in less than twenty minutes.

Whew! I made it. And I wasn't nearly as late as I thought I would be.

Punctuality, however, became the least of my worries as I searched for a parking spot outside of Union Station. That is when an overwhelming feeling of sheer terror seized me.

"It's too soon!" I said to myself while beating on the steering wheel. "I'm not ready for this!" My nerves were bad because I hadn't been in the game for so long; my dating skills were beyond rusty. I wasn't even sure if I still knew how to act around a man other than Roland.

You can do it, Tori. Just breathe . . .

I did a series of breathing exercises to keep from going into a full-blown panic attack.

Inhale for four seconds, hold for four seconds, and exhale for four seconds. Repeat. Then repeat again. And again. And again.

Several minutes later I walked into Union Station, my stiletto heels tip-tapping across the beige marble floors.

Outwardly, I may have looked confident, but inwardly I was silently praying for the best.

By the time I got inside Pierpont's, I was feeling a lot more confident. I walked straight to the long, dazzling bar, which is where Sean said he would be waiting for me. I did not see a tall black man in a red shirt right away, so I ordered an Amaretto Sour, and scanned the large after-work crowd that consisted mostly of white guys in button-down shirts and khaki pants.

To my left was a young Asian couple who were laughing and gazing into each other's eyes.

Way down at the opposite end of the bar, a group of five sisters were having a loud and heated debate on the fineness of Chris Brown versus Usher.

There was an older Hispanic man immediately to my right, who seemed oblivious to me and everything else going on around him. I watched as he slammed down two triple-shots of dark brown liquor, and I was wondering what his story was, when I felt a hand on my shoulder.

"Excuse me . . ." a deep male voice said. "Your name wouldn't happen to be Tori, would it?"

I turned around and my head went way back, because the man who tapped my shoulder was extremely tall.

"Sean?" I asked cautiously.

Sean nodded, and relief washed over his face as he wrapped me up into a huge bear hug. "You look just the way Yvette described you." He grinned.

I couldn't quite say the same for him. The photo he had posted online was clearly outdated. Up close and in the flesh, Sean was at least twenty-five pounds heavier, and I noted that he looked much older than thirty-nine.

Some people have accused me of being too judgmental at times, so I did not take points away from Sean for the two front teeth capped in cheap, 10-karat gold. While I was at it, I decided that I didn't really mind that he was wearing Ray Charles–type sunglasses. In the restaurant. At night. However, I was having a *little* trouble getting past the outfit.

In addition to the red shirt Sean said he would be wearing, he was dressed from head to toe in red alligator. The jacket matched the pants, and the belt matched the shoes.

Damn.

Aunt Vera's voice echoed in my head: *You can't trust a man who wears red shoes. If his shoes are any color other than black or brown—hit the damn door!*

And I was just about to do that, when Sean grabbed me around the waist. As if reading my mind, he said, "Come on, let's go find a table so we can talk."

I smiled weakly, and followed as a host seated us at a table in the Rose Room, which was much quieter than the bar area and main dining room.

Before leaving us, the host smirked at Sean's getup, and gave me a menu, along with a sympathetic smile.

It did not even occur to Sean to help me with my chair. Instead, he sat down at the table and gave me a quizzical look that read: *Why the hell are you still standing?*

See, that right there is why I blame the liberation movement for the problems between the sexes. Don't get me wrong, I think the women's rights era was very necessary in terms of women having the right to earn the same money as a man, and being able to go to work without being propositioned and sexually harassed, but when it comes to one-on-one relationships between men and women, the movement hurt things more than it helped. It confused things because women started refusing to let men treat them like ladies, and after a while, men started forgetting how to be gentlemen.

Those polite and respectful gestures that used to come naturally to men were lost somewhere along the way because women mistook chivalry for chauvinism, and began declaring, *No, you don't need to pull out my chair or open my door, I can do those things for myself. I am woman, hear me roar!*

And men started throwing up their hands and saying *Okay, fine. Do it your damn self!*

Despite Sean having no apparent manners or fashion sense, I silently resolved to keep a positive outlook.

"This is nice, huh?" He smiled, showing off his gold tee-fuss, just in case I hadn't already seen them. "You ever been here before?"

"Yes, several times," I said, taking a big gulp of my Amaretto Sour. Two minutes into the date, and I could already tell that I was going to need a buzz for this.

When the server came to take our drink orders, I asked for another Amaretto Sour, while Sean ordered a Budweiser draft beer and a double shot of cognac on the side.

One of the black women who were sitting at the bar when I came in, walked by our table on her way to the restroom. Obviously liking what he saw, Sean stared openly and lustily said, "Damn, that ass is fat!"

Positive outlook? Out the window.

"Hello!" I snapped. "Do you see me sitting here?"

"Why you tripping?" he asked, incredulous. "It ain't like we're married or something. I mean, damn. I just met you."

I shook my head, which was really spinning at this point.

Was I hallucinating?

Someone I have known all of five fucking minutes has never so blatantly disrespected me.

Not a minute later, Sean chuckled as if it were nothing more than a big misunderstanding. "Look, I apologize for all that," he said. "Can we start over?"

I looked at him through narrow eyes, not exactly sure where this weird sonofabitch was coming from.

"Hi, I'm Sean," he said, offering a handshake.

"Tori . . ." I replied, shaking his hand reluctantly.

When Sean said "start over" he wasn't kidding. For the next forty minutes, I was forced to feign interest as he told me his life's story from start to present.

I learned all about his whorish mother and abusive stepfather. The five-year bid he served in the early '90s "on some bullshit." The nervous breakdown (brought on by his recent, nasty divorce), his finances (which are in bad shape because of the divorce), and his bitch of an ex-wife (who hasn't let him see the kids in almost a year because of the restraining order).

Blahdy Blah Blah . . .

During the time Sean was rambling on and on, he kept ordering and downing drink, after drink, after drink.

Now, I'm all for people having a good time, but three Budweisers and four double shots of Hennessey in less than an hour is a bit much.

And the more alcohol Sean consumed, the more he talked.

The more he talked, the more agitated he seemed to get.

"So, what is it that you do again?" I asked, trying to steer the conversation in a lighter direction.

Sean glared at me as if he resented the question, and said, "I was in sales, but I'm transitioning at the moment."

"Transitioning? That's just a fancy way of saying you're unemployed, right?"

I didn't mean anything by it. It was just an innocent remark to keep the conversation going, but Sean took such great offense that he stomped off to the restroom without even excusing himself from the table.

Oh. My. God.

I was sitting at the table by myself wondering if I was caught up in the *Twilight Zone* or *The Matrix*, when Erin called on my cell phone with a question about the Carousel of Hope benefit next month. Right in the middle of telling Erin to contact the caterer to finalize the gourmet hors d'oeuvres selection, Sean came back from the restroom with a pee-pee track down the front of his pants. His fly was also unzipped, exposing the fact that he was not wearing boxers or briefs.

I couldn't help it. I burst into an uncontrollable fit of laughter.

"What in the world is going on with you?" Erin asked, over the phone.

It took almost a full minute for me to catch my breath, and I had to struggle to say, "I'll call you later . . ."

After ending the call, I looked over at Sean, who was staring at me with crazy all in his eyes.

It was a look somewhere between excitement and agitation, which confirmed for me that this man was indeed a couple electric shock treatments away from having a full deck.

"That is so goddamn rude," he said with cold disdain. "You could at least wait until we part ways before you start badmouthing me to your fucking friends."

"Wait a minute now," I said, keeping my voice low so that

Sean would take the hint and do the same. "That phone call wasn't even about you. Actually I was laughing because—"

"You know, you independent, highfalutin broads are all the same." He sneered. "Always putting a brother down instead of trying to lift him up."

I had no idea how to respond to that.

What do you say to a profoundly unstable man while he's on an alcohol-fueled tirade?

"I wasn't putting you down," was all I could think of, but Sean was so far gone, he just kept babbling as if he hadn't heard me.

". . . A man makes a few coins less than you do, and he ain't shit in your eyes. He's dispensable. And that attitude right there is why the majority of y'all are gonna die single, and why you bitches don't have no one to cuddle up to at night besides your goddamn vibrators."

I was offended on so many levels. First of all, I have never even owned a vibrator. Second, this mother-skunk just called me the b-word.

"Wait a minute, who are you calling a *bitch*?" I exploded, with Queen Latifah ferocity. "You *must* be off your fucking meds!"

The noise level in the room went down several notches as people turned to watch the unfolding ghetto drama.

"As a matter of fact, I am off my meds . . ." Sean said sarcastically. "*Bitch!*"

That was it. I was so done.

After emptying what was left of my drink on top of Sean's head, all eyes were on me as I grabbed my purse and headed for the exit.

Refusing for my exit to be viewed as a walk of shame, I pretended I was on a catwalk and treated the gawkers to my best Naomi Campbell impression: Chin up, with a my-shit-don't-stink strut, and a wry, kiss-my-ass smile.

Just inches from the door, I was horrified to see Roland's

brother, Gary, and his wife, Carlotta, sitting at a table near the entrance.

Shit!

I got to keep the wine collection, the red leather Natuzzi living room group, the contemporary art collection, the sixty-inch high-definition plasma TV, and even the state-of-the-art entertainment system, but what I did not get to keep was the handful of Roland's relatives that I had grown to love. Like his grandparents, Aunt Jean, Uncle Pee-Wee, and sister-in-law Carlotta.

We were all close at one time, but I have not seen or heard from any of them since everything went down, which is understandable.

With any breakup, friends have to choose sides. And I'm not surprised Carlotta chose Roland. After all, they are still family. And to keep the peace she has to fall in line with the rest of the clan, who have suddenly taken to treating me as if I have the bird flu. Like *I'm* the one to blame for this whole sordid mess.

Now here my ex-future-in-laws were, having a huge laugh at my expense.

That's just fucking great. It might as well have been Roland himself sitting up at that table because I had no doubt they would go back and provide blow-by-blow details of this whole fiasco.

What to do?

I smiled and waved at Gary and Carlotta, and didn't even break my stride.

I left Union Station, and sped south on Main Street like a demon was on my tail. I didn't think Sean was following me, I just wanted to put as much distance between him and me as possible.

Congratu-fucking-lations, Tori! You are officially back out there.

How ironic was it that my first date in many years, turned out to be *the worst* date I have ever had in my life?

I just hoped this was not a forewarning of what was to come.

This is what Sean's profile would say if he had written the whole truth about himself.

I am an overweight, binge drinking, old-school wannabe Mack Daddy with serious mental health issues. Instead of satisfaction, I can guarantee that you will wish you had never met me. If this sounds good and you think you are a match, hit me with an e-mail at Ittybittydick68@hotmail.com

I felt robbed. Like somebody owed me an hour of my life back.

On the way home, I called Yvette. "Good looking out," I said sarcastically, when she answered the phone.

I relayed the whole ordeal, which prompted Yvette to suddenly remember that Sean may have, kinda sorta been a *little* bit bipolar back in the day.

"But I thought he'd gotten over that," she said in her own defense.

"Yvette, being bipolar is not something you get over like a fucking cold!" I said through clenched teeth.

"So y'all going out again?" Yvette asked.

"What? Girl . . . bye!" I said, and hung up the phone in her face.

Nothing is at last sacred but the integrity of your own mind.
—Ralph Waldo Emerson

FRIDAY

And the lessons for today are:

1) Internet dating be damned! No matter how good their profile sounds

2) Yvette's taste in men absolutely cannot be trusted

What was I thinking, allowing Yvette to choose a man for me when she can't even find a decent man for herself?

After all, this is a woman who is so desperately seeking a husband that she's giving multiple dates to guys who should never have even gotten her phone number in the first place.

Damn it!

If things had worked out as planned, I would just be returning from my honeymoon in Aruba; tan, well-rested, and possibly pregnant. Instead, I'm here dealing with an alligator-in-ninety-degree-heat wearing, schizophrenic bozo that can't even piss straight.

Well, starting off this badly means things can only get better from here. They damn sure can't get any worse.

At least I hope not.

6

My team arrived at the Max Mara boutique at six o'clock this morning to get things ready for the grand opening scheduled for later this afternoon.

Event days are the culmination of months, and sometimes a year or more, of hard work and preparation. These days are what I live for, because it is so rewarding to see the client's fantasies come to life.

The headaches started right away.

The first mishap of the day came when two low-level members of the design team, broke one of the glass display cases while moving it during the setup.

"I'll take care of it," I sighed.

Three hours and many phone calls later, I was finally able to locate a glass company who could rush right over and replace the broken glass display case before the event started.

Next, I had to contend with Erin, who was having a major meltdown and could not focus on the tasks at hand. Apparently, she went home last night to find that her boyfriend John had just upped and hightailed it back to Omaha, taking the cat and most of her furniture along with him.

Erin wasn't the only one having problems at home, either. Demetrius, our in-house florist, had been on the phone arguing with his life partner, Burt, for half the day, but at least he was getting his work done, which was more than I could say for Erin.

"It's exactly like that old Gladys Knight song . . ." Erin sobbed, to no one in particular.

"Which one?" Steve, the lighting guy asked from across the room.

"The one where the guy couldn't make it in the big city and he had to go back to his old life with his tail tucked between his legs," Erin said, just standing around, not even pretending to be working.

"Oh, you mean "Midnight Train to Georgia?" asked Inez, a member of the design team.

"Yeah, that's it. I mean, there is absolutely nothing in Omaha, which is why we moved to Kansas City in the first place," Erin said. "What kind of life is he going to have now?"

Finally, I had to pull Erin's ditzy ass aside and remind her that this was not the time or place for her personal issues. "Erin, do you remember that conversation we had a while back, about emotions in the workplace, and what's appropriate and what's not?" I asked.

"Yes . . ." she said, wiping her tears with the back of her hand.

"So let's concentrate on kicking ass with this event," I said. "And afterwards we can go out for drinks and talk about John, okay?"

Erin sniveled, nodded, and got to work.

Jeez . . .

My specialty is behind-the-scenes chaos management.

Although I do know a few design tricks, Martha Stewart and B. Smith have nothing to worry about as far as I am concerned, because decorating is not my forte.

For years, I have worked hard on enhancing my skills in that area, but I have come to accept that I am not the type of event planner who can take two pieces of wood, some string, and a can of spray paint and turn them into something fabulous and beautiful. That is just not what I do.

But when push comes to shove, I can create stunning centerpieces, hot-glue appliqués, and dress a beautiful dinner table with the best of them. But that is where it stops. And that's okay, because at SWE we have design specialists for all of that—let them worry about décor.

I do the detail work of putting the whole thing together, and once it's game time I oversee everybody. Making sure everyone is on track, on target, and on time. I am the conductor in this zany orchestra filled with florists, wait staff, bartenders, electricians, lighting people, caterers, production people, and the list goes on and on. Depending upon the size of the event, I manage a cast of hundreds, and sometimes thousands.

I have been called a demanding, by the book, high-strung perfectionist, but I really don't see that as a negative. Usually, the only people who feel that way about me are the ones who fail to hold up their end of the bargain.

Despite the rocky start earlier in the day, the grand opening started on time.

I had instructed the production team to build an elevated catwalk right in the middle of the store, facing the front door, so window shoppers and passersby could see the goings-on inside. And what was going on inside, was a hot fashion show featuring killer summer fashions worn by gorgeous, ninety-eight-pound models strutting their stuff to hits like Jay-Z's "Change Clothes and Go" and "Beautiful" by Snoop Dogg and Pharrell.

The energy was high, and the cash registers were ringing.

Throughout all the activity, I had my eye on a woman who I instinctively knew was going to be trouble from the minute she walked in wearing generic jeans, a nondescript blouse, Payless shoes, and a platinum blonde weave that contrasted sharply with her dark skin.

Erin was outside greeting customers and working the guest list, but somehow she let this one slip through.

Gate-crashers and freeloaders are the pests at just about every event, and I know one when I see one. Sort of like roaches.

I went outside to school Erin on her mistake. "You see that?" I said, pointing the woman out to Erin. "That's what you call a liability. Just watch her for a minute."

Erin and I both watched from the storefront window, as Blondie pretended to shop for about two minutes, then went right to the food station where she grabbed two plates and piled them both high with gourmet hors d'oeuvres. After that, she went over and parked her behind at the bar where she started guzzling watermelon martinis like they were going out of style.

"See what I'm talking about?" I said to Erin. "Every cocktail and every single hors d'oeuvre has a monetary value. Nothing personal, I'm sure she's a nice woman, but if she consumes a hundred dollars' worth of food and drink and doesn't buy anything, what does that make her?"

"A liability," Erin said.

"Right! That's why you have to learn how to read people when you're working the door," I said. "Now what you should have said was *Sorry ma'am, this is a private event, invitation only. Please come back tomorrow when the store is open to the public.*"

"Got it," Erin said, sounding disappointed that she had failed at yet another simple task.

I turned on my heels and went back inside Max Mara's, where Blondie was now causing a ruckus.

"Where mine at?" she shouted at a passing sales clerk, who looked terrified and unsure of how to handle the situation. I went over to help out.

"What seems to be the problem, ma'am?" I asked pleasantly.

"The problem is, all these other heifers in here walking around with these cute little bags full of goodies. Where mine at?" Blondie said, sucking food out of her teeth.

"Ma'am, the gift bags come with a minimum seventy-five

dollar purchase," I said quietly. "Now, if you want one, you can start by paying for that."

A red silk blouse was not so discreetly tucked into Blondie's fake Louis Vuitton Murakami bag.

"How you know that ain't mine?" she snapped.

"Because the tag is sticking out for all to see, and it says Max Mara, one hundred and twenty-five dollars," I said.

"I can't stand bitches like you," said Blondie, nostrils flaring. "What the hell difference does it make to you, anyway? It ain't like it's your damn store!"

"It is for the day. And I understand the anger, sweetheart," I said with great sympathy. "But listen, why don't you click your heels two times and you just might find yourself back in Walmart. Okay?"

"Fuck you, bitch!" Blondie tossed the shirt in my face, and then stormed out of the boutique as if someone had done her wrong.

I love my job.

It took three hours for my team and me to put the Max Mara boutique back in its normal order. When we were done, we all went out for cocktails at Tomfooleries, our usual watering hole.

"I wanna propose a toast to Tori," said Inez from the design department. "The best senior event coordinator Sophie Wilkerson Events will *ever* see!"

"Hear, hear!" they all said in unison.

"Well, I just want to thank you guys for all of your hard work," I said. "Your creativity and input is invaluable to me in putting these things together, and I appreciated each and every one of you."

"Awww, we love you too!" Steve teased, which got a big laugh.

We were all seated around a large table. Erin was to my left, and had been talking my ear off for the last twenty minutes about John, her nutcase of an ex-boyfriend who, truthfully, she should be glad packed up and left.

"I mean, hopefully it's like Katherine Hepburn said in her A&E biography," Erin droned on. " 'I saw you could be happy, successful and loved without a husband.' "

"Yeah, well that is easy to say when you're being loved by someone else's husband."

"What do you mean?"

"The love of her life, Spencer Tracy, was a married man."

"He was?" The astonished look on Erin's face reminded me of the time I broke Junior's heart by telling him the Easter Bunny did not exist.

"Yeah, sweetie, he was." I patted her hand, hoping that I looked genuinely sympathetic. "And I know exactly what you're going through, but the thing is, you simply cannot dwell on it. The best thing to do is completely immerse yourself into something positive, and one of these days you'll wake up and say: John who?"

"That's right!" Erin said, suddenly optimistic. "I mean, look at you."

Yeah, look at me. Still faking it until I make it.

Colin, my caterer, came over and sat on the other side of me, putting an end to that conversation. Thank God.

"Excuse me, ladies, but did we kick ass today, or did we kick ass?" Colin asked, helping himself to my bacon cheddar-cheese fries.

I raised my glass in a toast. "As always, the food was the star of the show," I said.

"Yeah, great job, Colin," said Erin.

"A few appetizers are no big deal," he said modestly. "But getting to work with you, now, that's the icing on the cake for me."

"Well, I appreciate that," I said. "But you know I just love you and your staff to death. You guys make my job so much easier."

Colin and I have had a great working relationship for years, and he is a terrific guy who has come through for me in a pinch, time and time again.

In fact, Colin created the menu for the wedding fiasco, and was remarkably accommodating when things changed at the last minute. He certainly did not have to repack everything and send it all over to my place at the twelfth hour, but that is what makes him one of the most phenomenal chefs in the business. One who, at that moment, was flirting with me with no shame whatsoever.

Colin kept brushing his hand across my knee, leaning in extremely close, and staring into my eyes.

I have to admit that I have always found Colin attractive. A man who cooks well has always been a serious turn-on for me, and it doesn't hurt that he reminds me of Tupac with those gorgeous lashes and soulful eyes.

"Would it be too forward of me to ask to come up to your place tonight?" Colin asked softly in my ear.

"For?" I asked, being coy.

He licked his lips like L.L., and said, "My serving platters and chafing dishes."

I blinked, having no idea what he was talking about. Then I remembered. "Oh! From the day of—okay!"

Colin grinned at me, and the look on his face read *Gotcha!* when actually, the joke was on him.

Unfortunately, my guests took most of his serving platters and chafing dishes home after the packing party, and not one person has bothered to return them. Luckily, though, I still had a few of them to give back. I think.

I left the bar a full fifteen minutes before Colin, so as not to arouse suspicions of impropriety among my co-workers. I didn't plan on any hanky-panky with Colin, but I also didn't want to provide ammunition for someone to later be able to use against me. That is exactly how careers and reputations get ruined.

"Nice place," Colin said, examining my collection of hand-carved African statues that adorn the mantle over the fireplace.

"Thanks," I said, heading into the kitchen to search for the few things of his that I still had left.

It took awhile, but all I could manage to round up were three stainless steel platters, four chafing dishes, and the Sterno units that go with them. Oh, and about eight serving tongs.

Pitiful, considering that Colin had brought over at least fifty of each.

I was in the kitchen trying to formulate just how to break the news, when Colin crept up behind me and grabbed a handful of my ass.

Before I could even utter a word in protest, he braced his hands on the counter and started smothering the back of my neck with full, sensual kisses. I made a feeble attempt to move away, but Colin had me hemmed up against the counter so I couldn't get far even if I really wanted to, which I didn't, because it felt so damn good that my knees were buckling.

I turned around to face Colin, and he took the liberty of kissing me full on the lips.

"You taste good," he said, sucking on my bottom lip. "Now I want to taste something else."

Straightforward and to the point. I liked that.

"Don't go anywhere," I said, playfully pushing him away. "I'll be right back."

I went to the bathroom and took a quick shower using J'adore Bath & Shower Gel, then followed up with the lotion and a few spritzs of perfume. I rearranged my hair into a sexy coif, and I was ready for primetime.

Back out in the living room, Colin was checking out my Henry Dixon watercolor, *Vintage Grand Canyon Railroad*. That piece is the focal point of the room and I have had many a guest stand for hours, studying the intricate design.

Colin's back was turned to me, and he was so captivated by the painting that he didn't even notice that I had tiptoed up behind him and could see that he was digging all up in his nose. I mean, his finger was knuckle-deep. After a whole lotta digging, Colin finally retrieved a huge, slimy booger. He looked at it, rolled it around on his fingertips, and flicked the thing on my hardwood floor.

I gasped, and threw up a little in my mouth.

Ugh! What the hell?

Weird little kids pick their noses, not grown-ass men!

It was like letting all the air out of a balloon. The moment passed and I was back to my senses. I no longer needed, or wanted, to be touched by Colin. The trick at that juncture was how to graciously get his ass out of my condo without him putting his filthy hands on me.

I tapped Colin on the shoulder and backed far away from him before he had the chance to touch me.

"There you are," he said, wiping booger remnants on his pants. "It's about time."

"Sorry, but there's been a change of plans, boo," I said. "My period just started."

"That's alright," he said, reaching out to embrace me. "Nothing wrong with a little cherry sauce every now and then."

Okay, double-ugh!

Colin came towards me, and I avoided his touch at all costs. I was ducking and dodging, bobbing and weaving like I was in the ring with Holyfield.

"Colin, you really need to go," I said, leading him into the kitchen where I dumped his serving platters and chafing dishes right into his arms.

"Man," he said, totally bummed out. "I didn't expect the night to end like this."

"Neither did I," I said, opening the door for him and shooing him out like an annoying fly.

Meanwhile, Colin was trying to set up a second rendezvous where he could hopefully close the deal at that point.

"Do you think we can get together some other time?" he asked with so much hope that I almost felt sorry for him.

"I'll call you," I said, waving good-bye. "You be safe now, you hear?" I quickly closed the door in his face and breathed a sigh of relief.

And to think of all the food I have eaten that he's prepared. Yuck!

Colin may be good at what he does, but I definitely have to find a new go-to caterer, ASAP.

Learning to live in the present moment is part of the path of joy.
—Sarah Ban Breathnach

SATURDAY

I stopped by Costco early this morning to stock up on Red Bull and energy bars. As I was leaving, I ran into Tammy Hopkins, someone I had to put up with during my years at Jack & Jill, which is a social club for young adults.

Tammy and I lost contact years ago, so I wasn't able to send her an invitation to the "wedding," but evidently she had heard through the grapevine about what had taken place.

"Tori, it's so good to see you out and about," she said in that annoying, condescending way of hers. "If what happened to you had happened to me, it would be years before I'd show my face in public again."

Bitch. As if anybody asked you.

If Tammy weren't eight months pregnant, I would have dotted her eye for her real good. Mainly because I never could stand her ass. She was a snarky bitch then, and she clearly hasn't changed one bit.

"Jason is just the best husband in the world, and I know for a fact that he would never cheat, or humiliate me like that," Tammy said, all self-righteous and sanctimonious.

I had heard through the same grapevine that Tammy was married to a white man, so I said sweetly, "No, Jason would never cheat on you, Tammy. White men would just as soon kill you as divorce you. I don't know . . . if I had my choice, I'd rather be cheated on than smothered in my sleep, then dumped in the Missouri River!"

While Tammy was looking like she was choking on a chicken bone, I continued pushing my shopping cart in the direction of my truck. You know? Don't start none, won't be none.

But in all seriousness, it could just be the loneliness talking, but I miss Roland. I wish he would just call me, because there is a serious talk that we need to have in order to bring some type of closure to this whole situation.

Then again, maybe it is a good thing that there's been no communication between us, because the way I feel right now, if Roland answered all my questions in the right way, I just might take him back. Even after all that has happened.

And by the way, what does it say about me that I would even entertain the thought of taking him back after everything he put me through and all that he's cost me?

If that's wrong or stupid, then I'm sorry. I just cannot turn my emotions on and off like a faucet, and pretend I don't love Roland anymore, because I do. I never stopped.

7

I don't even know why I bother going all out for Father's Day. Daddy hasn't appreciated anything I've bought him since 1998, when I bought him a set of perfectly weighted, titanium golf clubs that set me back a couple of grand.

This year was no exception.

My father turned his nose up at three silk ties from Hermes, luxury box tickets to the Royals and Yankees series, and a fifth of expensive Scotch.

"You coulda kept this mess and just wrote me a check for ten thousand dollars," he barked at me.

Here we go again.

Ten thousand dollars is the amount of money that my father reluctantly gave me towards the wedding. It is a tiny fraction of the money I'm out of, but I can see where he's coming from; ten thousand dollars is a small fortune for a General Motors assembly-line worker.

"Daddy, do you recall saying: 'I know it's not much, baby girl, but this money is my weddin' gift to you.'?" I asked.

"I sure did," said Daddy. "But, no wedding, no gift. Everybody else got their little toasters and blenders back. Why should I be any different?"

I reached in my Michael Kors bag, grabbed my checkbook, and wrote my father a check for eleven thousand dollars.

"With interest," I said, handing Daddy the check. "Are you happy now?"

"Just as long as it doesn't bounce," he said, holding the check up to the light.

Daddy can be so ornery sometimes; he gets on my last nerve.

In addition to the Father's Day gifts I had given him, we were at Benton's having a one-hundred-dollar-per-person jazz brunch that I also paid for. It obviously wasn't much to Daddy, but it was more than his son bothered to do for him.

When I asked Junior to come along and pitch in today, he did what he always does, which is to pull the broke card. Not really all that surprising, since jobs are easier for my brother to get, than to keep.

It has been two years now, since NBA draft day came and went without Junior's name being announced. Since then, he has been drifting through life like he's waiting on some special announcement giving explicit instructions on what he should do with his life.

Unfortunately, my brother's chronic brokeness causes me, as the oldest child and only daughter, to have to pick up all the slack when it comes to doing things for our parents. Birthdays, anniversaries, errands, favors—everything falls on me. I don't mind, really, but the slap in the face is that my parents rarely seem to appreciate my efforts.

For instance, we were on the twenty-third floor of the Westin Crown Center Hotel, surrounded by over-the-top elegance, our own personal wait staff, and all the gourmet food you could eat, but my father still managed to find something to complain about. First of all, the restaurant was too bourgeois for Daddy's taste. He was not appreciative of the fact that there were servers standing over his shoulder, watching him eat, and anticipating his every need. As soon as any of us took a sip of raspberry iced tea, our glasses were promptly refilled back to the brim—something he loudly complained was pretentious and unnecessary.

And he hated the food. Being from the South, Daddy's taste buds are only accustomed to fried foods, collard greens, and pork fat. Oh, and barbeque. Daddy has never met a piece of smoked meat that he didn't like.

Mama, on the other hand, has a taste for the finer things in life, so she was enjoying every minute of it. Hell, caviar, lobster tails, and mimosas are the least of what the reigning vice-president of the local Ladies League deserves.

"So daughter," Mama said, daintily cutting a piece of beef Wellington, "are you seeing anybody right now?"

My so-called date with Sean was a joke, and Colin wasn't worth mentioning, so I said, "This soon after what I've been through?"

"Baby girl," Daddy said, "you've got to dust yourself off and get back out there. Haven't I always told you that one monkey ain't never stopped no show?"

"And I know that's right!" Mama said. "Now baby, what you need is a good man like Ethel Johnson's son, Lamar."

"Mama, please . . ." I sighed, looking out the window and suddenly becoming very interested in the goings-on over at the Liberty Memorial.

Ever since I turned eighteen, my mother has been trying to marry me off to one of the sons of the women in her social club. Which one doesn't seem to matter to her, just as long as his parents are Masons.

That's what happens in these clubs. There is a lot of intermingling of the families going on, with the parents of single daughters trying to marry them off to their friends' single sons.

Regrettably, I have learned the hard way that there is always something drastically wrong with any guy my mother tries to set me up with—usually a socially inept geek who still lives in his parents' basement.

Norman Harper was the son of Mama's bridge partner, Ida Mae.

I was lonely and in between boyfriends at the time, so in a moment of weakness, I agreed to go out with Norman.

When we met at Houston's Restaurant, I was impressed with how impeccably well-dressed Norman was. Then I found out he was a mortician down at Thatcher's Funeral Home, and that one of his corpses probably had more personality than he did. He was thirty-one, but looked fifty. His skin had this gray, waxy look to it, which made me wonder if he was doing a little something extra with the embalming fluid.

No. Norman was definitely not normal. In fact, I'm convinced that he was one chromosome away from being retarded, because he acted like he was on a thirty-second delay, or something. Seriously, I would ask him a question and it would take him around thirty seconds to formulate an answer; and even then, it wasn't always a coherent one.

After dinner, Norman and I went to listen to some live jazz. The music was good, but the company was unbelievably boring. So much so, that I fell asleep on his tired ass.

At the end of the night I told Norman I would talk to him soon, which loosely translated into *Have a nice life!*

I have heard it said that looking for love is the best way *not* to find it, which stands to reason since not one setup has ever worked out for me. I know, because I did a careful analysis of my dating history last night, and concluded that every meaningful relationship in my past came about serendipitously. It was not a fix-up, a blind date, the Internet, a nightclub, or a dating service. It was always a chance encounter that occurred during the course of taking care of my usual, everyday business: scouting venue locations, getting my morning caramel macchiato at Starbucks, or while standing in line at the bank or the grocery store.

In light of this concrete evidence, I'm going to send out an e-mail to Yvette, Cookie, Nadia, Mama, and about a hundred other people who all have someone that they're just dying for me to meet.

Please cease and desist all efforts to hook me up. I'm sure the guy you have in mind for me is as great as you say he is, but from here on out, I'll find my own man.

Or, hopefully, he will find me.

8

I finally decided to start doing something about the excessive pounds that have been rapidly piling up on my ass and thighs, the clear result of late dinners, midnight munching, and all those wine and cheese parties my neighbors like to throw every other week.

As soon as I got home from work this evening, I went and jogged for an hour at the fountain park near my building.

Afterwards, I walked over to Barnes & Noble to get myself an ice-cold lemonade, and to find something educational for my nephew's upcoming third birthday.

Junior's son, Trey, has tons of DVDs and video games, but not one book, which is a damn shame.

So there I was, sitting at one of those wooden tables, leafing through a stack of children's books. I have heard that bookstores are the new nightclub, but since I was dressed way down in workout gear, a sun visor, and no makeup, purposely attracting men was clearly *not* why I was there.

Yet, there he was, staring down at me with soulful brown eyes set in an attractive chestnut-brown face.

"Oh, Bother! Someone Didn't Say Thank You," he said, reading the title of the Winnie the Pooh book sitting on the table. "Wow! Not only is she beautiful, but she's an intellectual too."

Okay, who is this fool, and what is his angle? I thought, as this complete stranger took it upon himself to move my lemonade aside and sit his ass down in the chair right beside me.

"Ha, funny!" I said. "Actually, these aren't for me. I'm trying to find something for my nephew."

"Okay, cool," he said, trying to sound suave and sexy. "So what is your nephew's auntie's name?"

"No, no. Not so fast, slick," I said. "You came over here and made yourself comfortable, so I think it's only right that you tell me who you are, first."

"Oh, I like that!" he said with excitement. "Pretty, sassy and bold. Now I know I'm gonna fall in love with you!"

"Love? Ha! No way that's gonna happen," I said.

"And why not?" he asked, as if I had seriously broken his heart.

"Because you still haven't told me your name."

He flashed a wide smile, and chuckled. "You're a handful. I can see that already."

"So what's your name?"

"Anthony Matthews," he said, offering a handshake. "It's a pleasure to make your acquaintance."

Looking him over, I surmised that his style is shabby bohemian chic. He was sporting a plaid, thrift-store jacket over a green Jimi Hendrix T-shirt, baggy jeans, black-and-white converses, and the hair was an interesting combination of dreadlocks and a short Afro. Definitely a free spirit.

See? There's that serendipity I was talking about.

Cease to inquire what the future has in store, and take as a gift whatever the day brings forth. —Horace

WEDNESDAY

It has been a little over a week since I met Anthony, or Ant, as I call him, and surprisingly, we have really hit it off. He is a cool, neo-soul type brother who seems like he has a good head on his shoulders.

The two of us have talked on the phone every day since we met, and what I have learned is that he is a thirty-six-year-old aspiring comic. Ant was living down in Atlanta where he was just starting to make a name for himself, when his mom became gravely ill. Being an only child with no one else to care for his mom, Ant put his comedy career on hold and came back home to care for his sick mother.

I like him, I think. And I say, "I think" because Ant is always "on," which isn't a bad thing because he keeps me cracking up with his zany sense of humor. But at the same time, it is hard to tell if I am getting doses of his real personality or if what he's putting out there is all just an act.

Whatever the case, we have been getting along great, and I am really looking forward to our first date tonight.

Anthony said his Jaguar was in the shop getting new shocks and brake pads, so I agreed to pick him up at his mother's house, which turned out to be nestled in a quiet middle-class neighborhood not far from Swope Park.

Anthony came out of the house within a few seconds of me pulling into the driveway, and I breathed a sigh of relief that he didn't try to drag me inside to meet his mama.

"Damn, you look good!" he said, settling in on the passenger's side of my truck.

My look for the night was sexy-casual, with a black Zac Posen minidress and four-inch Gucci stilettos.

"You look pretty spiffy yourself," I said, noting that Ant was dressed in a slightly different variation of the bohemian chic ensemble he had worn when I first met him at Barnes & Noble. This time it was a tweed, thrift-store jacket over an orange Bob Marley T-shirt, baggy jeans, and orange Converse high-top sneakers.

Our date consisted of checking out Sheryl Underwood's standup routine at Stanford & Sons Comedy Club in Westport.

The comedy show was hilarious! Seeing Sheryl do her thing seemed to energize Anthony to the point where he could hardly wait to get home to write some jokes, and fine-tune his act.

After watching Sheryl act a fool, Anthony suggested we drop in on some friends of his who were having a little get-together.

"But I thought we were going to get something to eat," I reminded him, hoping he couldn't hear my stomach growling.

"We are," he said, playfully kissing me on the cheek. "Just as soon as we leave the spot."

Instead of giving me the address to where the party was, Ant just said, "Make a right here," and "Turn left up at the light."

That went on until we were East of Troost Avenue, and right in the heart of one of the most dangerous hoods in the city.

"This doesn't look like much of a party," I said, as Anthony instructed me to stop in front of a dilapidated house that looked like it would collapse if the wind blew too hard.

"Trust me, it's on and poppin'!" he said excitedly, then jumped out of the truck and ran around to open my door for me.

As I stepped out of my vehicle, it felt as if we had been thrust into Michael Jackson's "Thriller" video, with all these scary, zombie-looking folks coming out of nowhere.

I reluctantly followed Anthony inside, where the condition of the house was just as raggedy as the outside.

My first thought when we walked in that house was that I hoped nobody actually *lived* there because it was funky with a capital FUNK. The smell of ass, feet, mildew, and stale cigarette smoke was so powerful, it almost knocked me to my knees.

And there wasn't much of a party going on, either.

No music, food, or even a sip of Chardonnay to be found anywhere. Just six mean-looking cats playing Madden football on a big-screen television.

"Tori, this is everybody," Anthony said. "Everybody, meet Tori, my new woman."

His new woman? This was definitely news to me.

The fellas threw their chins up at me, and said "whassup?" through halos of ganja smoke.

"Have a seat," Anthony said to me before disappearing into a back bedroom, leaving me to fend for myself.

I looked around the small, shabby house, and the only place to sit was a worn-out recliner that smelled as if somebody had peed on it. No thanks.

Loud, animated voices were coming from the kitchen, so I wandered in, and was amazed at what I saw.

It was like a workshop. Several guys were sitting at the kitchen table using little digital scales to weigh, then bag up their product.

No. He. Didn't.

I could not believe that my date with Anthony had segued into a drug run, which at any given moment could turn into a drug raid.

The only other time I had been in a drug house was when I rolled with my date on prom night to get a dime bag of weed.

Now, here I was, a professional woman right in the middle of crack alley after dark.

It would have been just my luck for the cops to kick the door in at any minute.

Now it all made sense.

Laughing when nothing was funny, the red glassy eyes, frozen smile and overabundance of energy that kept him practically ricocheting off the walls—Anthony was always "on," because his junkie ass was always *high*.

I don't smoke cigarettes, but I said, "Damn! I left my Newports in the car," to no one in particular, and calmly walked out onto the porch where I took a much-needed breath of fresh air.

With keys in hand, I sprinted to my truck and burned out of there so fast that I left tire marks.

I was so furious I couldn't see straight. I decided that the best thing for me to do was to go home and decompress, then afterwards, maybe go to City Tavern for a late dinner.

I was waiting for the elevator to take me up to my condo on the ninth floor, still fuming about the Anthony situation, when a male voice said, "Whatever happened isn't worth having that pretty face of yours all scrunched up like that."

I whipped my head around like the girl in *The Exorcist* and had the evil eye ready for whoever just said that, but I softened when I saw that it was Nelson, the caramel-dipped cutie who lived directly across the hall from me.

"Oh, hey, Nelson," I said, calming down a bit. "You know, come to think of it he's not worth it. At all!"

"Uh oh. He? Why is it always a 'he' who's responsible for pissing you women off?"

"Good question! Maybe you can enlighten me."

Nelson leaned in front of me to jab at the up button, you know, to try to hurry the elevator along, and damn he smelled good! Once I got a whiff of his Issey Miyake cologne, I immediately started throbbing down in the panty region. That had been happening to me a lot lately.

I had gone without sex for so long, it didn't take much to get my juices flowing. It had been three months since I had been properly screwed, and three months is an eternity when you are used to having in-house dick, and getting it whenever you want it.

"I don't know," he said. "I think males get a bum rap the majority of the time because some of you women are just impossible to please. So, it's like we're damned if we do, and damned if we don't."

"That may be true," I said. "But since when did being sane and drug free become too much to ask for?"

Nelson laughed, and I noticed for the first time that he had this sliver of a dimple on the apple of his right cheek, and his teeth were so perfect it made me wonder if they were all his.

"You're right," Nelson chuckled at me. "Those things are never too much to ask for. Especially sanity."

Ding! The slow-ass elevator finally arrived.

Nelson and I got on, and we inadvertently pushed the 9 key at the same time.

The elevator doors closed and I leaned back against the mirrored wall, feeling my body relax for the first time since I got rid of Anthony's tweaking ass.

"So, just what did this idiot do that's got you so upset?" Nelson asked, shifting the grocery bag he was carrying to his other arm.

"He had me drive him to a crack house," I said.

"Oooh," Nelson winced. "Not a good look."

"I know, right? And what makes it so bad is that I was kinda digging this guy, too," I said. "Quirks and all."

"Well, that's the way it goes sometimes," Nelson sympathized. "But hey, when it comes to dating, men get the short end of the stick just as often as women do."

"Now, I have a really hard time believing that," I said.

"No, it's true!" he insisted. "Dating nightmares are a two-way street. Unfortunately, I've had some recent dates with women who didn't have any home training, either."

"Umph!" I said, genuinely feeling his pain. "It's hard out there, ain't it?"

"Most definitely," he said wearily, as the elevator delivered us to the ninth floor.

We stepped off the elevator and walked together in the same direction until we reached our respective doors.

I paused to sniff the air, and breathed in an aroma so delicious it made my stomach rumble. "Somebody's cooking something that smells good."

"That would be me," Nelson said, opening his door, causing the mouthwatering aroma to escape and assault my senses even more. "I was in the middle of putting dinner together when I realized I was out of a few things."

"Well, your dinner smells divine, that's for sure," I said, wondering if I had any turkey salami left to make myself a sandwich.

I put my key in the lock, and was just about to say goodbye when Nelson said, "Tori, listen. I'm sorry you had such a lousy evening, but on behalf of the entire male species, I would like to make it up to you."

"Really? And how do you plan on doing that?"

"Come have dinner with me," he said, his smile reminding me of sunshine breaking through on a cloudy day. "It's nothing fancy but I would really like to have your company."

As Nelson talked, an image of what he could possibly do to me with those smooth, luscious lips of his, popped into my head.

Bad Tori! I reprimanded myself. *Baaad Tori!*

As horny as I was, I could not entertain thoughts of sexing Nelson because first of all, I have a "Don't shit where you eat" rule, which means neighbors and co-workers are strictly off-limits.

This rule goes all the way back to college days, when I leased my first off-campus apartment.

Shane and I had met at the mailbox bank of our apartment complex. He was a six-foot-four premed major who introduced me to blunts, and taught me the art of French kissing. We would get loaded on Thai weed and spend afternoons in either his or my apartment, philosophizing on life, and making love. On one of these occasions, Shane's *other* girlfriend, whom he neglected to tell me about, showed up on his doorstep unannounced.

Long story short: there was an explosive confrontation, the cops came, and restraining orders were issued all around.

When it was all said and done, Shane ended up choosing the other girl over me, and I had to endure constantly running into the two of them, both at school and around the complex where I lived.

Hence, the DSWYE rule was implemented and has been in effect ever since.

"So, how about it?" Nelson asked, bringing me out of my reverie. "Will you come have dinner with me?"

He extended an arm to welcome me into his condo, and the smells of basil, oregano, and garlic rushed to greet me as I stepped inside.

I am nosy by nature, so I tried not to be a bad guest and do an overt inspection of the place, but overall, nice digs. The living room was surprisingly sparse, but what furniture Nelson did have was contemporary with very clean lines.

He had the usual hi-tech electronic gizmos that men love so much, and there was a black Brunswick pool table in the far corner of the room, which I thought was a nice touch.

The entire wall adjacent to the fireplace had been converted into a floor-to-ceiling bookcase, and the shelves were crammed with mostly hardcover classics by literary greats such as James Baldwin, Gloria Naylor, and Paule Marshall.

The infamous *Sugar Shack* painting by Ernie Barnes hung over the fireplace, which coincidentally is the same spot where *Vintage Grand Canyon Railroad* hangs in my condo.

"These are the most beautiful plants I've ever seen outside of a nursery," I said, fingering a Boston fern whose lush leaves seemed to go on forever. The fern was one of several houseplants that were all so healthy that there wasn't one brown spot on any of them.

"Thanks, but I can't take full credit," Nelson said, setting the grocery bag down on the island counter. "Those were Kara's babies, and her secret was Miracle-Gro mixed with used coffee grounds."

Kara was Nelson's deceased wife. The two of them had only lived in our building for a few months before her appendix suddenly burst, and she died in his arms.

That was almost two years ago.

A pretty, light-skinned woman with freckles and a wild

bushel of naturally curly hair, Kara was twenty-eight when she died. We only spoke in passing, but I knew her well enough to know that she was a sweet, spirited woman who loved her career as a pediatric nurse, and that she and Nelson seemed to be perfectly matched.

I followed Nelson into the kitchen where the first thing I noticed was a full set of those Japanese chef's knives that cost a minimum of one-hundred dollars each.

"You have to be a pretty serious cook to have even *one* of these bad boys," I said, examining a knife so big and sharp I'd be scared to use it, for fear I would lose one of my fingers. "Let alone a full set."

"I do a little sumthin' sumthin' every now and then," Nelson said, peeking into the oven to check on dinner.

"Hmmm . . ." I said, inhaling deeply. "Italian, right?"

"You win the prize!" Nelson looked me over with newfound respect. "I didn't know you were a foodie."

"Oh, from way back," I said with an air of casual nonchalance. It wasn't a complete lie. I do love food, but I am nowhere near as hardcore with it as are some of the self-proclaimed foodies who travel across the country just to eat the food of a particular high-end chef, or to dine in certain five-star restaurants. "So what's on the menu?" I asked.

"Oh, just a little Eggplant Parmesan, bruschetta, and Caesar salad," Nelson said, pouring two glasses of Pinot Noir and handing one to me. "How does that sound?"

"Sounds like my kinda meal," I said, taking a seat at the granite-topped island. "Italian food just so happens to be my favorite."

"Good!" Nelson washed his hands and dried them with a paper towel. "Because the whole point is to show you that we aren't all bad."

"Well I already know that," I said, taking a sip of wine. "My problem is that the good ones are so few and far between."

"Right . . . But like I said, that goes for *both* sexes," Nelson reiterated.

"Do you realize that's the second time you've made that point?" I asked.

"Yep! and that's because I just can't stress it enough, you know?" He topped thick slices of toasted Italian bread with a mixture of diced tomatoes and Italian herbs. "I just started dating again a few months ago, and man! I've met so many undesirable women that I'm starting to think dating isn't worth the effort."

Wow. If I could only choose one word to describe the edge in his voice, I would definitely have to go with "bitter."

"So how did you meet all these trifling women? Did you pick them or did they pick you?" I asked.

"Neither, actually," he said, starting to assemble the salad. "They were all setups by well-meaning people who insisted it was time for me to stop mourning, and get out there and start dating again."

"Well, I can definitely relate," I said. "But you know, for some reason I just can't picture you with anyone besides Kara."

The expression that came over Nelson's face was so pained, that I instantly regretted having said it.

"Well, every bad dating experience makes me miss her that much more, that's for sure," he sighed. "But, like my grandmother keeps telling me: 'You're gonna bounce back from this and get married again, baby, but it ain't gonna happen overnight. You just got to take the time to sort the good ones from the rotten ones.' "

Sounds like the truth, but hell, who has that kind of time?

It took me eleven years of my adult life to find Roland. So if love only comes around once every eleven years for me, then the search for Mr. Wonderful is such a needle in a haystack proposition that I had better put on some comfortable shoes, because it's gonna be a long-ass journey.

Over dinner, which was scrumptious by the way, the conversation was pleasant and flowed easily without too many awkward silences.

Nelson turned out to be a good listener, and seemed genuinely interested in what I had to say. We talked about food, music, books, and our favorite films (mine: *Claudine*, his: *Car Wash*).

I told him about my career, and he in turn filled me in on the work he does as food writer and restaurant critic for the *Kansas City Tribune*.

"You get paid good money to eat well, and to travel?" I asked, actually a little jealous. "I'm in the wrong line of business!"

"It's not a big deal," he said. "Everyone old enough to cut their own meat is a food critic."

"Maybe, but everyone doesn't get to fly first-class to Spain to cover their annual wine and cheese festival."

Being the humble guy that he is, Nelson shrugged off my admiration, and opened up another bottle of red wine. "You know, I heard what happened with Roland," he said, pouring more wine for himself. "I'm sorry things didn't work out for you two."

"Do *not* be sorry!" I replied cheerfully. "Everything happens for a reason, right?"

I don't really believe that shit, but at least it sounded good.

"Yeah, I guess it does . . ." Nelson's voice cracked, and it sounded as if he was on the verge of tears.

It was the second awkward moment of the night.

The only thing I could think to do to break the tension, was to raise my glass in a toast. "Hats off to the chef! And to the best home-cooked meal I've had in a really long time."

Nelson beamed, looking relieved that I changed the subject. "I'm glad you enjoyed it," he said.

"Did your mom teach you how to cook like that?" I asked.

"Nah, actually I kinda taught her. No disrespect, but my mom can't cook worth a damn." He laughed. "I started cooking for myself at about nine years old because she was always burning stuff up or making it too sticky, too salty, too bland, or too dry. You remember that song "Rapper's Delight?" Well my mother was the inspiration for that song."

I laughed out loud recalling the lyrics to the song where a mother ruins dinner by serving soggy macaroni, mushy peas, and chicken that tasted like wood.

"Do you cook?" Nelson asked.

"Actually, I am a better baker than I am a cook, but I do have a few specialties," I said.

"Like what? And please do not say spaghetti."

"What's wrong with spaghetti?" I asked.

"Nothing really, but everyone swears they make the best spaghetti in the world, and most of the time that's far from the truth."

"Well I'm not going to lie," I said. "Mine is bomb-a-licious! Okay?"

The look on Nelson's face indicated that he didn't believe me. "What do you put in yours?" he asked.

"A mixture of veal, Italian sausage, and ground chuck. Mix that with some portobello mushrooms, red bell pepper, and I make my own marinara sauce—from scratch."

"Not bad . . . You might be on to something," he teased, hating on my skills. "What's another one of your specialties?"

"Hmm . . ." I said, thinking it over for a minute. "Oh! I make a *banging* seafood enchilada. I serve it up with Spanish rice, *pico de gallo*, refried beans, corn cake—all that."

"Sounds like you really know your way around the kitchen," said Nelson, finally giving me my props. "What else can you do well?"

I was pretty buzzed from the wine, and in my state of mind, *What else can you do well?* sounded like a loaded question to me.

"I can show you better than I can tell you," I replied, and it wasn't too suggestive, but just enough to give him the option to take it however he chose to.

"Yeah," Nelson said, seeming to take my hint. "You're definitely gonna have to show me one of these days."

For dessert, Nelson served individual mango-lime tarts that he insisted he made from scratch. I didn't believe him for a second. Those things were so good; I was convinced that he bought them from one of the high-end restaurants in the area.

Once we finished eating, I helped clear the table and load the dishwasher despite Nelson's protests about me being a guest.

I like Nelson's style. Not only is he well-read and well-traveled, but the brother just lives extremely well, period. Everything he does is done with a high degree of style and sophistication, and he knows a helluva lot about food.

Kara was extremely blessed, that's for sure.

9

"High-rise luxury living within a renovated, historically preserved building" is the line the realtor used to sell us on the place, but Regency Park Place has actually turned out to be more like Peyton Place at worst, and Melrose Place at best.

Things can get wild around here sometimes, but I still love living here despite the drama that can come with a building full of young, hot-blooded professionals with plenty of disposable income.

What I pay to live here is pricey compared to what you can get for the money elsewhere in the city. But here at Regency Park Place, $400,000 will get you an underground parking garage, twenty-four-hour security, a state-of-the-art fitness center, indoor swimming pool, Jacuzzi, sauna, unobstructed bird's-eye views of the cityscape, and of course, this gorgeous rooftop deck that gets plenty of use for sunbathing, cookouts, and private parties.

"I didn't know Cuba Gooding Jr. married Tonya Harding," I said, flipping through the latest *In Style* magazine.

"He didn't," Nadia said, slathering suntan lotion on her arms and legs, being careful not to get any on the lounge chair, or her teensy-weensy two-piece Juicy Couture bathing suit.

"So who's this frumpy, cross-eyed white chick Cuba's all hugged up with?"

Nadia laughed. "Girl, that's his wife! They've been together since like fifth grade or something like that."

"Humph!" I took a closer look at the picture. "Well that explains a whole lot, doesn't it?"

Nadia and I were on the rooftop terrace of our condominium building, sharing a bottle of peach-flavored wine. The stuff is cheap as hell, but it actually doesn't taste too bad.

Nadia was living upstairs in 10E when I first moved into the building. I'd gone down to the fitness room one day to get my workout on, and there was this tall, pretty, multiethnic chic who was actually smiling while she went hard on the StairMaster. I don't know about you, but to me it was an indication that she had to be an extreme nutcase. I mean, really. How many folks actually enjoy strenuous exercise? So, I was all set to keep my distance from this kooky broad, but Nadia ended up disarming me with her bubbly, down-to-earth personality. It turns out that she is a bit on the nutty side, but then again, so am I.

We instantly hit it off, and it wasn't long before we were as close as sisters.

"That's all fine and good," Nadia said after I told her about my dinner with Nelson last night. "But what I really want to know is did you get some?"

"Is your mind always in the gutter?" I asked.

Nadia shrugged. "Pretty much."

"Well, sorry to disappoint you but Nelson was just being neighborly when he invited me over for dinner, and it wasn't even about trying to hook up or anything like that. He just genuinely wanted to get to know me."

"So let me get this straight: he's a writer who loves to cook, he reads, he's sweet, sensitive, and he didn't try to hit that? Girl, that brother is gay!"

"Now, there you go. Why can't a guy have all those qualities without his sexuality being questioned?" I asked. "Besides, the man happens to be a widower."

"*And*? I know plenty of gay guys who happened to be married to women."

"Nelson is not gay, okay? Trust me on that."

"Girl, I'm just messing with you," Nadia said. "So did y'all express interest in dating each other, or what?"

"Not hardly!" I scoffed at the very idea.

"Why the hell not? And please don't tell me it's about that tired ass 'don't shit where you eat rule' again."

"That's the main reason," I said. "But even if I did decide to violate my rule, Nelson has way more baggage than I'm ready to deal with at this point."

"And you don't?" Nadia said, raising an eyebrow at me.

"Please! You don't see me getting emotional and teary-eyed at the mere mention of Roland's name."

"No, but is there any reason in particular why you're sporting that ring?" Nadia asked, referring to the five-karat Cartier bridal set that I wore on my left ring finger.

"Oh, this little old thing?" I said, admiring the way the princess-cut diamond caught the sunlight and sparkled brilliantly. "It has no special meaning to me other than the fact that it's beautiful, and it really sets off my French manicure, don't you think?" I wiggled my fingers in Nadia's face so that she could get the full effect.

"Yeah, that sucker is pretty tight," Nadia said with a trace of envy in her voice. "But why would you even want to wear the ring of a man who disrespected you the way Roland did? *Knowing* what it represents."

Nadia can be a little slow at times, so I enunciated to make sure she got it this time. "This ring has no sentimental value to me anymore. It is just a ring! I put it on earlier just to look at and admire, I got busy cleaning, and just forgot to take it off."

"Humph! Well, the way I see it, there are at least three other fingers you could be wearing that thing on. Apparently, Nelson isn't the only one still emotionally attached to the past."

I sighed, wondering how in the hell I had been sucked into discussing any of this stuff in the first place. My intention when I came up here was to read *A Piece of Cake* by Cupcake Brown, and to relax in peace.

But just as I had been settling in, here came Nadia, the Wendy Williams of our building with a stack of fashion magazines, a mini-cooler full of Arbor Mist—oh, and as always, plenty of gossip about the neighbors.

"Oh!" Nadia said excitedly. "You'll never guess who that tramp in 1B is cavorting around with now."

"Who?" I asked, shifting my weight in the chaise to keep my butt from falling asleep.

"Eddie!"

I peered over the top of my Dior sunglasses to get a better look at Nadia. "You mean, the old-ass security guard that works around here?"

Nadia nodded adamantly. "Girl, yes! I was on my way down to the sauna when that old man came creeping out of 1B, zipping up his fly and sweating so bad I thought he was having a heat stroke."

Apartment 1B, also known as Ursula Jeffries, is one of the many single women in our building, and someone who Nadia is skeptical of because of the steady stream of male visitors in and out of her condo.

Talk about the pot calling the kettle black.

Ursula does have an unusually high amount of male company, but as far as being a real-live ho? I doubt it. More than likely, Nadia is just being catty.

All either of us knows about Ursula for sure, is that she

works for the *Kansas City Tribune*, and is what the old folks call "some-timey." Sometimes she will speak to you, and sometimes she won't.

"Maybe she's doing some kind of research," I said, trying to give Ursula the benefit of the doubt.

"Yeah, she's doing some *research* all right, and I hope she catches the crabs with her nasty ass!" Nadia said. "Speaking of nasty . . ."

Nadia's mood soured as Mitchell from 4C walked out, giving the guided tour to a slutty-looking redhead who wore so much makeup she resembled Bozo the Clown.

Fortunately, I don't know all of the gory details, but Nadia and Mitchell dated briefly last summer, which has now resulted in the two of them not being able to occupy the same space at the same time and be civil about it.

"Don't look now, but the cat done drug in something mangy again!" Nadia purposely said that loud enough for Mitchell to hear, which he did, because he immediately came over flashing that lopsided grin he's convinced is so irresistible to women.

Mitchell is one of our building's most eligible bachelors, and I'm not exaggerating when I say that he has boned just about every woman in the building, except for me. Even some of the married ones.

"Tori, you look as gorgeous as always," Mitchell said.

"Thank you," I said, graciously allowing him to kiss the back of my hand. "Looks like you have a nice tan going on there."

"Tina and I vacationed in Cabo last weekend, and we had tons of fun in the sun, didn't we, baby?"

Tina/Bozo giggled, as she and Mitchell proceeded to try and swallow each other's tongues.

I shielded my eyes from the disgusting public display of affection, while Nadia made loud retching noises as if she were vomiting.

"Still haven't gotten a handle on that little drinking problem of yours, huh?" Mitchell asked Nadia, finally acknowledging her presence.

"You know, I gotta give it to you, Mitch," Nadia replied, looking Tina over with a frown. "You are the only man I know who has this endless supply of blow-up dolls. Cheap ones at that."

"Tori, do me a favor and tell your friend to get over it." Mitchell said, then steered Tina back into the building.

"See," I told Nadia. "That's a perfect example of why you should never shit where you eat."

"Believe me," she said. "That's a hard and fast rule for me, from now on."

Twenty minutes later I was once again, deeply engrossed in *A Piece of Cake*.

"I kicked Byron's ass to the curb the other day," Nadia announced out of the blue. I thought she had fallen asleep while sunbathing, but apparently not.

I kept reading, pretending not to have heard her.

Nadia and my nerves do not always mix. She can be such high drama that you have to be in a certain mood to deal with her, because she will wear you out if you let her.

"I kicked Byron's ass to the curb!" Nadia said again, only this time she shouted close to my ear, making it impossible for me to continue ignoring her.

"What for this time?" I sighed, snapping the book shut.

"Because I warned him that if he didn't show up for my Grandma Lilly's seventy-eighth birthday party, then the two of us are finished. He didn't show up, so that's it. Finito!"

I would be applauding Nadia if Byron were a horrible bastard who treated her badly, but I like him. I think Byron is good for Nadia because he puts her on a pedestal and seems to have mastered the most important factor in dealing with her, which is giving her whatever she wants, and doing it with a smile.

"Nadia, the man's job transferred him to San Diego," I said. "You can't expect him to drop everything and come to Kansas City just to satisfy one of your whims."

"No, no, mami. This was not a whim. I told Byron about this months ago and he knew that this was something that meant a lot to me. Besides, he makes special trips to Kansas City whenever he wants to fuck me!"

The words "fuck me!" seemed to bounce off nearby buildings and echo throughout the entire city just as Jan and George, the conservative Republican couple from 4E, came out for a dip in the pool. The appalled expression on their faces was priceless.

Nadia is a mess, straight up and down. If she knew better, she would do better, but sadly she is thirty-one years old and still under the misguided delusion that every man she meets should be thrilled to have the opportunity to spoil her rotten. If not, she dumps the poor chump and moves on to the next unsuspecting sugar daddy, which besides being a massage therapist is how she was able to buy her condo in the first place.

I tell Nadia all the time that she suffers from a chronic case of the "next best thing syndrome." You know you are afflicted with NBTS when you're involved with someone, and no matter how much of a good thing you have going on, you are still constantly looking around for someone even better to come along.

Men suffer from it because music videos and Jermaine Dupree being with Janet Jackson has given them all hope that no woman is unobtainable. No matter what they themselves may be lacking in the looks department, they too, do not have to settle for anything less than their idea of perfection.

When it comes to women and NBTS, personally I think romance novels are responsible for the unrealistic notions of love and romance that some of us have.

I am really thinking about starting a petition to have those things come with warning labels, like cigarettes.

WARNING! There is a direct link between romance novels and NBTS. If you are not extremely careful, regular consumption may greatly impair your ability to distinguish fantasy from reality.

"So who's next in line?" I asked Nadia. "Knowing you, you already have another victim scoped out, and lined up."

"T.C." said she, with a glint of mischief in her eyes.

"As in Terrell Cunningham?" I asked in disbelief.

"That's the one," Nadia confirmed with smug smile.

Terrell "T.C." Cunningham is the Kansas City Chiefs' premier wide receiver, a six-foot-three-inch bi-racial cutie with a lean, perfectly muscular body, and the smoldering good looks of a young Rick Fox.

Several months ago, I headed up the Houghton Foundation's annual celebrity charity event, which benefits local disadvantaged kids. Nadia doesn't even like kids, but she literally begged me to put her on the guest list so that she could come rub elbows with some of the city's wealthiest bachelors.

I gave in against my better judgment, and Nadia showed up wearing five-inch spiked heels, and a risqué little Mariah Carey–type number that accentuated her ass and cleavage so much, mothers were literally covering the eyes of their children when she walked past.

Nadia's tactic worked, though, because guys swarmed around her that night like flies to sheep shit. She ended up giving her phone number to Terrell, who coincidentally had just signed a seven-year contract with the Chiefs, as well as a lucrative endorsement deal with Reebok.

"It was months ago when you met him," I said. "Why is he just now calling?"

"That's just how athletes are." Nadia shrugged dismissively.

"They travel all over during the off season, and come back to town right before training camp is about to start."

"I don't know, Nadia. If he was feeling you all that much, it wouldn't have taken him months to touch base with you."

"Will you stop knocking my hustle and just be happy for me? Terrell could really turn out to be the one."

"Poor T.C." I shook my head, genuinely sympathetic. "That boy has no idea that he's about to be eaten alive, does he?"

"Not a clue!" Nadia said, laughing wickedly.

I shook my head and sighed.

As I listened to Nadia lay out her sinister plans for Terrell, I wondered how it was possible that Oprah has been on the air for over twenty years, yet there are women in the world who are still this damn stupid.

The present moment is the only moment available to us, and it is the door to all moments. —Thich Nhat Hanh

SATURDAY

Back in my condo, I slip the ring off my left hand and stare at it for the longest time, before placing it back into my jewelry box under lock and key.

I wish I had the nerve to do something dramatic with it like they do in the movies.

I thought about sending it back to Roland along with a dead rat and a dozen black roses full of thorns. Tossing it out my car window while on the freeway, grinding it up in the garbage disposal, and even flushing it down the toilet.

But hell, five karats is five karats, and I am just not that courageous. Or that crazy.

10

Okay, I have to confess. I feel like a hypocrite right now, because I did not tell Nadia the whole story of what happened last night over at Nelson's place.

The version I gave her ended with dessert, and then me going home.

But what really happened was this:

Nelson and I polished off the mango tarts, plus that second bottle of wine.

After the Pinot was gone, we mutually decided that it was much too early for the night to end, so I ran my happy ass over to my place, and grabbed a bottle of champagne.

You know, ball till you fall, and all that.

We were in his living room, and I was admiring that nice, big Brunswick pool table of his, when he asked, "Do you play?"

"Not really," I said like a helpless damsel. "I've tried to learn, but I never could quite get the hang of it."

I was lying my ass off.

Actually, I'm pretty good at shooting pool. My father started teaching me the game when I was nine years old, and I've been perfecting my skills ever since.

"Are you up for a quick lesson?" Nelson asked.

"Sure . . ."

So I let him coach me as if I had never picked up a pool stick in my life.

I had mixed feelings about that at first, though, because I constantly tell my goddaughter Alicia that women should never dumb down for any man, but the reality is that there are a certain amount of innocent little games that have to be played in order to sway a man.

And make no mistake about it, I wanted that man.

Who wouldn't? Nelson is a tall, modern-day Adonis with golden brown skin, boyishly handsome looks, and the body of life.

DSWYE rule, be damned!

So there I was, flouncing around the pool table, trying to be as coy and cute as a drunk, horny woman could possibly be.

I chalked up the pool stick Nelson gave me, and positioned my body over the table just the way he showed me.

"That's it," he said. "Now lean into it a little more."

I complied, making sure to stick my ass way out where he could get a real good look at it.

"Good!" Nelson said, excited that I was catching on so fast. "Now, when you get the white ball lined up exactly where you want it, hit it as hard as you can."

I followed Nelson's instructions and broke the balls apart with a loud *Thwack!* Balls went flying across the table, dropping in pockets one after the other until only three balls remained on the table.

"Hot damn!" I said, trying to act surprised.

Impressed with my "natural" ability, Nelson pumped his fist like Tiger Woods, then gave me a high five. "Way to go, Tori!"

"I've got a very good teacher," I said, leaning across the table again with my ass in the air.

I was concentrating on dropping the six ball in the far left corner pocket when I felt a hardness brushing up against my backside, which I knew right away was definitely not his pool stick.

Nelson's obvious arousal gave me the courage to initiate a kiss. It was just a peck on the lips at first, but it quickly turned into a deeply passionate tongue-wrestling match that sent an overwhelming surge of throbbing heat straight down to my clitoris.

His lips were soft, and the kiss was good, but after a couple of minutes, I could sense Nelson's hesitation.

"What's wrong?" I murmured breathlessly.

"I can't do this," he said, backing away from me, looking flustered. "I'm celibate."

"What?" I blinked rapidly several times, looking at him as if he'd said he had a third testicle.

He repeated "I'm celibate" with no real conviction, so I didn't buy it for a second.

I don't know where she came from, but this aggressive diva suddenly emerged from inside of me, and she was not taking no for an answer.

I put a finger to Nelson's lips to silence him, and proceeded to plant kisses from his neck all the way down to his lower region where I unzipped his pants and pulled them down around his ankles. He stepped out of his pants while I reached inside his Calvin Klein boxers, pleased to find that what I was looking for was a very nice size and was every bit as hard as the Arabic alphabet.

"You sure you want to do this?" I asked, looking him in the eye as I took a condom from my purse and ripped it open with my teeth.

"Oh yeah . . ." he said softly. "This is exactly what I want to do."

Nelson squeezed the tip of the condom while I rolled it down over his magic stick.

Nelson pulled me to my feet, and unzipped the back of my

minidress, which immediately fell to the floor in a heap, leaving me standing there in my black lace La Perla bra and matching panties.

Nelson searched my mouth with his tongue, and this time the kiss was longer, and much more intense.

He unhooked my bra and voraciously sucked on my breasts, gently pulling at my erect nipples with his lips, and teasing them with his tongue.

I placed long, feathery licks from Nelson's shoulder blades up to his earlobes as he hoisted me on top of the pool table, slid my panties off, and dived head first between my thighs, devouring me the way a starving man would a five-course meal.

"My God, you smell like heaven!" he said, squeezing my ass and deeply inhaling the scent of my Bond No. 9 perfume, which seemed to be driving him to the brink of insanity.

We were both so caught up in the moment that I didn't even take time out to unbuckle my stilettos.

After what seemed like an eternity of having my honey pot licked, nibbled, and sucked, my body began to tremble almost violently.

Nelson sensed that I was about to climax and whispered, "Tori, look at me."

What? Why the hell is he talking?

"Look at me Tori," he insisted again, staring into my eyes. "Keep your eyes on me."

As I did, he went to work on my pulsating clitoris with even more focus and persistence.

The pleasure was so intense, I must have writhed over every inch of that pool table, and as Nelson requested, we were making direct eye contact when I reached my climax.

But that was only the beginning.

I came. Then again, and again, and again. Four times altogether and even then I had to beg him to stop.

Now I understood. Direct eye contact makes an orgasm so

much more intense. I have heard about tantric sex, but never thought I would actually find a black man who knows the fundamentals of it.

I was trying to catch my breath, and thinking what could possibly top that, when Nelson scooped me into his arms and carried me to his bedroom where he took control of my body like an expert.

We went from the bed, to the floor, back to the pool table, and back to the bed again. All the while, he was skillfully positioning my body in poses so erotic that they rivaled the Kama Sutra.

Whew! I have never experienced anything like it.

Roland's lovemaking technique was limited to predictable in-'n-out, in-'n-out thrusts. But Nelson swirled his hips, and put his back into it with the intention of hitting all the right spots.

And he certainly did just that.

The only negative was that there were so many pictures of Kara all over the place, that it felt like she was a voyeur of our sexual escapade, with her eyes following our every move.

Despite Kara's "presence," Nelson and I got it on until the wee hours of the morning, and when it seemed like it was finally all over, we just looked at each other and laughed, both of us giddy with satisfaction.

"Damn!" I said. "If I had known you had it like that, I would have been creeping across the hall a long time ago."

"Oh, yeah?" He smiled, trying to catch his breath, then rolled over on top of me again.

The count on the orgasms was something like Tori 4, Nelson 3. Just as Nelson was about to tie me, he screamed out "Kara!" and then climaxed.

I pushed Nelson off me with so much force, he almost fell backwards off the bed. "What did you just say?" I asked, already knowing what I had heard.

"What do you mean?"

"I'm not deaf! You do realize that you just called me 'Kara' don't you?"

Nelson leaned his back against the headboard, and looked up at the ceiling.

"Look," he said. "I apologize if I hurt your feelings, but it just . . . it just slipped out, alright? Jeez, I told you I was celibate."

"Oh, stop it with the celibate thing, okay? Let's just do away with that," I said, fighting the urge to pop him upside his head.

"Well it has a lot to do with what just happened here. I mean, the last person I made love to was Kara, and that was over two years ago. So—"

"So! How much of that was about you sincerely desiring me, and how much of it was about you fantasizing that you were having sex with your dead wife?" I asked.

"It's fucked up, but what do you expect when you sleep with someone you barely even know? What do you want me to say, I love you?" Nelson asked.

"Oh, now you got jokes!" I said. "No, I don't need for you to say you love me, but what I would have appreciated was for you to at least remember who it was that you were screwing."

Nelson scratched his head the way men do whenever they have been caught in the wrong. "Listen," he said, with compassion. "I just wanted to have dinner with you, but obviously, you had something else in mind."

"Whoa, hold up! Don't flatter yourself, homeboy. You rubbed your hard-on across my ass, so obviously you had something in mind, too," I said. "Come on, now. It's not like I just slipped and fell on your penis. And an *erect* penis at that!"

"It was the heat of the moment, and I went with it," he said. "But if you had been listening to a word I said tonight, it would be clear to you that I am still very much in love with my wife."

"Your *deceased* wife," I reminded him.

"Kara is still in my heart," Nelson said quietly. "Just as much now, as she was when she was alive."

Ah, damn!

I winced and rubbed my eyes as shame and humiliation washed over me. I wished there was a way that I could kick my own ass. To this man, I might as well have been a blowup doll.

"Well," I said, "don't let me be the one to come between you and your *wife*."

Nelson didn't say a word or even try to stop me as I slid out of his bed and gathered my things, which were scattered all over the place.

At a quarter to four this morning, I cautiously stuck my head out of Nelson's door, and looked both ways to make sure that the coast was clear. When I was certain that none of the neighbors would see me, I scurried my slutty ass back across the hall to my condo.

Just trust yourself, then you will know how to live. —*Goethe*

FRIDAY

I can't believe I played myself like that!

I get a few drinks in me, start carrying on like a co-ed gone wild, and end up violating my own DSWYE rule.

Nelson had been the perfect gentleman all night long, and I had to go and ruin the evening by behaving like the perfect slut.

I mean, I know that there is a sexual revolution going on where women are dating and having sex the way men do, with no emotions or strings attached. But sober and in the light of day, I am horrified that I allowed my body to rule over decency, morals, and good common sense.

Now you can see why I didn't share this information with Nadia. She's a good friend of mine, but shit, she doesn't need to know all my business.

And now, Nelson can add me to that list of trifling women he kept talking about so badly last night.

11

I was home alone on yet another Saturday night, when Nadia started bamming on my door like a damned fool. "Tori!" she shouted. "Open up!"

I did not budge.

Lackawanna Blues was on, and I was comfortable on the couch with a bag of Doritos, a king-sized Snickers bar, and a glass of white wine.

Besides, I was mourning the loss of my scruples, and I damn sure wasn't in the mood for company.

I sat real still and muted the volume on the TV, hoping that Nadia would eventually go away and leave me in peace.

"Tori! Girl, I saw your truck down in the parking garage, so I know you're home!"

I reluctantly unlocked the door, and the Cablinasian bombshell came bursting in, in all her hoochie-fied glory. Tonight's outfit consisted of a red, low-cut micro-minidress, and heels that were so high, they put her at around six-foot-two.

"What took so long to answer the door?" Nadia asked, doing a double take upon noticing my pink, Hello Kitty pajamas, brown Chip & Pepper moccasins, and raggedy ponytail. "Girl, you look a boiling hot ass mess!"

"And you look like you're on your way to the Skank Olympics."

"You're hating!" Nadia said, with a smile.

I swear, Nadia is the only person I know whose confidence and self-esteem levels are so high that she truly believes she farts gold dust and shits rose petals.

"Hating? Please. I'm always one to congratulate when congratulations are due," I said. "By the way, those bad-boys are fierce!" Being the shoe fanatic that I am, I was practically salivating over the silver metallic Giuseppe Zanottis that Nadia was sporting.

"Girl, you know GZ does not play," she said, kicking out her leg and arching her foot. "Suckers cost almost five hundred bucks, but I couldn't pass them up."

"Well, I'm not mad at you," I assured her. "They're definitely worth the investment."

"So," Nadia said, wiping Dorito crumbs from around my mouth. "What the hell is going on in here?"

"It's movie night," I said, flopping back down on the couch. "I'm chilling."

"Oh, hell no! I would not be a true friend if I let you go out like this," Nadia said.

"Like what?" I asked.

"Sitting around here moping, and looking like psych-ward Sally because you don't have a man."

"Chile, cut the drama," I said. "It is not that deep."

"Well why else would you be all cooped up in the house on a Saturday night . . . ?" Nadia snapped her fingers as a thought occurred to her. "You're sitting up here whinin' and pinin' over that tired ass Negro you almost married, aren't you?"

"Please! Why can't I spend an evening alone without you assuming I have the breakup blues?" I asked.

"Because truthfully, I think you do." Nadia tossed the Dorito bag onto the coffee table and sat on the couch beside me. "Look at you, Tori, this is not you! You're normally vibrant, fun loving, outgoing, and well put together," she said, flipping my ponytail with disgust.

"Unlike you, most of us are not all done up twenty-four seven, like we're waiting for our close-up," I said, taking a sip of Chardonnay.

"Well, that's something to look into," she said coolly. "And if it's not Roland you're yearning for, I sure as hell hope it's not Nelson."

I choked on my wine. The coughing got so bad, Nadia had to pat me on the back to help clear my windpipe.

"What does Nelson have to do with anything?" I croaked, still struggling to recover.

"Well, you know I'm not one to gossip, but just so you know, word around the building is that there's been some on-the-low creeping going on between you two."

"Lies and vicious rumors!" I said. "And where in the hell do you get this stuff, anyway?"

Nadia singsonged, "I'll never tell!"

Heifer.

"It doesn't matter," I said, hoping she couldn't tell I was lying, "because there is no truth to it, anyway."

"Good!" she said. "Because I also heard that old boy has been slinging the pipe to the tramp down in 1B, too!"

Nadia laughed, but all I could muster was a weak smile.

Nelson is sleeping with Ursula?

That son of a bitch played me like a violin with that celibate shit!

So much for his declaration that he's "One of the good ones." No, motherfucker, you are one of the *sneaky* ones. The lonely, bereaved widower act was all just a part of his game, and my gullible ass fell right into the trap.

Nadia and I went back and forth for about fifteen minutes before she finally took no for an answer, and left to go partying without me.

Afterwards, I was no longer in the mood for movie watching, so I grabbed my bathing suit and a couple of towels and went downstairs to meditate in the sauna.

I walked into the booth and was surprised to see Ms. 1B herself, sitting up in there like she owned the place. Ursula's head and torso were wrapped in yellow, fluffy towels, and she had a pair of Japanese spa slippers on her feet.

"Hello," I said, making sure to sound friendly, yet nonchalant.

Ursula said, "Hi . . ." without an ounce of energy or enthusiasm.

I wrapped a towel around my head and took a seat on the bench directly across from her.

I was tempted to strike up a conversation in order to find out more about Ursula—for instance, has Nelson cooked for her, gotten her drunk, and then screwed her on his pool table, too? But since her body language was screaming *Don't talk to me!* I didn't bother.

Unlike Nadia, I did not automatically dislike Ursula on first sight. Other than her being sometimey, I have never had anything specific against her. But now, in light of her stank ass attitude, I have to honestly say that I can't stand the bitch.

Ursula and I ignored each other for almost ten minutes, until Mitchell from 4C came in wearing only a pair of skintight Speedos.

"There you are . . ." he said to Ursula, and moved in for a smooch.

Ursula ducked away from Mitchell's kiss and nodded in my direction to let him know they were not alone.

"Hey, Tori," he stammered, surprised to see me. "What's up?"

"You tell me," I smiled, with innuendo in my voice.

Like I said, Mitchell has slept with just about everything with a pulse in our building, but this must be a new low, even for him.

I wonder if Nelson knows about this?

After a few awkward minutes of Mitchell and Ursula sneaking looks at me and whispering to each other, I made a mental note to bring Lysol and sanitizer the next time I come down to the sauna, then left those two freaks alone to do what they had obviously come to do.

How stank. Ursula really does get around like a bitch in heat, and the thought that we both have slept with Nelson makes my skin crawl.

A vision of Nelson freaking Ursula the same way he did me kept replaying in my head, and I couldn't get to sleep. It was nearly one in the morning, but I got up and took a long, hot, shower, then made myself a cup of hot chamomile tea. That did the trick.

A few minutes after I managed to drift off to sleep, I heard Nadia's special knock on my front door, which is her beating on the damn thing as if she were the Gestapo.

"Go away!" I moaned miserably, refusing to give up the sweet spot in my therapeutic mattress. I put a pillow over my head to drown out the knocking, which only got louder and more persistent with each passing minute. Finally, I got up and stomped to the front door with murder in my eyes, thinking whatever Nadia wanted, it damn sure better be an emergency.

"What is it?" I hissed, as I snatched the door open.

"I need to borrow a set of clean bed sheets." Nadia said, as if it were the same as asking for a cup of sugar.

"Sheets? What for?" I asked, noting that she looked very Zsa Zsa Gabor in a peach floor-length negligee, matching robe, and those high-heeled mules with the marabou puffs.

"I was giving T.C. a deep-tissue massage, he fell asleep and the next thing I know my mattress and sheets were soaking wet!"

"You mean wet, as in pissy?" I asked, incredulous.

Nadia nodded. "It's the steroids," she said in a whisper.

"They got him all fucked up, and this ain't the first time he's pissed on my expensive designer sheets, either."

"And you expect me to give you mine so he can piss them, too?" I asked, shaking my head, trying to clear it. I had to be dreaming that a six-foot, muscle-bound football player had actually peed in the bed, and now I was being asked to loan my 800-thread-count Pratesi linens, knowing those suckers ain't hardly cheap.

"He's not gonna do it again," Nadia assured me. "It only happens once every other night."

See, this is what happens when you get too friendly with the neighbors.

"Look, I don't know what the hell you have going on up at your place, but some things need to be left behind closed doors." I said.

"So, I can't borrow a set of your bed sheets, or not?" Nadia asked, indignantly.

"Hell no!" I exploded. "That shit is just nasty, Nadia, and I don't want any part of it. Now, you and Mr. Steroid are just going to have to work it out amongst yourselves. Now, good night."

Despite Nadia's protests, I firmly closed the door in her face, and stumbled back to bed.

12

Labor Day is always a big deal at my parents' house. Daddy gets started two days before by marinating everything that needs to be marinated, and that includes many pounds' worth of chicken, ribs, steaks, tri-tips, turkey, and pork tenderloin.

So many people show up every year that we might as well consider Labor Day our official family reunion.

The weather was forecasted to be hot and muggy for the day, so I put on a tan, lightweight sundress, and a pair of tan and gold Coach sandals.

I drove across the bridge to Kansas City, Kansas, where my parents still reside in the same three-story house Junior and I grew up in. Besides the deck they had built a few years ago, nothing else about the house has changed.

Visiting my parents is like walking into a time warp.

They have the exact same plastic-covered furniture and faux-wood paneling Daddy put up himself back in the '70s, and other relatives get a kick out of teasing me about my senior prom and high school graduation pictures, which my mother still has displayed on the fireplace mantle.

I pulled up in front of the house, and the thick cloud of smoke rising up from the backyard was an indication that Daddy had a good fire going in his heavy-duty six-rack smoker.

I got out of my Navigator and grabbed the two trays of crab-stuffed deviled eggs that Mama asked me to bring. I walked around to the backyard and found Daddy manning his station at the grill, with a pair of long tongs in one hand, and a can of Colt 45 in the other.

"What'cha know good, old man?" I asked playfully.

Daddy looked up and his eyes lit up when he saw me. "There's my favorite daughter!" he said.

"I'm your *only* daughter," I said.

"My one and only favorite!" he said, and kissed me on the cheek.

That's the way Daddy and I have been greeting each other since I was about fifteen.

"Smells like you have everything under control."

"Yes indeedy," he said, sipping his beer. "It's gonna be a wang-dang-doodle, today!"

My folks may have left Shreveport, Louisiana, over twenty years ago, but my father is still as country as a bucket of moonshine. For example, phrases like "wang-dang-doodle."

"Let me go in here and check on Mama," I said, walking up the few steps leading onto the deck.

"Alright, sweet pea," Daddy said, using a spray bottle to mist the meat with marinade.

My mother was putting a pan of peach cobbler in the oven when I walked into the kitchen.

"Hi sweetie," I said, kissing Mama on her cheek.

"Hey baby," she said, wiping her forehead with a paper towel. "Whew! I've been up cooking since last night. I think I'm gonna have to go take a power nap."

I put the deviled eggs in the refrigerator and grabbed a can of soda.

"Where is Aunt Vera?" I asked. "She's usually here helping you do all the cooking."

"Chile, she done up and ran off to Las Vegas," Mama said,

checking on a pot of greens. "*And*, with Brother Edwards from down at the church!"

"Whaaaat?"

"Ain't that some shit? I'm telling you, the older Vera gets, the ornerier she gets."

"Look who's talking!" I said. "I could say the same thing about you, with the way you've been cursing up a storm, lately."

"Shit, dealing with all the crazy folks in this family, I have to do something to let off steam."

"So who's making the five-cheese macaroni and cheese?" I asked, popping the top on a Red Cream Soda.

"I went ahead and made it," my mother said. "And since I know the recipe backwards and forwards, I doubt that anybody will be able to tell the difference.

I don't know . . . There was damn near a riot last Easter when Aunt Vera didn't feel up to making her legendary signature dish.

While my mother is an excellent cook, there are some traditions that you just don't dare mess with.

Mama's pecan rum cake is one, and Aunt Vera's five-cheese macaroni and cheese is another.

The backdoor opened and Junior walked in, followed by my nephew Trey. "Auntie!" Trey said, running over and wrapping his arms around my knees.

"There's my little buddy!" I said, scooping Trey up in my arms and kissing him on the lips.

"I miss you," my nephew said, reaching up to play with one of my gold chandelier earrings. I laughed because Trey is only three years old, and what he meant to say was, "I *missed* you."

"I miss you, too," I mimicked, and gave him a big squeeze.

"What's up, Tori?" Junior asked, attempting to cut himself a piece of rum cake, only to have Mama slap his hand away.

"Wash your hands first!" she said.

"So, how is Federal Express coming along?" I asked Junior, as he washed his hands in the sink.

"It's cool," he said. "My three-month probation is almost over, and I'm about to get full benefits."

"Congratulations!" I said, putting Trey back down on the floor. "So now that you're working steady, can I put you on a payment schedule to recoup some of the money you owe me?"

Junior's mouth was stuffed with cake at that moment so he held up a forefinger like an usher, and mumbled, "Wait a minute." Then he got a call on his cell phone, and left the kitchen without answering the question.

The problem with Junior is that he is well on his way to becoming a professional freeloader. Just like our Uncle Blue.

He's financially irresponsible, does everything half-ass, and is spoiled to the point that he is now handicapped and he can't even do simple things, like cook a decent meal, clean house, pay bills on time, or even wash a load of laundry without ruining everything.

Mama likes to believe that her baby boy is just trying to find himself. But the way I see it, Junior is living this prolonged adolescence where he gets to do whatever he wants to do, except be responsible and take care of business the way grown people do.

A few hours later, there were so many people coming and going from my parents' house, it was like being in the middle of Grand Central Station.

There were a lot of folks dancing to *The Best of the Blues* CD compilation Daddy had blasting on his Bose stereo, and there were several cutthroat games of spades and dominoes going on at different tables throughout the house.

At my table, Uncle Woody and I were partners, playing against Cookie and Uncle Blue.

"Umph! Gimme that!" Uncle Blue said, sweeping up the last hand of cards.

Cookie said, "Oh, Tori. I know what I forgot to tell you, girl."

"What's that?" I asked.

"I saw your girl Veronica at the casino last Friday night with some of her little raggedy-ass girlfriends."

"You saw her, but did she see you?" Uncle Blue asked Cookie before I could respond.

"Come on now, y'all know me," Cookie said. "I made sure that heifer saw me, by accidentally-on-purpose spilling my strawberry daiquiri right down the front of her white shirt!"

"Now you know you're wrong for that Cookie," I said. "Tell me you didn't do that for real."

"I sure did!" Cookie said.

"And what did she do?" I asked.

"What could she do besides stand there looking all kinds of stupid? Shoot, she's lucky I already have a case pending, otherwise I would have mopped her ass up all over Harrah's Casino."

"Watch your language . . ." Uncle Woody warned, studying his hand.

"Come on now, Uncle Woody," I teased. "You know you're the one who taught us all how to cuss."

"No I ain't neither!" Woody said, highly offended. "Don't you put that on me!"

"Well, come on, Unc," I said, displaying the big joker and winning the hand. "Let's set these fools!"

"Booyah!" Uncle Woody slapped the little joker down onto the table, causing us to beat Cookie and Blue for the third game in a row.

"Yeah!" I said, giving Uncle Woody a high five. "They can't handle this!"

"Whatever, y'all cheated," Cookie pouted, before getting up and leaving the table.

"Come on Tori, let's go cut a rug," Uncle Woody said,

grabbing my hand and leading me to the middle of the living room where everybody was dancing to "Let the Good Times Roll," by B.B. King and Bobby Blue Bland.

Despite being a very large man, Uncle Woody is an expert two-stepper, and I'm fortunate that he taught me everything he knows.

"For such a bad little girl, you actually turned out pretty good!" Uncle Woody said admiringly, as we twirled and bopped to the music.

I said, "With you for a godfather, how could I go wrong?"

Daddy came and cut in when Z.Z. Hill's "Down Home Blues" came on, and between Uncle Woody and my father, I danced the night away.

13

The day following Labor Day was business as usual.

The first half of the day was spent running around town getting things in order for The March of Dimes' five-hundred-dollar-a-plate fundraiser that is scheduled for next February. The day had been so hectic, it wasn't until two o'clock that my assistant and I managed to squeeze in time for lunch at the Peachtree Restaurant, located in the Power & Light District.

Our waiter was a good-looking black guy in his mid-twenties, with high energy and enthusiasm.

"You ladies ready to order?" he asked, filling our water glasses.

"I'll have the sweet tea, rotisserie chicken, and a house salad," I said, handing him my menu.

"And you?" he asked Erin, who was studying the menu as if it were a textbook.

"I've never had soul food before," she said. "What do you suggest?"

"Well, my favorites are the baby back ribs, macaroni and cheese, and sweet potatoes," he answered.

"Then that's what I'll have," Erin decided, and as she handed the waiter her menu, I noticed that the two of them were eyeballing each other flirtatiously.

While waiting for our food to arrive, I took out my iPhone to do some multitasking.

"Erin, I got an e-mail here from the Susan G. Komen Foundation, saying that they are still waiting to receive those vendor invoices."

"Oh!" she gasped. "I had so much going on this morning, it completely slipped my mind."

"That's unacceptable," I said. "Erin, you can't keep dropping the ball on important tasks. Do you know how unprofessional that makes us look?"

"I'm sorry," she said. "I'll take care of it as soon as we get back to the office."

"Okay, and what was the figure that Harrison Floral gave us earlier today?"

"You mean the first florist we visited?"

"Yes . . ." I said, trying to maintain the utmost patience. Erin is a nice girl, but being related to Sophie is the only thing that has kept her ass from being fired.

Erin flipped through her notebook, and looked at me like a two-year-old who had just pooped on herself. "I don't have that number here."

"Erin you were supposed to be taking notes."

"I know, I'm sorry," she said. "I'm going to get better at this, I promise."

"Don't be sorry," I said. "Just remember that in order to be successful in this business, you have to write everything down, then make sure you have everything in writing."

"Will do," Erin promised, holding up the Girl Scout sign.

After lunch, our hunk of a waiter brought us the check, and Erin whispered, "He's a cutie pie, isn't he?"

"Very nice," I had to admit. "But most restaurant servers are aspiring to be something else, and I prefer men who already know what they want to be when they grow up."

"I wasn't talking about for you."

"Uh, oh!" I said. "Is the little country girl from Omaha crossing over to the dark side?"

"Maybe . . ." she said with a sly wink. "I'm going to write 'call me' on my business card and leave it along with the tip."

"That's a bold move," I said. "But you know what they say about going black."

"That's what I heard," Erin said in such a sassy way, it made me wonder if there was more to my unassuming assistant than meets the eye.

Outside of the Peachtree Restaurant, Erin and I were walking to my Navigator, when we were accosted by a homeless man.

"Miss Ladies, Miss Ladies . . . anything you can spare would be a big help," he said, pitifully.

Erin gave the man a handful of change, but I rushed past him and said, "Sorry, I don't carry cash." As I did, our eyes locked for a split second, and I realized that there was something vaguely familiar about this guy.

I did a double-take, and so did he.

"James?" I asked, my jaw dropping.

"Tori Carter?" he asked with a rotten-toothed smile. James was my high school sweetheart and the first man besides my daddy that I ever loved with all my heart. He looked something like El DeBarge, left a lingering trail of Cool Water cologne everywhere he went, and was Kennedy High School's all-star wide receiver.

Neither of our parents approved of the relationship.

They tried numerous times to break us up and keep us apart, but like Romeo and Juliet, all that adversity made us love each other even more.

It was the two of us against the world, and no one was going to stop us from getting married right after graduation. In fact, I was so determined to become Mrs. Crawford that I was seriously considering turning down the full college scholarship I had earned so that I could stay in town close to my man.

James saved up his McDonald's paychecks to buy my ring. It was a quarter of a carat cluster—nothing but diamond dust really. But I thought it was beautiful.

Somehow, my parents got a whiff of my plans to ditch college and before I knew it, I was shipped off to Kansas University so fast I didn't even have time to pack properly let alone say good-bye to James.

I cried the ugly cry, all the way up to the Lawrence campus. "But, Daddy, I love him!" I wailed.

Daddy looked back at me in the rearview mirror, but was nonplussed. "That's okay, goddamnit," he said. "You'll get over it."

James and I put up a valiant effort to stay in touch, but the relationship eventually died a slow death.

Many years later, here I was face-to-face with my first love, who happened to be wearing a filthy plaid jacket, tattered jeans, and a pair of Air Force One Nikes that had definitely seen better days. "Damn girl, you got big!" he told me. "How many kids you got now?"

Life had obviously not been kind to James, yet it was amazing that he still had enough nerve to clown me about my weight.

Ain't that a bitch?

"Yeah, I packed on a few pounds," I said. "But what the hell happened to you?"

James's smile faded and his shoulders slumped.

"Life," he said stoically before walking away. "Life . . ."

No matter where you go, there you are. —Confucius

WEDNESDAY

Seeing James today drove home the point of an article I read in O Magazine recently. Or maybe it was Essence. Anyway, some psychologist was saying that whenever a breakup occurs, nine times out of ten, it is for the best. Yeah, it hurts like hell at first, but you should take some comfort in the fact that when the smoke clears, the next man you get into a relationship with is going to be a step up from the last one. For example, list every guy you ever loved in chronological order.

If you are truly learning and evolving as you should be, then you should be able to go down that list and see where each man in your past was always better than the one before him.

1) James

2) Shane

3) Vincent

4) Joseph

5) Roland

I can definitely see the pattern. Now, there wasn't always a huge step up from one man to the next, but it was a step up nevertheless.

14

It felt like déjà vu all over again. For the second weekend in a row, Nadia showed up at my door trying to convince me that hitting the town with her was the answer to what she perceives to be my depression over man troubles.

"Nadia, baby, I know you have ADD, but try to stay with me, okay?" I said, grabbing her face with both hands and looking her square in the eyes. "I'm fine, alright? I have a lot coming up at work this week, and I just want to relax and recharge my batteries. 'Kay?"

Nadia removed my hands from her face and said, "Bullshit! You can lie to me all you want, but at least have the dignity not to lie to yourself."

"Make that the last time you ever try and psychoanalyze *anybody*," I laughed. "Because you have the most issues of anybody I know."

"Don't hate me because I live an adventurous life," Nadia said defensively.

"Sweetie, you're thirty-one years old, and at your age, packing up everything and following some man wherever he leads is not adventurous, it's just plain stupid," I said.

The girl is like a gypsy. Eight cities in thirteen years is a horrible track record, but she goes wherever her heart leads her, which is usually influenced by some smooth-talking charmer she hasn't known for very long.

I had obviously struck a nerve, because Nadia haughtily flipped her long black hair, and gave me the stank-eye.

"Anyway!" she said. "We are not talking about me, we're talking about you, so come on and get dressed. We're going out."

"No!" I said, waving her off. "My hair is a mess, and I don't have a thing to wear."

"Now you know I know better than that. There's more designer shit in your closet than in mine, and that's saying something!"

"They're mostly work clothes, not party clothes," I said. "Which reminds me, when am I getting back my Armani blouse that you borrowed?"

"Soon . . . it's at the dry cleaners. Now, come on, because we're going dancing and we're gonna meet some men," Nadia said, doing a little two-step.

I wasn't stoked.

Meeting men in clubs is not a big draw for me. Mainly because I have exchanged phone numbers with lots of guys in many a club over the years, and have never had a decent relationship come from any of those encounters. I may have dated someone for a week or two, or even a month or two, but in the end, it never pans out.

So now, I am wise enough to know that you flirt with these guys and have fun with them for *the night*, and that's it. After the club, meet him at the Waffle House and let him treat you to breakfast, but you do not take him home with you, and you definitely don't go home with him.

It is never worth it.

"Nadia, I'm trying to avoid bullshit-ass men, not draw them to me. Besides, decent men don't hang out in clubs. Especially if they're over thirty-five."

"Normally that would be the case, but tonight we're going

where the ballers are," Nadia said, rubbing her hands with glee. "I'm talking about NFL, MLB, and NBA, baby!"

Nadia tried to pull me to my feet, but her little size-four body was no match for my solid 146-pound frame.

"Seriously Nadia, I'm sitting this one out," I said, firmly planting my feet on the floor. "Go 'head now!"

Nadia sighed, just as exasperated with me as I was with her. "What is it, movie night again?" she asked.

"Yep!" I said. "Tonight is a celebration of the musical. I got *Dreamgirls*, *Chicago*, and *Hairspray*."

"I thought you might say some shit like that. That's why I brought reinforcements." Nadia opened the door for Simone and Yvette, who were standing on the other side dressed to impress, and ready to party.

Initially, Yvette, Nadia, and Simone only knew each other through me, but now the four of us are such a cohesive unit, it feels like we all grew up together.

"Diva squad to the rescue!" Simone said, wafting in wearing her usual colorful, neo-soul garb. Tonight she wore an ethnic-inspired sundress, matching head wrap, and ballerina flats.

"That's right, so off your ass and on your feet!" Yvette ordered, and I had to blink a few times to get my eyes adjusted to the rock-star getup she was wearing.

It looked like Yvette had gone on a shopping spree in Macy's junior's department. Her outfit consisted of low-rise jeans, high-heeled clogs, a rhinestone belly chain, and a tight midriff T-shirt that said "Hot Chick" across the front of it. Clearly, she had forgotten that she is thirty-four years old and that her size (eighteen) equals her daughter's age.

It was useless to continue arguing. Not only was I outnumbered, but Nadia was already popping the top on one of the many bottles of Veuve Clicquot Champagne I had left over from the wedding; and once that girl gets in party mode it's like trying to stop a freight train with a caution sign.

"Okay, everybody listen up!" I said. "I will agree to go out with you heifers on one condition—"

"Which is?" Simone asked.

"That there be no talk about Roland, weddings, or anything related to any of the above," I said.

"Deal!" they shouted in unison. Probably because I have already talked their ears off enough about that whole situation.

"We will definitely drink to that," Nadia said, handing each of us a glass of champagne. "Let's just enjoy the night and each other, okay, ladies?"

"Agreed!" the four of us said, as we clinked glasses.

My only thought as the divas ushered me into my bedroom to help me get dressed was that it was going to be one *hell* of a night. These women were already high energy enough, but when you added alcohol to the mix, watch out! Ain't no party like a diva squad party 'cause a diva squad party don't stop!

We all said that we were down for whatever, and Yvette took full advantage of that by insisting that we go to Club Heifers, her favorite nightspot. The number one rule at Heifers is that you have to be at least a size fourteen to get in, hence the name.

This weight requirement was not a problem for Yvette, but I'm a size twelve. Nadia and Simone are sizes four and eight respectively, which added together don't even add up to fourteen.

"Sorry ladies," a bald, hulking doorman said to Nadia and Simone. "Fourteen and up, only!"

Yvette sidled up to the guy, and purred, "Come on, Eugene. These are my girlfriends."

Eugene pocketed the twenty-dollar tip Yvette gave him, and violà! We all gained entry past the velvet rope.

Inside Club Heifers, the ratio was around two hundred

women to twenty men. And they weren't even quality men at that. The chubby-chasers were all either over fifty, overweight themselves, unattractive, short, nerdy, creepy, or some combination of the above.

Nadia, Simone, and I might as well have been invisible. The only attention we got was from some of the other heifers, who kept shooting us dirty looks, angry that skinny bitches were infringing upon their territory.

Yvette, on the other hand, was the belle of the ball up in there. She was out on the dance floor doing her signature dance move, which is to twirl her wide hips in a suggestive manner, and spank her own ass.

No sooner had she finished dancing with one guy than another would come and take his place.

"Look at her," Simone said with distaste. "Carrying on like that old bitch in the club, who we all said we'd never be."

"She's just making up for lost time," I said. "She'll be alright once she gets it all out her system."

Yvette became a mother at seventeen, and now that Alicia is on her way to college in the fall, Yvette is going through a phase where it is all about her.

After dancing six songs straight, Yvette finally left the dance floor and joined us at our table.

"Why am I the only one out there dancing?" she asked, patting her perspiration with a cocktail napkin.

"Because these men are here to get their big girl fantasies fulfilled," I said. "And nothing else will do."

"You got that right!" Yvette laughed facetiously. "Skin and bones ain't on the menu up in here, baby!"

"Whatever!" Nadia said, taking offense. "All I know is that I'm picking the next spot."

"Okay, this is what we're going to do," I said. "Tonight, each of us gets to pick a spot."

"That could take until the wee hours of the morning," Simone protested.

"Well, we're out here now, so we might as well make it an all-nighter," I said, surprising everybody, including myself.

"Uh oh, listen to you!" Yvette said. "It damn near took an act of Congress to get your ass out of the house, and now you wanna party all night long."

"My girl!" Nadia said, slapping me a high five. "Let's get out of here, and let me show you ladies how I get down."

The four of us jumped back into my Navigator, and ended up downtown at Club Suede, where the atmosphere was so festive we all came to the unanimous decision that no other stops would be necessary; this was where we would be partying for the rest of the night.

Club Suede is a nightspot that prides itself on being the plushest club in the city, which caters exclusively to the grown and sexy. The club is practically Nadia's second home, and she led the way to the VIP area where we were seated in a plush, semicircular banquette.

"Jill, could you start us off with a round of mai tais please?" Nadia asked the hostess.

"You got it, girl," Jill answered, and was back in less than three minutes with a tray of frothy, fruity concoctions served in super-sized glasses.

The drinks were so strong that not even ten minutes later, Yvette suddenly shouted for no reason, "Roland is a goddamned fool!"

"There she goes . . ." Simone said, referring to the fact that Yvette was becoming increasingly agitated, which is how she always gets whenever she's had too much to drink.

"It's okay, baby." I patted Yvette's hand, trying to calm her ass down. "Let it go."

"I mean, I wonder what possesses a nigga to do some stupid, disrespectful shit like that?" Yvette said.

I looked at Nadia and Simone, incredulous. "Didn't we agree not to make this a topic of discussion?"

Nadia shrugged and rolled her eyes. "You know how she is when she gets to drinking."

"*She* has been drinking, but *she* ain't that damn drunk. Stop talking about me like I ain't here," Yvette said, and then belched.

"Hell, we know you're here with your loud ass mouth," Nadia shouted over the music.

"Never mind all that," Simone said to me, raising her glass in the air. "Tori, my sister, here's to strength, courage, and the birth of possibility."

We all toasted to that. I thought it was sweet, but Yvette snickered and shook her head.

"Girl, you need to light an incense and go meditate somewhere." Yvette laughed in Simone's face. "That Sister Souljah unity act is getting on my *last* nerve."

"All right now," Simone warned. "Don't let me get started on you."

"You know better!" Yvette snapped. "Anyway, Tori, you would have been better off if you had married James. Now, *that* motherfucka loved your ass to death! He would have never shit on you the way Roland did."

"Oh, it's ironic that you brought James up," I told Yvette. "I ran into him outside of the Peachtree the other day, and guess what? He's a fucking bum! Literally!"

"For real?" Yvette said. "Damn, that's messed up."

"That just goes to show that all things in the universe are in divine right order," Simone said. "And every breakup is God's way of saying that he has something better for you somewhere down the line."

"And that's exactly why I don't sweat none of these knuckleheads," Nadia said. "If you wanna go, go! 'Cause I'm gonna make damn sure that the next man is better than you anyway!"

"Hear, hear!" Simone raised her glass in agreement.

"Ooh! Y'all let me out, I gotta pee!" Yvette said, scooting her way out of the booth, which caused me and Simone to have to jump up and let her out.

"Can't take her ghetto ass nowhere!" Nadia said.

"I don't know about you ladies, but I feel like dancing," I said, rocking to the beat of a T-Pain remix.

"Me, too!" Nadia said. "Come on, let's go."

Simone opted to stay at the table to wait for Yvette, while Nadia and I walked down to the common area, where it was so jam-packed, I was sure some kind of fire law was being violated. The swell of the crowd swept Nadia and me in separate directions, and I spent the next five minutes drifting in a sea of sweaty bodies.

I finally made it to the edge of the dance floor, just as Missy Elliott went off and a slow jam came on. Some random guy grabbed my elbow and gestured to the dance floor, but I turned him down because I wanted to dance to something up-tempo, and wasn't in the mood for bumping and grinding with a total stranger.

So I squeezed, turned, and maneuvered my way through the crowd, until I finally made it to the bar for a cool, refreshing drink. Once I got there, I was surprised that my shoes had only been stepped on twice.

I told the bartender, "A mai tai, please," and slid fifteen dollars in front of him, as he slid the drink in front of me.

Since it was so crowded, I did not want to take the chance of spilling the drink on me or anyone else, so I hopped up on an empty stool and scanned the bar area, searching for a guy to get my swerve on with. While I was searching, Simone emerged from the crowd and joined me at the bar.

"There you are!" she said, taking my drink from my hand and taking a sip.

"You having fun?" I asked.

"I'm having a ball!" she said, grooving to Kanye's latest hit song. "I just got through dancing with a cutie that almost made me forget that I have a man at home."

Simone has had a man at home for the past nine years, though they haven't gotten around to getting married yet.

Rasheed is a poet, playwright, painter, musician, and just an all-around renaissance guy who does everything except bring home a steady paycheck. The two of them are neo-soul cute and very *Love Jones* together. And because Rasheed loves Simone so thoroughly, she doesn't mind being the sole breadwinner while Rasheed pursues his creative endeavors.

"Oh, there's Reggie from my writer's group!" Simone said, pointing out a good-looking guy with horn-rimmed glasses. He looked to be in his mid-thirties, and wore a New York Yankees baseball cap, with a charcoal gray Armani suit and crisp white Air Force Ones.

"What else do you know about him?" I asked, and Simone was all too eager to fill me in on Reggie's background as far as she knew it.

Apparently, he is a screenwriter who recently completed a fellowship with the Academy of Arts and Sciences, and has been making the rounds in Hollywood, where there is talk that Columbia Pictures wants to buy one of his scripts for John Singleton to direct.

"Come on, I'm gonna hook you up," Simone said, ushering me over to Reggie's table despite my efforts to stop her.

Reggie smiled big when he saw Simone approaching.

"Simone! What's up, girl? I haven't seen you in a long-ass time."

"Too long, right?" Simone said, giving him a hug. "I hear you've been taking care of business, though."

"Oh yeah, got to, got to . . ." he said, while looking me up and down. "Aren't you going to introduce me to your friend?"

"I most certainly am," Simone said, pulling me front and center. "Reggie, meet my best girlfriend, *Miss* Tori Carter. Tori, Reggie Tyler."

"Nice to meet you," I said, offering a handshake. "Congratulations on your success."

I felt naked as Reggie's gaze roamed from my feet to my head.

"Tori," he said, gazing into my eyes. "A beautiful name for a beautiful woman."

You would think that after thirty-three years, I would know how to take a well-deserved compliment, but I was grateful that the room was dark so that Reggie could not see the flush in my cheeks.

I told him, "Thank you," and when I looked over to my right I noticed that Simone had conveniently disappeared, taking my mai tai along with her.

Reggie shooed one of his buddies away, and offered me the vacant seat next to him.

"Would you like some champagne?" he asked, referring to the bottle of Ace of Spades that was chilling in an ice bucket.

Reggie turned one of the flutes that came with the setup, right-side up, and poured me a glass.

"I hear you're on the verge of selling a script," I shouted over the loud music. "What's it about?"

"Oh, it's about an ex–Black Panther who tries to restart his life after serving almost twenty years in prison. The title is *The Revolution Was Televised*."

"Hmm, sounds like it might be controversial," I said. "I can't wait to see it."

"Yeah, it's definitely going to rattle some cages and get people thinking, you know? If all goes well, it should be released in about a year or so."

"Good luck!" I said, crossing my fingers for him. "I've heard how hard it is just to get a toe-hold in the film industry; especially for black folk."

"Oh, most definitely," he said. "That goes without saying. But once I get all the way in there, my goal is to somehow open the doors even wider for other minorities to come in after me."

"Bravo!" I said, clapping for him. "I respect that. Not saying any names, but some of us forget to keep paving the way, which is partly why we don't have more power and control than we do in this day and age."

"Sad, but true," Reggie said, refilling his champagne glass. "But you know, Spike Lee is one of my mentors in that respect; but it's unfortunate that as much as he's done to advance opportunities for us in Hollywood, it's still not enough."

"Well, just do me a favor and keep consistently writing brilliant roles for our veteran black actors, because Lord knows they deserve better roles than they're being given," I said.

"I like you!" Reggie said. "You have what is the dopest combination in the world to me, and that's beauty *and* brains. Do you have a man?"

"As a matter of fact, I don't," I said.

Reggie leaned in close to me. "Well, we're just gonna have to change all that, huh?"

"Maybe so," I smiled. "But then again, you're moving to L.A. soon, aren't you?"

He shrugged. "That's why they have frequent flyer programs, right?"

Hey, now!

Mary J's bouncy new tune came on, and there was a rush to the dance floor.

Reggie asked, "Would you like another drink?"

"No, thank you, but I would like to dance," I said.

"Let's do it," he said, taking my hand.

I felt safe and protected as Reggie effortlessly navigated the crowd and guided me out to the dance floor.

He turned out to have pretty good rhythm. We danced and flirted with each other for four songs straight until the music slowed down to a Mariah Carey ballad.

I turned to leave the dance floor, but Reggie gently grabbed me by the waist and pulled me closer to him. "Just one more dance. Please?"

I nodded, and allowed Reggie to envelop me in his arms

while I wrapped my arms around his back. My head came up to the middle of his chest, and he held me just right: not too far away and not close enough where I could feel the outline of his package. I deeply inhaled the scent of his Burberry cologne, and sighed.

15

If I never see another bottle of champagne in my life, it will be too damn soon.

I woke up this morning—or rather this afternoon, feeling like I had been beaten up and tossed out of a moving vehicle at a hundred miles an hour. My head, my neck, my back—everything hurt. It didn't help that I had forgotten to close my blinds last night and now the living room was bathed in sunlight, which was torturing my eyes.

The last thing I remembered clearly was all four of us coming back to my place where we drank, laughed, and bashed no-good men, until the wee hours of the morning. It was fun. At least it was at the time. But now, I'm paying for it. Big time.

I knew a cold washcloth would do my throbbing head some good, but it took a few minutes for me to work up the strength to get my ass up off the couch. When I finally did, I almost tripped over Yvette, who was camped out on my stowaway futon. My girl was knocked out and snoring so loud that I placed a pillow over her face to drown out some of the noise. It didn't work.

I went into the bathroom, and loathed what I saw in the mirror. Bloodshot eyes, wild hair, and smudged makeup. Not a good look. Especially since I heard that every time you go to bed without washing makeup off your face, it ages your skin seventeen days. This aging is irreversible and it adds up, so if you go to bed 30 times without washing the makeup off you have aged yourself almost two years. Ugh! I quickly washed my face with Neutrogena and cold water, hoping that it wasn't too late to deduct a few days off that seventeen.

When I went back into the living room Yvette was sitting up on the futon, trying to get her bearings.

"Tori's got a man . . ." she teased as she stretched.

"Puh-leeze!" I said, but secretly wished it was true.

"Shit, I was checking you out with ol' boy last night," Yvette said. "You still got game, girl!"

Reggie and I had flirted and danced the night away, then exchanged numbers, agreeing to keep in touch and go out sometime.

I must admit that I like Reggie. A lot. Not only is he attractive, but he also has an aura about him that makes him irresistibly sexy.

I don't want to get ahead of myself like I have sometimes been known to do, but I can definitely see myself with a rich, famous screenwriter for a boyfriend.

"Where is Simone, by the way?" I asked, starting to clean up some of the mess we made last night.

"Girl, you know she had to run home before that fool put out a missing persons report on her," Yvette laughed.

"Shoot, you just wish you had a man to keep tabs on your whereabouts."

"I do, I'm not gonna lie, but I'll be damned if I juggle two and three jobs and foot all the bills while he plays the starving artist role," Yvette said.

"Well it works for the two of them," I said. "And that's all that matters."

"I'm baaa-aacck. Wake up, wake up!" That was Nadia, letting herself in the front door. Unlike Yvette and me, Nadia had showered and looked well-rested.

"Alright ladies, here it is." Nadia said, placing a clear plastic bowl of what looked like gumbo on the island counter. "My mother's surefire hangover remedy."

Yvette and I joined Nadia at the island. She removed the lid from the bowl and a foul, funky stench filled the room. The smell was so repulsive it gave me the dry heaves, and if I had already eaten something, it surely would have come right up.

"Ooh, girl, don't nobody want that shit," Yvette said, covering her nose.

"Try it before you knock it," Nadia said, shoving a heaping spoonful of the concoction into Yvette's mouth.

"Mmmm!" Yvette said, helping herself to another spoonful. "Mama Chen can throw down!"

"I told you!" Nadia said proudly. "Come on, Tori, try it. Why do you think I'm so perky right now? And I probably drank the most out of all of us."

I was still skeptical. Not only did it stink to high heaven, but there were also too many unidentifiable objects floating around in there for my liking.

"No offense to your mama," I said, holding my nose and fanning the air with my latest copy of *Gourmet* Magazine. "But what's in that stuff that makes it smell like week-old assholes?"

"That, my friend, is an ancient Japanese secret," Nadia said, mysteriously.

Ancient *Korean* secret is probably closer to the truth.

Either way, I wasn't about to eat that mess.

But my stomach had other plans. It made this loud, weird grumbling noise that I've never heard it make before.

"Damn, Tori!" Nadia said. "You're obviously hungry, so you might as well try it."

"It really is good, girl," Yvette told me, slurping her bowl and reaching for yet another helping.

"Well, if Yvette said it's alright . . ." I sampled the concoction, which was so tasty, I went ahead and fixed myself a big bowlful. The taste reminded me of hot and sour soup, and I had eaten half of it before asking, "Nadia, what is this spongy, noodle-looking stuff?"

"That's tofu."

"No this . . ." I said, brandishing the spongy, noodle-looking thing in question.

"Oh, that?" Nadia said casually. "That's just cow brains."

I am at least grateful that I made it to the bathroom without throwing up all over myself.

Nadia's hangover remedy worked like a charm for Yvette. But because it was nearly four in the afternoon, and I still felt like stir-fried shit, I was forced to place the dreaded phone call to let the folks know that I wasn't coming for dinner.

It is an official rule in my family that the only acceptable excuses for missing Sunday dinner at my parents' house are:

1) You are dead
2) You are working
3) You are on your deathbed

It took nearly twenty minutes to convince my mother of the latter, and before I knew it, Junior was beating down my door, sent over by Mama with a plate of food and a get-well kit, which consisted of 7Up, a bag of oranges, and a jar of Vicks VapoRub.

My brother noticed right away that I wasn't fever-and-chills sick, just hung-over sick.

"Ah, damn!" Junior said when I opened the door for him. "I can smell the booze seeping from your pores!"

"Well, you ought to know what it smells like," I said. "Weren't you king of the frat boys?"

"For three years straight," he said with pride. "Q-Dogs in

the house!" And he topped it off with those loud, irritating barking noises.

"Alright, settle down, Rover," I said, popping two more Advil and swallowing them dry.

Junior put the bag in the kitchen for me, then immediately made himself at home by flopping down on my couch and putting his feet up on my glass coffee table.

"So, you kicked it last night, huh?"

"Just a little bit." I put my fingers up to represent an inch.

"Well, I don't know what you told Mama, but she was running around acting like you were on your deathbed, or something."

"I sure feel like I am."

"And you look it too," he joked, ruffling my hair even more with his huge mitts.

"Who-all showed up for dinner?" I asked.

"The usual: Uncle Woody, Aunt Rita, Aunt Vera, a few of the cousins; plus I had my little soldier with me for the weekend."

"Oh yeah? How's my nephew?"

"Ah, Trey's cool. I just dropped him off with Ashley."

"You two getting back together?" I asked.

"Nah, it's over for good this time. I'm not trying to be with somebody who calls me a nigger every time she gets mad."

Fucking with them white girls! Like Chris Rock said in his routine, it just doesn't pay off in the end.

Junior is twenty-five, and has had a rocky on/off relationship with Ashley since he was a star athlete at Kansas University. I liked the girl initially, but I soured on her when it became clear that she was only with my brother because it looked like he was on his way to making millions in the NBA. After Junior blew out his knee and wasn't picked for the draft, it was all downhill from there. By that time, Ashley was already pregnant with Trey.

Junior reached into his back pocket and handed me a couple of envelopes. "Here, I brought your mail up."

"Thanks," I said, taking the mail and sorting through it. "But I want my keys back, Junior, and I'm not playing."

"Come on, sis. You never know when I'll need them again," he said, trying to keep the keys out of my reach.

"You'll never need them again," I said. "Believe that!"

Junior is my heart, but the eight months he lived with me and Roland was a hellish experience that need not be repeated. Ever!

The boy is just trifling for no reason.

During the time Junior stayed with us, he didn't help buy groceries or contribute towards one bill. His nickname was Captain Couch Potato, because he slept well into the afternoon, and didn't budge an inch when I cleaned or vacuumed around him.

But aside from all that, trifling was taken to a whole new level when Roland and I came home a day early from our Jamaican vacation and walked in on Junior and Ashley screwing in our bed like wild monkeys.

And I *know* Mama and Daddy raised him better than that.

"You think you're slick, don't you?" I said. "Mama already warned me that you are on the verge of losing yet another apartment, so don't even try and butter me up for a place to stay."

Junior picked up the remote control and turned the television to BET. "That's what you said last time. And the time before that, and the other time before that."

"Well I mean it this time, because I can't afford you anymore," I said. "It's time for you to finally get yourself together, and stand on your own two feet for more than just a few months at a time."

Junior waved me off. "I ain't trying to hear all that, Tori!"

"Well that's just too damn bad, because you're gonna hear it," I said, holding my hand out. "Keys please!"

"You don't even have to do me like this," Junior said, giving a wounded hound-dog look before dropping the keys in my palm. "We're family, man."

"It's called tough love," I said, knocking his feet off my coffee table. "Get used to it."

16

It's true. There is never any rest for the weary.

Later on that night, I was finishing research for an initial consultation that I have coming up this week. Eugene Campbell, better known as "E-Money," is an up-and-coming local rapper who wants to throw an album release party.

Being a jazz, neo-soul, and R&B girl, I personally have never heard of E-Money, but this is a project that Sophie dropped in my lap last week, giving me the usual spiel about me being her number one superstar and the only employee she can trust to pull this off.

My plate is full enough as it is, but I don't mind this last minute addition because if all goes well, E-Money's record company will hopefully contract with SWE exclusively to put on all of their future events.

Cha-Ching!

My knowledge of hip-hop is limited mostly to the old-school artists I grew up listening to, so I called Yvette's daughter Alicia, and asked what she knew about the guy.

"Hey, Auntie Tori!" is the way Alicia answered her cell phone, and if I didn't know better I would have sworn she was white.

"Hey sweetie," I said. "I need a favor . . ."

Aside from thinking E-Money's single "Pop Dat Boo-Tee"

is "Tha bomb!" the only other information Alicia knew about him was that he was an "ex drug-dealing gang banger who was shot fifteen times and lived to tell about it."

That didn't tell me much since that happens to be the bio on half the rappers in the music industry. I did a Google search on E-Money and wrote down a few notes.

1) Signed to Bullet Hole Records, a local label that is making a name for itself with other acts such as the Red-Headed Step-Chillren, and a female rap group who call themselves the Princess Posse.

2) Lengthy criminal record with a case pending for felony assault against a former business associate.

I got a phone call while conducting my research and, ironically, the caller ID read:

Kansas City Missouri Police Department

I almost didn't answer, thinking my cousin June Bug was just shit out of luck this time. However, my curiosity got the best of me and I answered the call.

It was Junior.

"Tori, I need for you to come and get me," he said, and I distinctly heard a trace of fear in his voice.

I sighed. "What kind of trouble have you gone and gotten yourself into?"

"I ran into Roland."

Enough said.

The waiting room down at the Police station was noisy and filled mostly with concerned relatives and apathetic, gum-popping baby mamas who were letting their hardheaded kids run wild. I signed my name on a stack of documents and handed over eight-hundred dollars in cash.

"He should be processed out, any minute now," said the clerk behind the bulletproof glass.

I took a seat on one of those hard, plastic chairs and picked up a copy of *People* magazine to kill the time.

"Any minute now" turned into three hours, and counting.

While reading an interesting article about Michael Jackson and his comeback, I heard a familiar male voice say, "Hey . . . How's it going?"

It was Roland. Standing there in front of me sporting a big black eye.

"Hey, yourself," I said, struggling to keep the laughter out of my voice. "What happened to you?"

"I was on my way up to the condo when I ran into Junior and his fists." Roland winced, and placed a can of cold soda on his eye.

Atta boy, Junior! I hope you got a punch in for me, too.

But I was also thinking that even with his right eye discolored and almost swollen shut, Roland is still one sexy M.F.

"Look, I don't agree with what Junior did and I hope you don't think that I put him up to it," I said with all sincerity.

Roland shrugged it off. "Your brother always was a loose cannon. Not to mention a freeloading loser."

"Now see, it wasn't even necessary for you to go there," I said with an angry edge in my voice.

Awkward silence. I mean, *really* awkward.

Finally, Roland sat down next to me and asked, "So, how are you doing these days, Tori?"

It was such a simple question, but I smiled when he asked me this because it had been such a long time since he had.

"Good," I said. "How about yourself?"

"I can't complain. Well, you know, except for . . ." Roland gestured towards his eye, which was turning blacker by the minute. No small feat for someone as dark as he is.

"Is there any particular reason you were on your way up to the condo?" I asked, trying not to sound too hopeful.

"Well for one, I'm pretty sure my BlackBerry is still around there somewhere."

"Well, I'm pretty sure I packed up all of your things," I said. "Where do you think it might be?"

"It could be under the bed, or else in the nightstand on my side of the bed."

My side of the bed. Something about that made my heart sink into my shoes, because even though I had been secretly hoping for reconciliation, it could quite possibly never be his side of the bed again.

"No, Roland, I can't say that I have seen your BlackBerry," I said. "But if I find it, I'll be sure to send it over to your office."

"And how is that?" Roland asked, glaring at me with his one good eye. "Damaged, just like you sent all the rest of my valuables?"

I didn't appreciate his sharp tone of voice or the evil way he was eyeballing me, so I gave Roland a wicked smile and said in a cutesy way, "Damaged valuables? You need to check with the shipping company about that, because I have no idea what you're talking about."

"Look Tori, I know I didn't handle things the way I should have handled them with you, but I have a lot of important information stored in that BlackBerry, so please don't do anything childish and petty."

"Childish and petty? Like breaking up with someone on their wedding day via text message because you were too chicken-shit to let it be known that your *friend* was actually your baby mama?" I said it all in one breath, my anger rising by the second.

"Nuh-uh, no he didn't!" said a young woman sitting across from me. "Niggas ain't shit!"

"Listen," Roland said, now conscious of the fact that we had an audience. "Now is really not the time or place to discuss all of that. I would just appreciate getting my BlackBerry back in good, working condition, okay?"

"And I would have appreciated not being made a fool of the way I was for three years, but there's not much I can do about that now, is there?"

"Come up off of the victim role, Tori. You're a big girl; you knew what time it was."

I knew that he and Veronica were sleeping together?

That statement was so fucking absurd that it was comical as hell. He was obviously grasping at straws, trying to come up with any excuse to make himself feel better about being such a coward.

"That's the best you can come up with?" I asked, and laughed until tears came to my eyes.

Meanwhile, Roland just sat there looking at me as if I had completely flipped the fuck out.

My laughter only seemed to enrage him. The politeness he had displayed at the beginning of our conversation evaporated into thin air.

"Don't fault me for your own stupidity. You would have to be naïve as hell to fall for that good-friend-of-the-family bullshit," Roland sneered at me, venom dripping with each word he spoke. "I'm glad things went down the way they did, because I am exactly where I want to be, which is with Veronica, raising *our* daughter."

The cold, callous look in Roland's eyes sent a chill through my soul, and he suddenly became extremely repulsive to me.

What in the hell was it that I ever saw in this man?

At that moment, I felt as though I never really knew him, that he never really loved me, and the Roland I thought I knew was just a figment of my imagination.

I was just about to get up and move to the other side of the room, when Junior finally appeared from behind a closed door. He looked no worse for wear, but immediately noticed the tension between Roland and me.

"Is there a problem here?" Junior asked me, while looking Roland dead in the eye.

"No, tough guy, there's no problem," Roland replied calmly. "But that attitude of yours is part of the reason why your scrub-ass didn't make it to the NBA."

Uh-oh. Roland knew good and well that that subject was a sore spot for Junior.

"Man, you's a little bitch!" Junior tried to lunge at Roland, but I stood between them, holding Junior back.

"See a bitch, smack a bitch," Roland said.

"I already did that, remember?" said Junior. "And I don't have a problem cold-cocking your ass again, either, punk!"

"Whatever, *boy*," Roland said, looking like a chump. "According to the restraining order you're fifty feet too close, so back the hell up out of my face."

Everyone in the waiting room was tuned in to the commotion. I pushed Junior towards the exit before anything else could pop off. "Come on, Junior, let's go," I said, not wanting to be the next one to have to call somebody to come bail me out of jail.

"It was a pleasure to see you two again!" Roland taunted, suddenly brave now that Junior and I were headed in the opposite direction. "Oh, and Tori, you can send that ring right along with the BlackBerry, too."

"Sure thing," I said, with a smile on my face. "You got that coming."

Just as soon as there is peace in the world.

I have held many things in my hands, and I have lost them all;
but whatever I have placed in God's hands, that I still possess.
—Martin Luther

SUNDAY

Seeing Roland tonight reminds me of two important tasks that have yet to be completed.

The first order of business was to call a 24-hour locksmith to come change these locks, and to add an extra deadbolt for good measure.

While waiting for the locksmith to show up, I grab the thick photo album from under the coffee table, and toss every picture with Roland in it into a trash bag. Three years' worth of Christmases, Thanksgivings, birthdays, vacations, and just happy times in general.

Or, what I had always thought were happy times.

Looking at Roland's face in those pictures, I can see the deceit written all over him. The emotionless eyes, the hardness of his jaw, and the cocky smile all add up to a lowdown snake that was harboring a deep, dark secret.

Why couldn't I see this before?

The locksmith showed up to do his job, and nodded knowingly as I cut Roland's image out of picture after picture. Now I'll bet he has some fucking stories to tell.

It takes me almost two hours, but when I'm done, I haul the trash bag down to the incinerator where my sincere hope is for that bastard to burn in hell.

With that done, I start searching for that damn BlackBerry. I find that it had fallen behind the nightstand on Roland's side of the bed, and is still connected to the charger.

After fishing it out, I promptly drop it into the toilet. The thing hums, vibrates, and buzzes all at the same time. I watch as the lights flicker on and off, displaying these weird patterns and symbols. Then it just goes dead, which to me, symbolizs our relationship.

The greatest discovery of my generation is that a human being can alter his life by altering his attitudes of mind. —William James

MONDAY

I woke up this morning feeling more refreshed than I have in months.

Why?

There are so many reasons to celebrate the absence of Roland and his many trifling-ass habits, like:

1) Blowing his nose at the table while I'm eating.

2) Often forgetting to flush after #2.

3) Clipping his crusty-ass toenails in bed and leaving them for me to clean up.

4) That extreme lactose intolerance of his that chronically flares up in the middle of the night.

5) The globs of toothpaste splattered all over the bathroom sink, along with disgusting remnants of his last meal.

6) Being startled awake by his sharp toenails piercing my skin.

What's more, being unattached comes with freedom and a few other perks, such as:

1) More drawer and closet space.

2) I can cook and eat what I want, when I want.

3) I can go anywhere I want, and stay as long as I want without having to answer to anybody.

17

E-Money showed up two hours late for our consultation meeting.

I was just about to write him off and go on with my other afternoon commitments, when a lanky brown-skinned guy bopped into my office reeking of marijuana and munching on a bag of cheddar-cheese potato chips.

"What up?" he said to me, and then flopped down in the chair across from my desk, offering no apologies or explanations for wasting a huge chunk of my day.

Still, I welcomed him with a polite smile. "You must be Earl Campbell," I said.

"Earl is my government name. I like E-Money better."

"Okay," I said courteously. "E-Money it is."

Mr. Money was sporting a beige Gucci sweat suit with the hat and sneakers to match.

He also had the nerve to bring eight hulking and sulking guys along with him. As they filed into my office and made themselves at home, my one and only thought was that Sophie had thrown me to the wolves.

What the fuck was this all about?

Rule number sixteen in the SWE handbook clearly states

that it is against policy to associate ourselves with clients whose derogatory reputations could tarnish the company's image.

Example: The grand wizard of the Ku Klux Klan would be turned away if he came in here requesting help with the next Klan rally.

It must be the money. Rappers are notorious for their lavish spending habits, and nothing turns Sophie on more than the almighty dollar.

I waited until the entourage was all settled in before speaking. "Is this it?" I asked. "Or are we expecting more people to show up?"

"Nah, this it," E-Money said casually, as if traveling with a three-ring circus is something we all do. "We can go 'head and get started."

"Alright, so why don't you tell me how you envision your album release party," I said. "What elements do you absolutely have to have?"

"Okay . . . You know how my boy Diddy got the white party, right? Check it, I wanna do the *black* party, where everybody is dressed like they going to a funeral and shit!"

I rubbed my temples where a migraine had already kicked up. "I see . . ." I said. "Because the funeral aspect ties in with your image and the theme of the album, right?"

"Yo! 'Cause I'm killing mu-fuckas with my lyrical content, ma!"

Church!

I didn't know how good a rapper he was, but E-Money was certainly colorful and animated. He would be a handful to work with. I could tell that I would constantly have to rein him in, but the bright side was that he probably has a small fortune set aside for the party, and I was going to come out of this with a nice, fat commission check.

I let E-Money rattle on for ten minutes, telling me his vision of the event, which is what I expected of a newly rich, uneducated Negro: Extravagance to the point of gaudiness. He wanted exotic pole dancers, cages for women to dance in naked, naked shadow dancers, a couple of crap tables, juggling flame-throwing bartenders, and a swimming pool filled with cold champagne.

I jotted all his requests down on my notepad, but E-Money wasn't finished yet.

"I want Bengal tigers walking around in that joint, too. And I gotta have a big-ass buffet with nothing but shrimps. Fried, steamed, broiled—all that shit Bubba was talkin' about in *Forrest Gump*."

The entourage laughed on cue, all agreeing that the big-ass shrimp buffet was the best idea yet.

"And," E-Money continued, "I want a six-foot-tall ice sculpture with my name spelled out in block letters. And we gonna need like thirty video projectors, pyro, explosions—all that shit, ma. Feel me?"

"I definitely feel you," I said, patting my heart. "So, let's start with the budget. How much do you have to spend?"

The biggest member of the posse pulled out a Crown Royal bag, and tossed a fat wad of cash onto my desk.

I recoiled as if a snake had just landed in front of me.

The money looked damp and sticky, and I didn't even want to know where it came from, or how it was earned.

"And you are?" I asked the big man.

"Ace," he practically shouted at me, then folded his arms. "I'm E-Money's business partner, manager, bodyguard, and accountant."

"That's ten thousand right there," E-Money said proudly. "Do what you do, ma—make it happen."

The meeting was going downhill fast. Bigger budgets equal bigger commissions, but small, shoestring budgets equal a waste of my damn time.

"Listen, Mr. Money," I said as diplomatically as I could.

"The way it usually works is that ten-thousand dollars is the *deposit* down on the event, not the entire budget."

"Ah, so what chu saying?" E-Money asked with a scowl.

"That I would love nothing more than to bring your vision to life, but I'd say we need upwards of one-hundred thousand dollars—"

"A hundred G's!" the posse shouted in unison.

"At least," I said.

"Lady, you must be out cho damn mind!" Ace yelled at me.

"Can't you get the record label to help offset the cost?" I asked E-Money, beginning to fear for my safety.

"Naw," E-Money said, a little deflated. "Ain't nobody got no hundred G's for no party. Especially when we can take just 5 G's and get it on and poppin' in a penthouse suite at the Ritz."

"Then that is exactly what you should do," I said, edging the stack of money away from me with an ink pen.

"Oh, it's like that?" E-Money said, nodding his head like he was listening to a drumbeat. "Aye y'all, come on! Let's be out."

E-Money bopped out of my office the same way he came in.

Ace shook his head at me, snatched back the wad of cash, and the entire posse bounced up outta my office.

So much for having money to throw away. "Pop Dat Boo-Tee" may be a hit, but as of yet, E-Money hasn't earned the type of cash he needs to throw a SWE party.

18

I know I knocked back my share of drinks that night I went clubbing with the girls, but damn, how drunk was I?

That was the question I asked myself when Reggie the screenwriter reintroduced himself to me. When we met for lunch at P.F. Chang's, the man that stood before me in no way resembled the man I remember meeting and dancing with at Club Suede.

First of all, he had somehow shrunk from five-foot-eight to about five-foot-four, which was irritating because I'm five-foot-six, and I would prefer that a man be at least that tall in order to get on this ride.

Not to harp on the matter, but Reggie was so short that I could see clear over the top of his head, and I had to fight the urge to ask him if he knew a bald spot was forming right on the top of his noggin.

We were seated at one of the large wooden tables at the center of the room.

"What took you so long to call me?" Reggie asked with a smile that revealed spaces between every one of his teeth.

Whoa! He looked like Biz Markie in the mouth.

Sober and in the light of day, Reggie is not what you would call classically handsome. Not that it matters. Looks aren't everything. Like Aunt Vera always says, "You can't take fine to the bank and cash it," meaning looks should not be the primary criteria by which you choose a man. Besides, I have dated enough pretty boys with serious issues to know that looks aren't everything.

"What do you mean, what took me so long to call?" I said. "We just met a week ago."

"Like I said, what took you so long?" he asked. "I would have called you, but I misplaced your number and I've been literally waiting by the phone for you to call."

"That's sweet of you to say," I said, although I knew it was just game.

The server came to take our orders. Lettuce wraps and marinated sea bass for me, and Reggie chose the orange-peel beef.

"So, how's the film project coming along?" I asked.

"Pretty good, actually. My agent told me that they will start casting for the film in a few weeks and we will be going into production in about six months or so."

"You're about to blow up!" I said. "I'll be sure to keep you in my prayers."

"I appreciate that," he said with a grin, flashing that jacked-up grill of his again.

I excused myself and went to the ladies' room to call Simone for more information on Reggie. For the most part, she told me what I already knew, which was that he belongs to one of her writers groups and is also a friend of Rasheed's.

"I know he's not Mr. Universe," Simone said. "But he's a good guy, Tori. You should definitely give him a chance."

Back at the table, our food had just arrived and Reggie had moved to my side of the table so that we were sitting side-by-side.

"You had to call and get the rundown, huh?" he asked, giving me a knowing look.

"Yes, I did," I said. "And I'm happy to report that you passed with flying colors."

"That's good to hear." He leaned over and kissed me on the tip of my nose.

So what if Reggie is vertically and facially challenged?

He is still a nice, interesting guy that I wouldn't mind getting to know better. He asked for a second date. I said yes.

To travel hopefully is a better thing than to arrive.
—Robert Louis Stevenson

THURSDAY

After having lunch with Reggie, I went back to work this afternoon feeling optimistic and energized.

In fact, I had so much surplus energy at the end of the day, that I put myself through a grueling two-hour workout this evening. I was down in the fitness room going from the treadmill, to the Lifecycle, to the StairMaster, to the free weights, like a mad woman. And I have to admit, I felt good afterwards because I am starting to see some results. My ass is no longer spreading like wildfire, and my thighs don't jiggle half as much as they used to.

For weeks, I have been going out of my way to keep from running into Nelson by taking the stairs instead of the elevator, looking through the peephole before venturing out into the hallway, and avoiding common areas where residents congregate to socialize.

I got back up to the ninth floor after my workout, and the moment I have been dreading finally arrived: my door and Nelson's door swung open at the same time.

My heart jumped into my throat, but I calmed myself by reasoning that if I was woman enough to spread-eagle for this man, then I should be woman enough to look him in the eye and be halfway civil.

I held my head up high, and braced myself for the confrontation, only it was not Nelson who stepped out into the hallway. It was Ursula. And she was wearing a slinky, black slip dress and a pair of black high-heeled sandals. Her long hair hung loose and was disheveled. Like maybe she just got through boning something.

This is exactly what happens when you violate the DSWYE rule. You have to put up with shit like this.

19

I did something this morning that I have never done in my life. I asked a man out on a date. Don't ask me where the courage came from, but I called Reggie the screenwriter and boldly asked him to go out with me tonight for dinner and a movie.

"Yeah, that's what's up!" he said with excitement in his voice, and agreed to meet me outside Cinemark Theater at eight p.m.

My day at work was uneventful. I sat in on a couple of meetings, then went out to the Kansas Speedway to take a tour of the venue with a client who wanted to surprise his racing-fan wife with an anniversary party. He never showed. Instead, I received a tearful phone call from him an hour later saying that his homebuilding business was failing due to the mortgage crisis, and he could no longer afford the big extravaganza he had planned for their eighteenth wedding anniversary. It was sad. I felt so bad for the guy that I had to cheer myself up with some retail therapy at the nearby Legends shopping district, where I bought a nice leather jacket from Wilson's Leather, and a couple pairs of boots from Off Broadway Shoes.

I found a chic, pinstriped pantsuit at Ann Taylor, and a cashmere sweater and several cute tops at BCBG.

Once I got home, I decided that fun and flirty would be my

look for the evening. I went with a long, sleek ponytail with a Mohawk center, House of Deréon jeans, and a kimono-style top.

The Cinemark Theater was extra packed, but it did not take long for Reggie to find me standing by the ATM machine where I said I would be.

"Hey, beautiful," he said, giving me a warm hug. "You just keep getting sexier and sexier every time I see you."

"Thanks, and I'm digging your look, as well," I said, referring to his retro '80s gear, which consisted of Cazal glasses, a Polo shirt with an upturned collar, jeans, and black-and-white shell toe Adidas.

"Alright, so let's see how much of a movie buff you are," Reggie said, as we stood in the mile-long line for tickets to the latest Will Smith flick. "*Birth of a Nation*, did you love it or hate it?"

"Hated it!" I said.

"*Friday*, with Ice Cube and Chris Tucker?"

"Oh, that's easy," I said. "Loved it! That's a classic."

"Johnson Family Vacation?"

"Eww . . . I'm a Cedric the Entertainer fan, so I'll just say: it wasn't my cup of tea."

"*The Great Debaters*?

"Love it!" I said. "It was incredible."

The long line in front of us moved a bit, and we inched closer to the ticket window.

"Okay," Reggie said. "*Hustle & Flow*?"

"Hmmmm . . . Truthfully? It just didn't live up to the hype for me," I said. "I mean, really. A pimp and three ho's all living together, and they're still doing bad?"

"Yeah, they should have named it *Hustling Backwards*, instead," Reggie laughed. "But at least it wasn't as ridiculous as *The Cookout*."

"Oh! I don't even understand how movies like that get

made," I said. "Now, somebody at the studio should have put that shit on the grill and burned it!"

"You got that right." Reggie casually draped his arm around my shoulder. "When I get in there, I'm gonna elevate—change the whole game!"

As Reggie and I were talking, some crazy-looking woman ran up on us, foaming at the mouth. "Just what the fuck is going on here?" she shouted, spit flying everywhere.

I was confused. I had never seen this woman before in my life. I gave her a "talk to the hand" gesture, and said, "Excuse me?"

"Oh, you're excused, because I wasn't even talking to you!" she said, then turned to Reggie. "You're foul. You're a foul mutha-fucka, Reggie, and you best believe that my sister is going to hear all about this!" Psycho chick whipped out her camera phone and took a picture of Reggie standing next to me looking like a deer in headlights.

"Enjoy your movie, because your ass is grass now!" she laughed, then disappeared in the crowd.

"Someone you know?" I asked.

"Somethin' like that," Reggie said, wiping sweat from his brow. A minute later, his cell phone started blowing up with back-to-back calls.

"Look," I said. "I don't know what the drama is all about, but I think you need to go take care of that."

"Everything's cool, but you're right. I do need to straighten something out right quick." Reggie gave me thirty dollars and said, "Go on and get the tickets. I'll be right back."

Five minutes passed, and the writing was on the wall.

There was a white couple in their fifties in line behind me. The woman tapped me on the shoulder and whispered, "You're better off, honey. You can do better than that."

Instead of going home to brood about it, I bought one ticket, then went in and watched Will try to save the world, and looking mighty damn fine while doing it.

I had a great time too, mostly because I don't mind going to the movies by myself. It's dining alone that's difficult for me. But, after the movie was over, I decided to tackle that fear head-on by keeping the dinner reservations I had made for two at the Golden Ox.

Word on the street is that mobsters opened the Golden Ox back in 1946, but true or not, the décor surely hasn't changed much since then. It is a cozy, romantic little place with dim lighting, dark, wood-paneled walls, and an open kitchen.

My waiter was an older brother, early fifties maybe, who made my first solo dining experience entertaining and pleasant.

"What do you name a baby girl with one leg shorter than the other?" he asked, removing my lobster tail from its shell for me.

I didn't know the answer.

"Eileen!" he said, "and her nickname would be Tippy!"

Corny, but I still appreciated his efforts to make me feel comfortable. In fact, I enjoyed my meal and the service so much that I didn't even think about Reggie or that he'd had the audacity to abandon me on our date. In fact, that idiot didn't cross my mind until I was spooning up the last of my tiramisu. That's when my cell phone rang, and Reggie's name and number popped up on the caller ID.

"Can I speak to Tori?" a woman's irate voice demanded on the other end of the phone.

"This is Tori speaking."

"Hi Tori, this is Shonda. Are you the one Reggie went out on a date with tonight?"

"If you want to call it that, then yeah."

"Well this is his *wife*, and I really don't appreciate the fact that your phone number is stored in my man's phone!"

"And how is that my problem?" I asked.

"Bitch, it's gonna be your problem if I catch you messing around with Reggie. Now, this was just a courtesy call, but if there should be a next time, bitch, that's gonna be your ass!"

"Look, you really need to check yourself," I said, "because there's not a man alive who is worth all that aggravation."

After that, I couldn't get a word in edgewise.

Old girl was really trying to get live.

Yelling, and calling me everything but a child of God.

She kept asking questions like, "Where you know Reggie from?" "How did y'all meet?" "Have y'all slept together?" and "Did he tell you that we're engaged and have two kids together?" but she didn't pause long enough to get the answers.

Sister-girl was on such a rant that I could have hung up the phone and she wouldn't have known the difference.

Then things really got hilarious when she put Reggie on the phone. "I'm really sorry about all this, Tori," he said. "I should have told you I was already with someone."

Reggie sounded like he was genuinely sorry about the whole situation, which caused Shonda to go off even more in the background. "Tell that bitch you can't see her anymore!"

"I can't see you anymore." Reggie squawked like a damn parrot.

"Tell her you're in love with me!" Shonda demanded.

"I'm in love with Shonda . . ." Reggie repeated.

Squawk! Polly wanna cracker! Squawk!

I ended the call and did the only thing I could do under the circumstances, which was have a good laugh about the whole thing.

The minute you settle for less than you deserve, you get even less than you settled for. —Maureen Dowd

FRIDAY

My new dating record is now 0–3. Man, I really thought I was a better judge of character than this. Then again, this is what dating and "kissing frogs" is all about.

I always said I would never be one of those women who fran-

tically run around trying to find a husband like a chicken with its head cut off. Well, never say never, because here I am.

The truth is, single women in search of their soul mates want every man they date to be "the one" because it is a long process and we don't want the process/road to be long or particularly painful. So we try to circumvent the process by projecting all our hopes and dreams on one poor, unsuspecting guy who just wants a good meal, good conversation, and hopefully a good lay.

Just like Yvette told me the other day, They ain't all gonna be winners, but there is at least one guy out there that has your name on his heart. You just gotta keep going until you find his ass.

20

The day following my "date" with Reggie, Simone and I met for green tea and sushi at Kato's Teahouse.

The restaurant is a magnificent specimen of architecture that always makes me feel as if I've been miraculously transported to Okinawa, Japan, and the zen atmosphere is calming to the spirit, something I definitely needed after last night's misadventure.

As is customary for Simone, she wasted no time relaying third-hand information that she thought I could use.

"I told Fatima about the trouble you've been having and she told me to tell you that it's way too soon for you to be out there."

For the past year-and-a-half, every other word out of Simone's mouth has been "Fatima said this," and "Fatima said that."

Fatima is a life coach who Simone swears is a godsend, but personally, I think the woman is a fraud.

Simone introduced Fatima to me at a party once, and I'm sorry. I just do not trust a woman who wears open-toed shoes and hasn't even bothered to get a pedicure. That right there suggests that the woman doesn't have good, sound decision-making skills.

Why should I trust her to tell me how to go about handling my life?

"Wait a minute," I said, taking a bite of my shrimp tempura roll. "Why are you discussing my personal, *private* business with a woman I don't even know?"

"Fatima's a licensed therapist," Simone snapped, obviously irritated that I don't revere Fatima as much as she does. "And she said it takes at least six months for every year you were together to truly get over a breakup."

I did the math: Three years . . . six months . . .

"So I shouldn't date for eighteen months?" I asked.

"At least that long."

"Hell no! First of all, pleasuring myself has long since stopped being pleasurable, not to mention frustrating as hell," I said. "And at this point, it's not even entirely about orgasms anymore. I need intimacy, too. You know? Someone to hold me, and a warm body to snuggle up to in the wee hours of the morning."

"No," Simone said. "What you need is to give your heart time to heal so that you don't take old emotional baggage into a brand new relationship."

Now she tells me.

"Well if that's true, why in the hell did you introduce me to Reggie?"

"Because the last I knew, he was single!" Simone said. "And besides, you were already back out there meeting the same type of fools you were dealing with before you settled down with Roland—not that he was such a great catch, anyway."

"Of course it's easy to say that in hindsight," I said.

"Well, truthfully, I knew all along that you and Roland wouldn't last. And it's only because ever since I've known you, Tori, you have consistently made bad choices in men."

"Don't we all?" I asked, thinking that Simone was sitting just a little too high on her moral throne. After all, Rasheed is extremely gregarious and has the tendency to be a little too touchy-feely with other women at times.

Me included. He will kiss you on the cheek, put his arm around your waist, rub your shoulders, hold your hand, and Simone thinks absolutely nothing of it.

"Rasheed is just an incredibly passionate man who loves and admires women," Simone told me once. "Nothing more, nothing less."

I don't know . . .

I've been at parties where I saw Rasheed getting a little too close for comfort with other women, but I never said anything to Simone because knowing her, Rasheed and the woman in question would actually have to be in the act of fucking before she would even consider that it was not completely innocent.

Not saying that Rasheed is a cheat, just that I have learned the hard way that it is never a good idea to be *that* trusting of any man.

"Of course, choosing the wrong guy is something we've all done," Simone said, dousing a rainbow roll with soy sauce. "But the problem with you, Tori, is that you are led by your hormones and your emotions, instead of using your head. You only thought Roland was the one, because the sex was good, and because he wasn't always stealing money out your purse like some of the others in your past."

"That's not entirely true," I stammered. "Roland had some other . . . good qualities."

"Like what?" Simone asked, crossing her arms like she couldn't wait to hear this.

"Well, he was extremely affectionate for one thing."

"Affection doesn't count, because it goes back to your hormones. Try again."

"Let's see . . ." I searched my mind for Roland's good qualities, but drew a prolonged blank. Finally, I said, "Fuck it! The truth is he was a conniving, selfish, immature mama's boy, who was a fraud from Jump Street. Is that what you wanted to hear?"

"There you go! Now that is the stuff you should have taken the time to find out before you declared you were in love. Instead, you did what you have always done, which is to fuck first and ask questions later."

"Wow!" I said, completely offended. "That wasn't very nice."

"But it's the truth. And as we all know, the truth ain't always pretty," Simone said. "But if you really want to get deep, you should schedule some couch time with Fatima."

"No, thanks," I said. "Everything ain't for everybody. Besides, I don't need Fatima, when I have you to so lovingly point out my faults and shortcomings."

Exasperated, Simone gave me a "you didn't learn a damn thing" look, drank the last of her tea, and signaled for the check.

21

Sophie breezed into our status meeting twenty minutes late. Gucci sunglasses shielded her eyes, and she was holding her ever-present venti mocha latte, all evidence of a long night with her latest twenty-something Italian boy-toy.

The meeting got underway with Sophie offering no apologies or excuses for her tardiness.

Just rude and inconsiderate. And just one of the many perks of being the boss.

"Tori, how is the planning for the upcoming breast cancer benefit coming along?" Sophie asked.

"Everything is all lined up, and under control," I responded. "We have the models for the fashion show, the caterer, the DJ, the gift bags, and Kay Barnes has been confirmed several times to emcee the event. So, as of right now, there are no foreseeable worries or delays."

Sophie smiled at me. "I knew you'd be on top of things, which is why I choose you, Tori, to be in charge of a surprise sweet sixteen bash for the daughter of a wealthy businessman. Sky's the limit on the budget, which means your commission will be astronomical."

Cha-Ching!

Now that's what I'm talking about. Big money, plus a chance to redeem myself.

The first sweet sixteen party Sophie put me in charge of was years ago, back when my career first started. The event was such a complete disaster from start to finish that I was nearly fired because of it.

That particular event was held in the main ballroom at the Hyatt Regency hotel. The guest of honor was the mayor's bratty, overindulged daughter, who insisted on a Caribbean theme in the middle of November when most things tropical are out of season. On the day of the party, it was all of nineteen degrees outside and the weatherman was predicting several feet of snow, three of which had already fallen. The palm trees, flowers, and pineapples that we did manage to round up were droopy and not of the best quality, but décor would prove to be the least of my worries.

Shortly before the party was to start, one of the lighting technicians was electrocuted and had to be rushed to the hospital, and then I found out that the caterer accidentally brought the wrong food.

Meanwhile, the birthday girl was up in the penthouse suite with some of her closest friends, having a pre-party celebration, which I later found out included marijuana and a couple bottles of Grey Goose vodka. Come party time, the girl was so loaded that when she leaned over to blow out the candles on her birthday cake, she kept leaning forward . . . kept leaning forward . . . kept leaning forward . . . until SPLAT! Little Miss Princess was facedown in the cake—passed out cold.

Ah, man . . . That debacle was the talk of the town for months, and to this day is the one and only blemish on my otherwise spotless reputation.

So of course I'm looking forward to redeeming myself with this one.

"This family is the crème de la crème of high society," Sophie was saying. "So we want to impress these people, and have it be shock and awe all night long."

"Got it," I said, writing it all down. "Just keep the good times rolling and make sure this turns out to be bigger than the prom at her school."

"Exactly!" Sophie agreed. "Which is why this is your baby, Tori. You know what the trends are, and I trust that you have enough creativity and resourcefulness to bring this one home."

"Will do," I said with a smile. "When is the initial consultation?"

"Three o'clock this afternoon."

"And the client's name?"

"Vincent McKinney."

I kept smiling, even though hearing that name was the equivalent to being whacked upside the head with a Louisville slugger.

Vincent McKinney, (aka "super freak") is the owner of a chain of twenty-four-hour fitness centers, and someone with whom I had a steamy on-again/off-again affair, back when I was young, dumb, and full of you know what.

He was thirty-four, I was twenty-one, and for me Vincent was that one liaison everybody eventually has where you learn not all that is good *to you* is necessarily good *for you*. The relationship was doomed right from the beginning. He was married for one thing, and was cruel enough to wait until I was hooked on him before confessing that he was married with three children.

Vincent made it clear to me that he did not intend to leave his wife, but he certainly wasn't against sexing me on the side every chance he got.

Unfortunately, when you are young and naïve, there is always someone willing to take advantage of your youth and inexperience. This is exactly why older men love younger women, because they know you don't know enough to realize when you are being mistreated. Being the dum-dum that I was at the time, I went along with Vincent's infidelity because hey, getting good head is a hard habit to break, and I didn't see any reason to go cold turkey just because he happened to be someone else's husband.

It wasn't the healthiest situation to be in, to say the least. The affair went on for almost two years, and towards the end, I was feeling so guilty and insecure that I could hardly stand myself. Simone suggested therapy, but I took Mama's advice and just prayed on it. It took awhile before I finally wised up, but I eventually recovered my self-esteem, and found the courage to break it off with Vincent completely.

At ten minutes after three, I walked down the hallway towards the conference room, and I could smell Mr. Vincent McKinney before I actually saw him. His signature Fahrenheit cologne never failed to get me in the mood, which is exactly why I did not want to be alone with him in my office, where most of my client meetings are usually held.

Erin was supposed to attend the meeting to take notes and serve as a buffer between Vincent and me, but she was running late getting back from dealing with the florist on another event. Vincent had already been kept waiting for ten minutes, so I had no choice but to start the meeting without Erin.

Before entering the room, I paused in order to calm my nerves, and to gather up the determination to remain detached and professional towards Vincent, as if I had never laid eyes on him before.

I walked into the conference room with my defenses up, and there he was, still fashionably on-point from his Gucci cuff-links and spit-shined Salvatore Ferragamo dress shoes, to his impeccably tailored Purple Label suit with a silk Hermes pocket square and matching tie.

Vincent obviously makes use of the gyms he owns, because even at forty-four, he still has the chiseled, muscle-bound body of life. His smooth, brown face is as handsome as ever and he hasn't lost that mischievous glint in those sexy, dark-brown eyes.

Overall, time has been good to Vincent McKinney.

The only apparent change is that his hair and goatee have bits of gray here and there.

"Good afternoon, Mr. McKinney," I said, offering a handshake. "My name is Tori Carter, and I understand that you want to throw a sweet sixteen party for your daughter."

"You look beautiful, Lolita," he said, opting for a hug instead of the handshake.

Lolita was Vincent's pet name for me, and hearing him say it now really pissed me off.

I quickly backed out of the embrace. "The name is Ms. Carter," I stated firmly.

"Oh, well, excuse me. *Ms. Carter* it is."

"Thank you," I replied coldly, taking a seat across the table from him. "Now, why don't you tell me what you have in mind?"

"Well, Dawn will be sixteen on November second, and I want this party to be a complete surprise for her."

"And your wife?" I asked.

"We're divorced," he said, rather pointedly.

I folded my arms and shot him a look that said, *As if I care two-shits about your marital status!*

"I *meant* does you wife—or ex-wife—know about the party for your daughter?" I asked.

"She does, but Brenda won't be involved with the planning, which is why I need your help, *Ms. Carter.* Word of mouth is that you are exceptionally good at what you do, and I was hoping you could work some of your magic on me," Vincent said, his voice dripping with lust.

I shifted in my seat to keep from getting all worked up *down there.*

"Why don't you tell me about your daughter's likes and dislikes, and we can take it from there," I said, opening my Louis Vuitton portfolio to the notepad.

"Well, Dawn is a typical teenager. She likes to shop, listen to music, eat, run up her cell phone bill, and hang out with her friends."

"Okay . . ." I said, writing it all down.

"And like most girls her age, she seems to have a new infatuation every other week," he continued.

"So what is it this week?"

"Dorothy Dandridge, Eartha Kitt, and all that old Hollywood stuff."

"By 'stuff' you mean glamour, style, and sophistication?"

"Right. Just that whole era is what she's into. The way they dressed and carried themselves . . ."

As I zealously jotted down notes, I could feel Vincent's searing gaze damn near burning a hole in my forehead. I looked up and sure enough, he was staring at me.

"Yes?" I said, more rudely than I should have.

"I was just admiring your beauty," he said. "But aside from that, I have to ask: Do you treat all of your clients in such a rude and ungracious way?" Vincent looked and sounded so wounded, that I felt terrible for treating him so badly.

"No." I let my guard down. "But then again, it's not every day someone I used to love walks through the door and wants to do business with me."

"I can understand that," Vincent said, again with that wounded look. "But I'm not that bad guy that you obviously remember me to be."

He was making me feel lousy, but self-preservation is the first law of nature, and I had to ensure that I wouldn't end up being wounded by this man again.

I decided to put it all out on the table.

"Look Vincent, we're going to be working closely together for the next couple of months so I just want to let you know right now, that I'm not interested in rekindling what we had."

Vincent gazed at me silently for a beat, and then laughed as if I had just told a really good joke.

"Wow! You're quite full of yourself, aren't you, *Ms. Carter*?"

"I wouldn't say that, but I'm certainly not lacking in self-esteem the way I was when we were together."

"Listen, let me clear the air by saying as good as we were together, that is all in the past. The only agenda I came here with was to enlist your help with my daughter's birthday party."

"There are other event planners in town to choose from," I said. "Why did you come here, knowing that this is where I work?"

"Like I said, I know how good you are at what you do. Besides, never underestimate the power of word-of-mouth. I'm always hearing how such-and-such an event wouldn't have turned out so well if it weren't for you," Vincent said, so sincerely that it dissipated my apprehension towards him.

And just like that, the tension between us was gone.

Do you see what I'm dealing with here? The man is such a smooth-talking charmer; he was able to disarm me in less than five minutes. And as further proof of Vincent McKinney's charm and power of persuasion, I am having dinner with him tonight.

It's just a business dinner, though. No big deal.

After all, there are a million-and-one details that have to be hammered out for Dawn's big day, and there is no time like the present to get started.

22

After leaving work, I headed straight over to McCormick & Schmick's Restaurant, where Vincent was already waiting for me in the lobby. Once we were seated at a table, and had ordered cocktails and appetizers, I pulled out my notes and started painting a vivid picture of my vision for Dawn's Old Hollywood–inspired sweet sixteen party.

I planned to recreate a 1930s supper club in the same historic country club mansion where I was to have had my wedding reception. The kids will be dressed to the hilt in elegant eveningwear. I envisioned the birthday girl dripping in diamonds, with marcel waves, and a fur stole.

There will be a red carpet, klieg lights, dozens of photographers, and a fleet of antique Rolls Royce limousines for the guests to arrive in.

Inside the venue, roving waiters will serve hors d'oeuvres, while a live band plays onstage. Soft lighting, tons of cream satin, and a special VIP room for Dawn and her closest friends.

"There should definitely be a classy, sit-down dinner, and even restroom attendants offering gum, mints, lotion, and perfume," I said.

As I talked, Vincent stroked his goatee and nodded his approval as he could see it all playing out in his head.

"It's going to be very Gatsby-esque," I assured him, taking a sip of my mojito.

"That all sounds good, Tori, and I'm sure Dawn is going to love it," he said, caressing my legs up under the table. "But you know something? I'll bet you haven't had multiple orgasms since the last time I gave them to you."

Cocky bastard. With Nelson being the exception, the sad part is, Vincent is absolutely right. Roland wasn't bad in bed, but let's just say that being older, Vincent has much more *experience*, as well as a special talent for going downtown.

"I see you still consider yourself God's gift to women," I retorted, having a flashback of the way he rolled his tongue like an ocean wave and used the tip of it to tease my clitoris with light feathery licks.

"Not *all* women, but I am God's gift to you." Vincent grinned with confidence. "And what's more, I would really like to eat you out right here, right now." He moistened his lips with that extremely long tongue of his, and despite vowing to never have any more sexual dealings with this man, I felt my honey pot getting hot and moist with the anticipation of Vincent's familiar touch.

The chemistry between us was so strong that nothing else needed to be said. I finished what was left of my mojito, while Vincent left more than enough money to cover the bill. We practically raced each other towards the exit.

Vincent left his car at the restaurant, and rode with me for the short drive over to my place. We got in my Navigator and before I could even buckle my seat belt, his hands were all over me and his tongue was swirling around in my right ear.

Vincent ripped my leopard-print Donna Karan blouse open, and went to work nibbling on my breasts as if they were two long-lost friends that he was extremely happy to see again.

I wasn't worried about anyone seeing what was going on inside my vehicle because my windows are tinted, but I was concerned about getting into a car accident.

"We're almost there," I said, pushing Vincent away while trying to stay focused on the road. "Can't you wait?"

"No . . ." Vincent said, putting a hand up my skirt and going straight to my clitoris, which he gently massaged with his fingers. "Tori, you just don't know . . . I have been dreaming about being with you again for so long, that I would fuck you right in the middle of rush hour traffic if you would let me."

"We can't do that," I moaned, as he plunged his fingers deeper inside me.

McCormick & Schmick's is less than five minutes away from my building, but it seemed like it took an eternity to get from the restaurant up to my condo. Once there, we started stripping off each other's clothes right in the foyer. I grabbed Vincent's penis with eager anticipation, and was alarmed to find that there was no magic in his magic stick. Instead of being rock hard and standing at attention, his penis was shriveled as a prune, and as soft as pudding.

"Just let me taste you," he said apologetically. "That should have me ready in no time."

Vincent did his thing, and his skills brought on the multiple orgasms that are his specialty, but he never did get it up. Hot oil massage, pleasure balm, honey dust—nothing worked. I was so embarrassed for Vincent that I didn't want to embarrass him further by asking him the cause of his impotence.

Instead, I was understanding and supportive.

"Don't worry about it," I said, rubbing his back. "I'm more than satisfied."

Truthfully, I was hugely disappointed.

I'd had a couple of explosive orgasms from the foreplay, but damn it, I wanted to close the deal. Especially after all of that anticipation.

Vincent admitted that he had purposely sought me out, and that he wanted to be back in my life for the long haul.

The timing was wrong before, but maybe we could make it work at this point in our lives.

"I'm so happy to have you back in my arms again," Vincent said, while lovingly caressing my face.

"I'm happy too," I said, wrapping both arms around him and squeezing him tight.

And we stayed that way for a couple of hours, until I took him back to the restaurant to get his Jaguar and we parted ways from there.

I see us in a real relationship this time.

Minus the game playing, the wife at home, and all the lies. Just him and me. Straight up, with no chaser.

23

Two weeks after Vincent and I became reacquainted, Yvette, Nadia, and I met for happy hour at the Kona Grill to unwind and catch up. Unfortunately, Simone couldn't make it because she was working one of her many jobs.

The latest is that Alicia is down in Atlanta, loving college life, and after eighteen years of dedication and service, Yvette will be out of a job soon because more cutbacks are on the horizon over at AT&T.

Nadia is progressing steadily with Terrell, aka Mr. Steroid, despite the fact that he said in the latest issue of *Sports Illustrated* that he considers himself to be "very single and looking for that one special woman."

"That's like a slap in the face," I told Nadia. "Essentially what he is saying is that you are good enough to screw around with, but not good enough to marry, or at least introduce to the public as his girlfriend."

"It's not that serious," Nadia said, immediately digging into the appetizers that had just arrived at our table. "Terrell just said that to make himself more popular with his female fans. I know where his heart is."

Yvette and I looked at each other and shook our heads. Clueless should be Nadia's middle name.

"I wish Simone was here," Yvette said to Nadia. "She would be all over your ass right now."

"I know," Nadia replied. "And I wonder what she would say about Terrell offering to pay to get my boobs done."

Yvette and I gasped in unison.

"That's not a good sign," Yvette said. "I mean, you practically just met this man and he's already trying to change you."

"He's a boob man, and if I want to land the big fish, I gotta do whatever it takes to make him happy, right?" Nadia sounded like she was trying to convince herself more than Yvette and me. "Besides, I was already thinking about getting them done anyway."

Ever since I've known Nadia, she has always been self-conscious about the small, A-cup mosquito bites she has for breasts. But still.

"Nadia," I said. "I know you're hoping that somewhere down the line Terrell will ask you to marry him, but it's not smart to make such a drastic change at the request of a man that's not your husband."

"That's right," Yvette chimed in. "You're trying to be a trophy wife, but the shelf-life for trophy wives is extremely short. Once things start sagging, wrinkling and not looking so cute, it's over. On to the next young babe."

"And now you're talking about mutilating your body?" I asked Nadia, feeling deeply sorry for her. "Whatever happened to being happy with how the good Lord made you?"

"You hypocrite!" Nadia said, wagging her finger in my face. "Tori, you're forever complaining about saddlebags and cellulite. Now you want to front like there isn't anything about yourself that you'd change."

"There isn't!" I said. "Especially not if I had to have surgery to change it. Now, if I could just get a shot or pop a pill, then yes, I'd try something. But do you actually know how breast implant surgery is performed? Girl, they cut your nipples off and put them on the table!"

"Ewww!" Yvette said, covering her breasts as if they hurt from just the thought of it.

"Well, I don't really care," Nadia said. "As long as they look good afterwards. I think I'm gonna go with like, a 38 Double-D."

"Oh, you're going for the stripper tits," I said, snatching up the last piece of calamari before Yvette could finish off the whole platter by herself.

"That's right," Nadia said. "Go big or stay home."

"Well, I don't see anything wrong with cosmetic enhancements," Yvette said. "But I would never get breast implants, though. I've heard way too many horror stories."

"That's easy for you to say," Nadia retorted. "You already have big, bodacious tah-tahs."

"Yvette's a size eighteen," I said. "She's supposed to have big boobs."

"I'm a sixteen now," Yvette snapped. "Thank you very much!"

"All I know is that if you keep this weight loss up, you're not going to be able to get into Club Heifers anymore," Nadia told Yvette.

"And that's just fine with me," Yvette said, striking a model pose. "They're just gonna have to be one heifer short!"

"Okay, okay," I said between bites of my Maui taco. "Who's got the dirt?"

"Ooh! I do! I do!" Nadia said, like a sugar-crazed third grader.

I rubbed my hands in anticipation. "Well, let's hear it."

"Well," Nadia said dramatically. "A certain somebody who shall remain nameless, but is sitting at this table, has recently been spotted in the company of a handsome, older gentleman who creeps in and out of her place at all times of the day and night."

Damn that Nadia with her nosy ass.

I gave Yvette a puzzled look. "Is it you?" I asked.

"Shit, I wish!" Yvette said. "I could use an old sugar daddy in my life, especially with Alicia's college tuition bill kicking my butt the way it is."

Silence fell over the table for a few minutes.

I kept my eyes on Yvette's face and could almost see the wheels turning in her head.

"Wait a minute . . . So if it's not me or Nadia," said Yvette, slowly putting two-and-two together, "that leaves you, Tori!"

"Bingo!" Nadia said happily, sipping her sangria.

I was nowhere near ready to discuss Vincent with anyone just yet and certainly not Yvette, who hates him with a passion because of the way he treated me back in the day.

All eyes were on me and inquiring minds wanted to know.

"So what's his name, girl?" Yvette asked me, all excited.

"That's not important right now," I said, glaring at Nadia. "I didn't bring it up to you guys because the relationship is so new, I don't want to jinx it." I busied myself trying to fish the maraschino cherry from my Long Island iced tea.

"What does this guy look like?" Yvette asked Nadia, suspiciously.

"He's on point, I'll tell you that. He's tall, good looking, and built solid for a man in his forties," Nadia said. "*And* judging by that red Jaguar and the way he dresses, the man definitely has his bank account up."

"You better say it ain't so," Yvette interjected, looking like she wanted to reach over and slap the taste out of my mouth. "Just please tell me Nadia is not talking about who I *think* she's talking about."

"Who, Yvette?" Nadia asked, excitedly.

"Just some ole no-good married sonofabitch who drug Tori's heart through the mud for a couple of years and then stomped on it."

"Oooh!" Nadia said. "Scandalous!"

"Don't you think you're jumping the gun a little bit?" I asked Yvette. "I mean, the man in question could be someone entirely different for all you know."

"Is it Vincent?" Yvette asked me, almost threateningly. "Yes or no? It's a simple question."

"Okay! Yeah, *and*?" I said. "*So*?"

"*So* what the fuck are you thinking?" Yvette said loud enough for people to turn and stare. "You have got to be stuck-on-stupid and double-parked-at-dumb to get hooked up with that bastard again, Tori. Have you forgotten all those times I sat with you while you cried enough tears to drown in, over his sorry ass? Because I sure haven't."

"Look, that's all old news, okay? Now can we please change the subject, because really, when it comes down to it, it's no one else's business."

"Bull*shit*!" Yvette snapped. "The people I love are my business and somebody needs to pull your coattails until you get it through your head that you don't dip back, *ever*."

"Even I go by that philosophy," Nadia agreed, giving me a *shame-on-you* look.

"That's right," Yvette said adamantly. "When it's over, it's over."

"Oh, that's rich as hell coming from Miss I'm-still-sleeping-with-my-ex-husband-even-though-he-divorced-my-ass-and-married-someone-else," I said to Yvette.

"No you didn't!" Yvette said. "You don't want me to get started on your situation, Tori."

Meanwhile, Nadia was shocked. "You and Ant still get busy from time to time?" she asked Yvette.

"Me and Andre have a daughter together."

"So that entitles him to a lifetime supply of coochie anytime he wants it?" I asked.

"Look, I cut that creeping-with-my-ex shit out a long time ago," Yvette said. "And Tori, if you're smart, you'll do the same thing and not let that sneaky son of a bitch worm his way back into your heart and your panties again."

Yvette was so upset that I didn't have the heart to tell her that Vincent had already done just that.

24

"Work it, baby,"Vincent said, enjoying the seductive striptease I was performing for him in black lacy Agent Provocateur lingerie.

While I danced, Vincent sat on the bed wearing just a pair of burgundy silk boxers and a robe to match. He put his glass of Merlot on the nightstand and said, "Get your sexy ass over here so I can suck those luscious titties."

I sauntered over to him and rubbed my breasts across his face. "You want some of this?" I asked, pushing him back on the bed.

"Baby, I want all of that," he said, pulling me down on top of him.

I put my hand inside the opening of Vincent's boxers, and lo and behold, we had signs of life down there.

Hallelujah! Now we were finally going to consummate our renewed relationship.

Just as I was about to straddle Vincent, his doorbell rang.

"Sweetheart, I have to go get that," he said, gently pushing me aside. "I'll be right back."

"Don't be too long," I said, striking a seductive pose across the bed.

Vincent tied his robe closed and shut the bedroom door behind him.

While he was gone, I took the opportunity to do a little snooping. A quick look in his nightstand drawer revealed a stack of porno magazines, a nearly empty bottle of baby oil, an X-rated video, condoms, and a prescription bottle of Viagra that he had filled at CVS/pharmacy earlier today.

Well, now. I couldn't take all the credit for putting magic back in the magic stick, after all.

I quickly closed the drawer as the bedroom door opened, and Vincent walked back in with a woman trailing behind him.

"Tori, I want you to meet a friend of mine," Vincent said, referring to the scantily clad, cosmetic surgery-enhanced Amazon who looked like she just got off a pole down at Bazookas strip club. "Rosalyn, meet Tori. Tori, Rosalyn."

"Nice to meet you, Tori," Rosalyn said in this Betty Boop meets Minnie Mouse voice.

I tentatively shook Rosalyn's outstretched hand, not sure where all this was headed, especially since Vincent and I were both half-naked, and his Viagra-induced boner was protruding right through his robe.

"Sweetheart, you are just in time to join the party," Vincent told Rosalyn as he started massaging her shoulders.

"I can see that," Rosalyn said, looking me over. "She's just as gorgeous as you said she was."

"She is, isn't she?" Vincent said. "Look at those lips . . . and that ass! Oh my goodness!"

Screech! Hold up. Now, I may be a little slow to catch on at times, but I would have to be intellectually disabled not to see what was going on here.

"Nuh-uh! You got me so twisted!" I told Vincent as I jumped up off the bed and started putting my clothes back on.

"I thought you said she was down for whatever," Rosalyn said to Vincent, looking disappointed.

"Trust me, she is," Vincent assured her. "Tori is very open-minded and experimental. Aren't you, Lolita?"

"I am?" I asked him, surprised to find this out about myself.

"Obviously you don't know me as well as you thought you did, because this is some sick shit."

"Why?" Rosalyn asked me. "Because you don't want to do it?"

"Bingo!" I said sarcastically. "Despite whatever Vincent may have told you, I like my sex the old-fashioned way, which for me, is one man and one woman!"

"Listen," Vincent said impatiently. "I didn't think I would have to go this far to get you to try new things, but do you think your boss would appreciate you losing a client who was prepared to spend at least a couple hundred grand with her company?"

My mouth damn near hit the floor. "I hope you're not implying what I think you are implying, Vincent."

"I don't want to play hardball with you Tori," he said, rubbing a hand across his erection. "But I want this so bad that if it has to come down to 'no ménage, no party,' then so be it."

"Oh my God . . ." I said, completely in awe. "You're still the same selfish, sex-addicted motherfucker you always were, aren't you?"

Vincent casually shrugged off the accusation. "I love pleasing women," he said. "Hell, it's not like you didn't benefit from it."

"So, essentially what you're saying is that you expect me to be your sexual slave in exchange for your business?"

"Sounds like a fair exchange to me," Vincent said, nonchalantly sipping his Merlot. "How about you, Rosalyn?"

Rosalyn nodded, then turned to me and said, "Give it a chance. You'll be in good hands, I promise."

By then, I was fully dressed. I slipped my pumps back on, and stuffed the lingerie into my python leather Prada bag.

Vincent ran over and blocked the doorway to keep me from leaving. He got down on his knees and buried his head between my legs. "Let us show you how good it can be," he pleaded, the heat from his breath stimulating my clitoris.

It was hard, but I forcefully pushed Vincent away from me and said, "I'm leaving now, and don't you ever call me again, you limp dick motherfucker."

Vincent threw up his hands in frustration as I walked out of his apartment and out of his life forever.

25

The next morning, my mother called just as I was leaving for work, all up in arms about walking in on Aunt Vera having sex with Brother Edwards, a widower from down at the church.

This morning, Mama had gone to check on Vera like she does every day, and there they were, two old geezers going at it right in the middle of the living room floor.

"Ooh!" Mama said, disgusted. "I just can't get that nasty-ass image out of my head!"

Aunt Vera has always been tougher than a two-dollar steak, and completely incorrigible. Even at seventy-four, she can still teach any sailor a thing or two about cursing, and then turn around and drink his ass right up under the table.

Usually, as people get older they begin to repent, and cling closer to religion. But not Aunt Vera. She's still doing the same stuff she was doing in her thirties, which is frequenting blues clubs, drinking, gambling, smoking, and apparently, having sex.

"Well, like I keep telling you, Aunt Vera is grown," I laughed. "And if she can still get busy at her age, then I say God bless her and more power to her!"

Mama did not see the humor. "The woman is five years older than dirt, and I would think she would have more decorum than that!"

"So what did Aunt Vera have to say for herself?" I asked.

"Nothing much," Mama said. "Just told me to go back out the same way I came in, and next time use the doorbell."

"You two didn't fall out, did you?" I asked.

"You better believe we did!" she said. "Which is why I need for you to do me a favor and run your auntie around this afternoon."

Aunt Vera and Mama are forever arguing over something petty, and I'm always the one caught in the middle.

"Mama, I am extremely busy with work these days," I said. "What about Junior?"

"Oh, that's what I meant to tell you! Do you know that boy is about to get his car repossessed? The repo man came over here today looking for him."

"The car that I cosigned for?" I asked.

"I guess so . . ."

Great, just what I need. Another financial mess of Junior's to clean up after before it adversely affects my credit.

"So will you take Vera to run her errands for me?" Mama asked, ever so sweetly.

"Yes, ma'am." I said dutifully, even though I had no idea how I would find the time.

"Thank you, sweetheart," she said, happy to have gotten her way. "I appreciate cha!"

Uh-huh.

No one is useless in this world who lightens the burdens of another.—Charles Dickens

TUESDAY

When it comes to my loved ones, I always say yes even when I really want to scream no!

Remember that old song, "Superwoman"?

Well, because I have the ability to multitask like crazy, and cram a lot into a single day, Superwoman is exactly who most people think I am. That's a ton of weight to carry every day. It's like, once people know that you're competent and reliable, you can never get a moment in edgewise for yourself because your to-do list is always filled up taking care of other people's business.

I love my family and all, but sometimes I feel so put-upon that I fantasize about running away from it all. I'm talking about just straight-up packing up, and checking out.

Like that businessman I heard about on the news last month. I forget his name, but let's call him Jack Suburbia. Jack lived a routine life with his wife and kids until one morning he left for work and never made it to his job as an accountant. Everyone thought Jack had met with foul play since his bank account had been emptied and his car was found abandoned in a city park.

As it later turns out, Jack was found alive and well in Lubbock, Texas, where he was working as a convenience store clerk. Jack admitted to the news camera crew that tracked him down that he just needed a break from his life. Plain and simple.

Not that I would actually do that, because my family means the world to me. But sometimes, I just need a break from all the madness.

26

My day at work was all about gearing up for the annual Firefighter's Ball, which is always one of the most anticipated social events of the year. My meeting with the design team lasted all day, because everyone had conflicting ideas on how to make this year's event bigger and better than the previous ones.

At the end of the day, my brain was fried and my patience was thin, yet I still had Aunt Vera to contend with.

My aunt's home of forty-plus years is located in a South Kansas City enclave that is considered prime real estate for affluent black professionals.

As I pulled up into her driveway, my eyes were drawn over to the Robinsons' front porch, where I saw this unbelievably gorgeous guy, who had a Michael Ely–vibe going on. I waved hello. He waved back, and smiled. I could feel his eyes follow me as I walked up to Aunt Vera's porch, where I rang the doorbell, and waited.

My aunt never locks her front door, but I was scared to let myself in unannounced like I normally do, for fear that she would be in there bumping and grinding with Brother Edwards again.

"There's my shuga!" Aunt Vera said, opening the door for me.

"Hey, Auntie!" I said, giving her a hug. "Don't you look nice and colorful today?"

"Thank you, baby," Aunt Vera said, graciously accepting the compliment.

Colorful is actually an understatement. My aunt was sporting a velour, leopard-print tracksuit with gold metallic tennis shoes, gold fanny pack, and a metallic gold sun visor.

Just styling, okay? And despite all of her sinning ways, Aunt Vera looks good for her age. She is only slightly overweight, and her smooth, sand-colored skin is a testament to the fact that good black will never crack.

Told one too many times that she resembles Lena Horne, Aunt Vera is so vain that she won't leave the house or even answer her front door without full makeup and a nice wig.

"A lady is a lady at all times. Even when nobody is looking," she always reminded me whenever she caught me drinking out of a bottle or a can, or sitting without crossing my legs.

After helping Aunt Vera up into my SUV, I jumped behind the wheel and the strong smell of Blue Grass perfume made me sneeze four times in a row.

"Here you go, baby." Aunt Vera reached down into her titty bank and pulled out three crumpled and soggy dollars. "A little something for your gas tank."

"Little" is right. But bless her heart. Aunt Vera has never owned a car, or even learned to drive, so she has no understanding that three dollars doesn't do a thing for my gas tank.

Unfortunately, Lincoln Navigators aren't the most fuel-efficient vehicles on the market, and in the two years that I have owned mine, complete strangers have taken every opportunity to remind me that Jesus would not drive such a gas-guzzling monstrosity. Maybe not. But since I have no authority to debate what Jesus would or would not do, my only defense is that the truck is roomy, has a great GPS system, and comes in handy when it comes to hauling loads of stuff for events.

"So, where we headed?" I asked Aunt Vera, as I backed out of her driveway.

Aunt Vera rattled off a long list of places she needed to go:

1) Bank of America: Cash social security check ("But ain't nothing *secure* about it!")

2) Optometrist: Pick up new eyeglasses

3) Walmart: Pick up prescription from pharmacy and get miscellaneous items

4) Price Chopper: Grocery shopping

5) Home Depot: A couple bags of mulch, plants on sale for $7.99

6) Liquor store: A six-pack of Miller High Life and a pint of Canadian Mist

7) Bunny's Wig Emporium: Get some new hair

It was almost nine o'clock by the time Aunt Vera and I made it to Home Depot, which was, thankfully, our final destination. The two of us were searching for the best-looking Yucca plant, when I heard a male voice say, "Excuse me . . . don't I know you from somewhere?"

That's original.

I turned around and came face-to-face with Nelson.

Damn.

It was just my luck to have successfully avoided him for almost three months, only to end up running into him halfway across town.

Nelson had a box of Miracle-Gro in his hand, and wore beige khaki shorts, black Havaiana flip-flops, and a black touristy T-shirt that said "New Orleans" across the front of it.

"Hey!" I said, with a surprised smile. "Long time, no see."

"Yeah, it has been a minute, hasn't it?" he asked.

"Yep . . ." was all I could think of to say, while simultaneously having flashbacks of all the nasty acts we engaged in the last time we saw each other. Acts that I am now so embarrassed to have committed that I could feel my face flushing hot.

My one-time lover smiled that dazzling smile of his, and did not look to be nearly as nervous and uncomfortable as I was at that moment. "So," Nelson said. "Just out doing a little plant shopping?"

"Yeah . . . among other things . . ." I stammered, looking everywhere but directly at him.

Aunt Vera cleared her throat, waiting for an introduction. "Oh, I'm sorry . . . Aunt Vera, meet Nelson Tate, one of my neighbors. Nelson, this is my aunt, Mrs. Vera Hayes."

"Pleasure to meet you, Mrs. Hayes," Nelson said, giving Aunt Vera a warm handshake.

"Same here," Aunt Vera said. "You seem like such a nice young man. Are you married?"

"Yes ma'am," he said, and then caught himself. "I'm sorry, I mean, my wife passed away a little while ago."

"Oh, what a shame!" Aunt Vera said. "I'm a widow myself, you know."

Nelson started to say "I'm sorry" but Aunt Vera cut him off.

"Don't be sorry," she insisted. "That man was one of the *evilest* bastards who ever drew breath. Nothing to be sorry about!"

Aunt Vera patted Nelson on the back, and went back to looking over the yuccas. Meanwhile, I still hadn't thought of anything substantial to say to Nelson, who was starting to look just as awkward as I felt.

"Well, I'm not going to hold you up any longer," he said. "But, um, we definitely should get together soon to catch up."

"Sounds good!" I lied, with a smile on my face.

Catch up on what? We know little more about each other than what we look like naked, and the last thing I need to do is be reminded of what a slut I can be without even really putting my mind to it.

* * *

Back at Aunt Vera's house, I climbed out of the truck and popped the hatch open. Just as I was about to start unloading my aunt's purchases, the Michael Ely look-alike approached.

"Good evening, Miss Hayes." He waved to Aunt Vera. "Do you mind if I help you ladies with all of this?"

It was a rhetorical question because without waiting for permission, he hefted two large bags of mulch, and followed Aunt Vera up to the house.

Umph! Strong and fine.

"You can set everythang down right inside the door, baby," Aunt Vera said, unlocking the door and going inside. "We can manage from there."

"Yes ma'am," he said politely, obeying her command.

Meanwhile, I was still at the back of the truck separating the few items I picked up for myself, from Aunt Vera's things. The Michael Ely look-alike rejoined me, and was so forward as to place a hand on the small of my back.

"You know, I see you visiting from time to time and I swore to myself that the next time I saw you, I would come over here and introduce myself."

"And what's your name?" I asked, flirting with a demure smile and lots of eye contact.

"Chris Jenkins. The Robinsons are my godparents."

"Chris, I'm Tori," I said, extending a hand. "Nice to meet you."

"Likewise," he said, shaking my hand.

After having placed all the bags right inside the door, like Aunt Vera told him to, Chris stood at the front door, waiting to be invited in.

Aunt Vera noticed. "Chris, baby, I sure appreciate you helping us with these groceries and thangs. Tell Vydella I said 'hey' and not to forget that red velvet cake she's supposed to make for the pastor's anniversary dinner on Sunday."

"Yes ma'am," was all Chris was able to get out before the door closed in his face.

"Aunt Vera!" I protested. "How can you be so rude? That man just did us a favor."

"Just saving you some time, chile," she said, snatching her wig off and scratching her scalp. "That is exactly the type of man you *don't* need."

"Did you *see* him?" I asked, flabbergasted.

" 'Course I did. I see him nearly every day, 'cause he's always down to Vydella and Herbert's borrowing money and eating them outta house and home. He's probably on that stuff, you know."

"And what stuff is that, Aunt Vera?"

"That dope, girl!" she said. "Why you think I didn't want him in my house? Boy be done came back in here and robbed me blind."

I was skeptical because Aunt Vera is forever accusing people of being "on that stuff," which is just another one of her many eccentricities.

Then again, she is a retired nurse who knows something about everybody in town. If she doesn't know anything about you, you can bet she knows something about your mama 'nem.

"Auntie, are you sure? Because he didn't smell, he had all his teeth, and—"

"Yeah, I know. He was what you call 'fine,' wasn't he?" she said, giving me a wink. "What you outta know by now is that fine is, as fine does. Look at Roland. He was fine too, and he didn't turn out to be worth a damn."

Touché.

Aunt Vera has a way of dispensing advice and wisdom, yet making you feel like a fool at the same time. I felt like I was sixteen again, with her warning me that nothing was open after midnight but legs and liquor stores.

Aunt Vera has been married and divorced several times over, which indicates that her judgment when it comes to men is not much better than mine, but her being seventy-five does count for something.

When an elder speaks, one damn sure ought to listen. Which is why when I left Aunt Vera's house and found a scrap of paper with Chris's phone number left under my windshield, I didn't think twice about tearing it in half.

27

Nelson's silver Cadillac Escalade was the first thing I saw when I pulled into the parking garage of my condo building. Clearly, he was at home, which meant that I had to go into stealth mode.

I took my keys out of my purse while I was on the elevator, so that I didn't have to fumble for them in front of my door. I didn't want all that jangling to alert Nelson.

I tiptoed to my door, feeling like a thief about to break into my own place. Just as I put my key in the door, Nelson's door creaked open, and he stepped out into the hallway.

"You weren't trying to avoid me, were you?" he asked, in a teasing way.

"No! Of course not!" I laughed nervously.

"Good, because I would like to talk to you if you have time."

I sighed like I was being put upon, which I was. "Right now?"

"No, the day after tomorrow," he joked. "Yeah, right now. That is, if you can spare me five minutes."

I followed Nelson into his condo, and noticed the devilish glint in his eyes when he asked, "Would you like a glass of wine?"

"No thanks," I said tersely, and watched while he poured himself a glass of Chardonnay.

Looking at his body language, the way he suddenly tensed

up and became anxious, it all became clear to me. Nelson got sprung on my poonanny, and has been fiending for a hit of Tori ever since. Poor thing. Now I had to crush his hopes by letting him know that he and I can never be.

I felt so badly for him, I wanted to hug him. But I refrained, deciding it would be a nice touch to save the comforting hug for after I broke his heart.

Nelson offered me a seat on the sofa, and sat down beside me. "I've been thinking about that night we spent together," Nelson said, taking my hand.

Ohmygoodness, he's about to propose marriage!

I know my honey pot can be addictive, but damn. This is much too soon.

"I like you a lot, Tori," he continued, gazing at me intently. "And I just want to clear the air by offering you a sincere apology for what happened, and for how things were left off between us."

A shocked "What?" escaped my mouth before I could stop it.

My face cracked in a million pieces, and I hoped it didn't show, but I knew it did.

Well fuck you then! I screamed at Nelson in my head. It wasn't like I was ready to order the invitations and call the florist, either.

"Is something wrong?" Nelson asked, looking very concerned.

"No, not at all!" I said, recovering nicely. I hoped. "I was just thinking that no apologies are needed because that night, we were two consenting adults who had too much to drink and then went with the flow of things, you know? No big deal. No hard feelings."

"You sure?" he asked, with a smile.

"Positive!" I said, reaching out and giving him a reassuring hug. "And you know what, Nelson? I am so glad you wanted to put this out on the table because the truth is, there is someone special in my life now, and I can't even tell you how deeply I regret that night we had. I seriously wish it had never happened."

I got a degree of pleasure watching *his* face crack into a million little pieces. After picking his face up off the floor, Nelson offered me a handshake. "Friends?" he asked.

"Friends."

The beginning is always today. —Mary Wollstonecraft

WEDNESDAY

I woke up this morning thinking about the conversation that I had with Nelson last night, and I realize now that I should have gotten some clarification on that. Is that friends with, or without, benefits?

And just what is his angle anyway?

One minute he's celibate, the next he wants to fuck, and the minute after that, he just wants to be friends.

Can men and women be friends once they have already had sex? It depends. If you have two individuals who are extremely mature, well-adjusted, and who have no hidden agendas, then maybe it can work. Otherwise, I don't think straight men know how to be "just" friends with women. The very best they're able to do is bide their time by putting you in the "I'll-catch-you-at-a-vulnerable-moment-and-tap-that-ass-when-the-time-is-right" category.

Men like to play the sensitive, caring brother for a certain length of time, but getting the coochie is always the ultimate goal. Of course, he's not going to tell you this. Nevertheless, that's the deal.

It's too soon to tell if this is where Nelson is coming from. All I can say for sure, is that I am not going to be his across the hall booty call, someone he can screw, with no strings attached, whenever he's feeling horny.

28

I walked into my office Monday morning, to find a bouquet of flowers, a gift basket, and a note of apology from Vincent that said: *Call me if you think we can get past this. If not, I will understand*.

Negro, puh-leeze!

How stupid does he think I am?

You can't try to blackmail me into having a threesome and then expect me to forgive you.

I tore the note card in pieces, then gave the flowers and gift basket to the first person who walked by my office, which happened to be Demetrius.

"For me?" he squealed, as if I had just crowned him Miss Gay America.

"For you, darling," I said. "Enjoy!"

After that, I walked down to the conference room for our daily status meeting. When Sophie asked, "Tori, what's latest on the Dawn McKinney sweet sixteen party?"

I had with no choice but to announce that it was a no-go. Sophie nodded and, thankfully, continued the meeting without probing any further, but the second the meeting was over, she pulled me aside and said, "Tori, my office. Right now!"

I followed Sophie into her plush corner office, which puts all the other offices in the company to shame.

If things work out as planned the office will be mine someday, with its leather furnishings, expensive paintings, hideaway wet bar, mini-fridge, TV, and floor-to-ceiling windows that offer spectacular views of downtown Kansas City.

"Have a seat," Sophie said, closing the door behind us.

I sat in the wing-backed chair across from her massive glass desk and waited anxiously for whatever it was she had to say.

"So," Sophie began. "Mr. McKinney has decided not to work with SWE after all?"

"Unfortunately, that is correct," I said.

"Well I'm confused, because the way I understood him before he met with you initially, was that it was pretty much a done deal. What the hell happened?" Sophie asked, with a look of suspicion on her face.

Think fast . . . Think fast . . .

"After some discussion, Mr. McKinney decided it would be better to buy his daughter a new car and send her on a first-class trip to Paris in lieu of the party," I lied.

Sophie's facial expression relaxed a little, and she seemed to buy it.

"And what about the album release party for Eugene Campbell?" she asked. "Why didn't that work out?"

Now that one was easy.

"Because as great as I am, Sophie, I am not a magician," I said. "There is just no way to put together a decent event for five hundred guests on a measly ten thousand dollar budget."

"Tori, I know you're used to clients with unlimited budgets, but one of the first things I taught you about this business is that nothing is impossible. Granted, you had your work cut out for you, but you could have humbled yourself by finding a way to make it work."

"Well, let's not forget that the man is a rapper," I said. "The cost of insurance and security that we would've needed would have been twice the amount of that measly little budget."

Sophie folded her arms and gave me a look that said, *Have you lost your rabbit-ass mind?* "You blew it! That young man is going to be incredibly rich and famous one day," Sophie said. "And when he can afford to throw parties in excess of one-hundred thousand dollars, he's going to go somewhere else because he'll remember that we told him his money wasn't good enough for us. I can't tell you how disappointed I am in you, Tori."

I quickly wiped at the beads of sweat that had suddenly popped up on my forehead, and silently thanked God for the melanin in my skin. If I were a few shades lighter, I would have been fire-engine red at that point, because I was definitely in the hot seat.

"Well, I guess we'll just have to agree to disagree," I said in my own defense. "It just could not be done, Sophie. And I will stand by my decision, even if it means losing my job."

Sophie smiled at me as if I were an exasperating brat.

"That's a commendable stance to take, especially since you have lost two potential clients, and managed to alienate one of our best caterers. All in six months' time."

My mind raced, trying to backtrack and pinpoint which caterer I worked with recently that I could have pissed off. Then it came to me.

"Colin?" I asked tentatively.

Sophie nodded, confirming my suspicions. "That's right. He called me a few days ago, requesting that he not be paired with you on any future events he should contract to do with SWE."

That nasty motherfucker.

I had not planned to use Colin's services anymore anyway, but I definitely would have told Sophie about his booger habit if I had known that he would turn the tables on me like this.

Now it looks as though *I'm* the problem. I had no choice but to launch a counterattack.

"Sophie, the situation with Colin is that I walked in on him picking his nose."

Sophie looked unfazed. "Under what circumstances?" she asked calmly, as if we were talking about the weather.

"I'm sorry?" I asked, not quite comprehending the question.

"Under what circumstances did you catch Colin picking his nose? Was he actually in the kitchen cooking at the time of this alleged nose picking?"

"No, he wasn't cooking at the time," I admitted, feeling like I was on trial. "But it's still a disgusting habit for a chef to have. I mean, I can't conscionably use Colin's services again, knowing that he has such a disgusting habit."

"Let me get this straight: you caught Colin picking his nose *one time*, and that *one* instance led you to believe that he would be so unsanitary as to pick his nose while he was in the kitchen cooking?"

It was a surreal moment. Two grown, professional women having a conversation about boogers.

"All I'm saying is that it's a possibility," I said. "And when it comes to providing the best catering services for our clients, that is a chance I am just not willing to take."

Sophie leaned back in her swivel chair, and started tapping her pen against the desk, something she does when weighing a tough decision.

After a long moment, she finally said, "Tori, nose picking, just like farting, is something we all do from time to time. Now, I have to tell you I think your reasoning is way off on this matter, and frankly, you have been uncharacteristically ineffective since April third."

That was an extremely low blow.

April third was the day I was supposed to have married Roland.

"Just what are you alluding to, Sophie?" I snapped. If I was going to be fired, I refused to go out like a punk.

"Simply that you need to take some time off to recharge your batteries," Sophie said. "Consider it the time you should have taken after your relationship fell apart, instead of coming right back to work as if you were Superwoman and Wonder Woman all rolled into one."

"Do I have any say in the matter?" I asked.

"No," Sophie said firmly. "And if it were anyone else besides you, they would have been shit-canned." She snapped her fingers. "Just like that! Now, you can call it a sabbatical, a mental health break, or just a plain ol' vacation, but I want you to take six weeks off."

I opened my mouth to protest, but Sophie shut me down with a hard look that indicated she had given this a lot of thought, and her mind was already made up.

And just like that, I was temporarily unemployed.

I left the building feeling like I had just been fired.

From my office all the way down to the parking lot, Sophie's voice echoed in my head.

Call it a sabbatical, a mental health break, or just a plain ol' vacation . . .

Of the three, vacation sounded best.

In the years I've spent building my career, the words "time off" mysteriously vanished from my vocabulary and "vacation" was something I viewed as overrated and unnecessary. Mainly because there's no money in it.

We get vacation pay, sure, but bonuses and commissions are my bread and butter. They account for over half of my yearly income, which is a hefty amount of money to miss out on. And for what? Rest and relaxation?

Shit, I need to make this money while I can make it, because one thing's for certain, I'll get plenty of rest when I'm dead.

But all of that is neither here nor there. I couldn't go back to work even if I wanted to, because Sophie confiscated my employee ID badge and the electronic access card that allows me to gain entry to the building.

All growth is a leap in the dark, a spontaneous unpremeditated act without benefit of experience. —*Henry Miller*

THURSDAY

Being home in the middle of day feels so strange, I don't even know what to do with myself.

Today, I slept in until almost 10 o'clock, had breakfast, and then tuned in to The Young and the Restless *while I cleaned up my place.*

I first got hooked on Y&R the summer I fell out of a tree and broke my leg in two places. While I was recuperating, Mama would drop me off with Aunt Vera during the day while she went to work, and the two of us would have a ball eating bon bons and watching "the stories," as she called them. I was nine years old that summer, and for me it was all about the romance between Cricket and Danny Romalotti. We got to see graphic footage of Katherine Chancellor getting a facelift, and Aunt Vera loved to hate Victor Newman, who at the time was an abusive bastard that kept his first wife locked up in a closet.

During my college years, sisters Drucilla and Olivia were dealing with their crazy-ass mama, Lillie Belle, while also vying for the affections of the Winters brothers. Today though, I just could not get into my once-favorite soap opera because the only characters I recognized were Nikki and Jack Abbott.

Soap operas may not be as titillating as they used to be, but there is still plenty of daytime drama to go around, thanks to the court shows. I never realized there were so many scandalous, low-down people in the world until I got acquainted with judges Judy, Mathis, Toler, Brown, and Hatchet.

After a full day of watching these shows, I figured out there are mainly two types of cases, and I was over it.

1) Exes suing over money and unpaid bills.
2) Ex-friends feuding over unpaid, ridiculously high cell phone bills.

The bottom line is to never loan money to anyone, and never under any circumstances get a cell phone in your name for your friend to use. Hello! If their track record is that bad where they can't get a phone in their own name, chances are, you're getting stuck with the bill.

No wonder I'm bored already. And to think, five-and-a-half more weeks to go. Yahoo!

29

I throw birthday parties for each of my parents every year, and Daddy's fifty-fifth birthday is less than two months away. Because I never wait until the last minute to put things together, I had a menu tasting with Chef Pierre Jean-Claude Basquiat this evening at Rembrandt's, a fine dining establishment that specializes in European fare.

Chef Basquiat is from France, and I chose him to cater Daddy's birthday party because the James Beard Foundation has named him "Chef of the Year" for the past seven years in a row, which makes him not only the best chef in town, but the best in the entire country.

What better gift to my father than to have a five-star gourmet chef serve all of his favorite foods?

Set back off of Barry Road approximately one-hundred feet, the two-story restaurant sits on a sweeping fifteen-acre estate. I drove down the long entry drive lined with well-pruned foliage and white-barked sycamore trees, and was awestruck by the serene beauty of the place.

Inside, the restaurant exuded an old world charm.

Original oil paintings by Rembrandt, hung in the foyer and were illuminated by opulent handmade chandeliers.

"Chef Basquiat has been anticipating your arrival," said a charming hostess as she escorted me back to the kitchen.

"Ah, Mee-sus Carter!" The chef greeted me with open arms. "So good to see you again. Please, sit."

I sat down at a table, and the chef proceeded to serve me sample after sample of foods that were far from what I had requested he prepare.

There is no love lost between black folks and European food. Pizza and pork chops, we know. Foie gras and escargot—not so much. And the portions. It might not be so bad if they at least served you enough to get full and satisfied, but the entrée-the-size-of-a-deck-of-cards thing does not work for us.

Nevertheless, I tasted everything that was put in front of me, and pretended to like it whether I did or not.

Mostly not.

"This is the last dish," Chef Basquiat raved in his heavily accented English, "and it is the highlight of the entire meal!"

He presented me with something that resembled a steaming pile of horse manure in a butter cream sauce, then wrung his hands in eager anticipation of my assessment.

I gave him a halfhearted smile, and took one for the team.

It was so utterly disgusting, I couldn't bring myself to swallow it. Instead, I spit the stuff out into a napkin, wiping the look of anticipation right off of Chef Pierre Jean-Claude Basquiat's face.

"Problem?" he asked, gravely concerned. "You no like mushy pan goat?"

The chef has a reputation for flying off the handle at the drop of a hat, so I kindly and delicately said, "What happened to the customized menu I gave to your catering manager?"

"Ah, your list we cannot do," he said. "I changed it, and made it much, much better. Yes?"

Uh, no.

Daddy despises highbrow frou-frou food, so I was thinking an upscale twist on all his soul food favorites would be a great idea. Instead of creating a full menu, I wrote down a list of suggestions, like smoked barbequed chicken, brisket, macaroni and cheese—stuff like that, but apparently the chef was utterly offended to have been asked to prepare something as lowly as fried catfish.

"Do you happen to have the menu I faxed over?" I asked.

Basquiat instantly copped an attitude. He dashed into a small office off the side of the kitchen, and came back waving a sheet of paper.

"Ah! Here it is!" he raged. "This is no good—stuffed pork chops, and chitterlings, no! Mushy pan goat, yes!"

"And what exactly is mushy pan goat?"

"No, no, no . . ." He said it again slowly, and then spelled it.

"Oh! Mushrooms and goat!" I said.

"Yes, yes! Zat is my spe-cial-ty, *not* barvecued shee-ken!"

Chef Basquiat's eyes were bulging, and spit was flying all over the place. I thought I was stressed and uptight, but this guy really needed to relax.

"No disrespect, Chef," I said. "But I know my father, and we're just going to have to start all over and try and come to some sort of compromise."

"No! Zat is something you will have to do with someone else," he said, ripping my list of suggestions in half. "Finished! Now go!"

"You can't do this to me," I said, on the verge of panic. "What about my deposit?"

"Laydee, it has already vin done!" Basquiat said, handing me back the five-thousand-dollar check I had written him six months ago "Bonjour!"

Chef Pierre Jean-Claude Basquiat banished me from his kitchen so fast that I didn't have time to tell him to take his mushy pan goat and stick it up his French-fried ass.

★ ★ ★

To lose your caterer at the eleventh hour is the worst thing that can happen to an event planner. Without good food, you might as well call the whole thing off.

What's worse, it is extremely difficult to get a quality caterer at the last minute because every single chef worth his salt is booked up for months in advance, even a year or more in some cases.

The thought of calling Colin crossed my mind, but I quickly banished the thought. I was desperate, but not so much that I'd chance someone finding a booger in their food.

Think . . . think . . . think . . .

Got it!

I jumped up, ran across the hall, and knocked on Nelson's door. After all, food is his passion, and he knows everybody who is anybody in the culinary world.

Hopefully, my new friend could help me out.

"I'll tell you what," Nelson said, after I explained my dilemma. "Give me a couple of hours to make some phone calls. We'll have dinner at Le Dome's at eight o'clock, and I'll let you know then what I was able to come up with."

"Thank you so much!" I said, breathing a huge sigh of relief.

"Not a problem," Nelson said, patting me on the back. "Anything for a friend."

"By the way," I said. "I like the way you just slid that in there, asking me to dinner without really asking."

"Hey," he shrugged, "we both gotta eat, right?"

"True . . ." I said. And I probably should have left it at that, but I just had to ask, "You sure Ursula won't mind you having dinner with me?"

He looked confused. "Why would she mind?"

"Well, I saw her using her own key to go in and out of your place on several occasions, so I just assumed that you two had something going on."

Nelson threw his head back and laughed. "First of all, Ursula and I are co-workers," he said. "Plus she and Kara were good friends, so I would never— Anyway, I have an arrangement with Ursula that whenever I'm out of town, I let her *borrow* my key so that she can keep the plants watered for me. I would have asked you, but it was like you had disappeared from the face of the earth."

"Oh," I said, hoping I didn't look as molded as I felt.

"You weren't jealous or anything, were you?" he teased.

"Of course not. Who you screw—I mean, what you do is none of my business."

"Well, just for the record, there has never, nor will there *ever* be, anything between me and Ursula. Trust me; she has more than enough irons in the fire already."

I felt a huge sense of relief, and was confused as to why. Nelson is not my man, and I shouldn't care one way or the other if he was getting it on with the neighborhood jump off.

After all, we are just friends.

30

It was a little after six-thirty. Time was short, so I had to make a quick decision as to what to wear.

Technically my dinner with Nelson was not a date, but Le Dome's caters to an elite clientele, so I definitely didn't want to walk in there looking like a slump-a-dump.

After much debate, I finally decided to go with a look that was classy and elegant, but not too much: A navy blue Yves Saint Laurent pants suit, set off with silver accessories and a pair of silver Valentino stilettos. I did my makeup, then swept my hair into an updo with a few loose, wavy curls framing my face.

By the time I finished getting dressed, it was ten minutes past eight, and I was late.

I stepped out into the hallway to find Nelson waiting patiently for me, wearing black slacks, black Kenneth Cole loafers, and a black Ralph Lauren blazer over a white button-down shirt.

He tapped his watch when he saw me, as if to say, *What took you so long?*

"I know!" I said. "Sorry I'm late."

"That's alright," he said, locking his door. "The reservations are for eight-thirty, so we have plenty of time."

The restaurant is not far from our building, so Nelson and

I decided to walk and save ourselves the hassle of trying to find a parking space, which is always hard to find on the Plaza.

"Have a good evening, folks." Eddie, the security guard, waved to us as we passed through the lobby.

The sun had begun its descent towards Kansas as we walked out of our building and into the hustle and bustle of the high-end shopping district.

"Man, I love living down here," Nelson said, deeply inhaling the commingled aromas coming from dozens of nearby restaurants. "I wouldn't trade it for any other place in the city."

"Yeah, you can get a decent meal around here, but it's the architecture and the fountains that I love seeing everyday," I said, as we strolled by a life-sized statue of Benjamin Franklin. "It never gets old to me."

"I know, right?" Nelson said, as he held open the door to Le Dome's for me. "It kind of reminds me of New Orleans a little bit, with all the different influences from around the world."

Inside the restaurant, the bar lounge and vestibule were crowded with people waiting to be seated. It was my first visit to Le Dome's, but I had heard that the waiting list is often booked months in advance, and that there can be a long wait for a table, even with reservations.

The maitre d' greeted Nelson with a wide smile, and a cheery "Welcome back, Mr. Tate!"

"Good to see you again, Chauncey," Nelson said.

And the other waiting patrons looked annoyed as hell that Nelson and I were immediately whisked to a large, round table in the center of the main dining room.

If Nelson was trying to impress me, he had already succeeded. We had been in Le Dome's all of three minutes, and already we were being treated like royalty.

Nelson held my chair out for me, before sitting down across the table.

"This is quite a place," I said, feeling as if I had been warmly welcomed into someone's home.

"Yeah, and the food is amazing, too," he said. "The executive chef is doing some really innovative things with food here."

"So, Mr. Food Critic, what do you look for when you review a restaurant?" I asked, opening my menu and taking note of the exorbitant prices.

"A little bit of everything," he said. "Décor, service, atmosphere, what you ordered and expected versus what you actually got."

The sommelier came to the table, and decanted a bottle of Rothschild Pinot Noir, 1978, with a flourish. He poured a sample for Nelson, who held the glass up to the light and inspected it.

The sommelier waited patiently as Nelson swirled the wine, smelled it, and then took a small sip. After a long minute, Nelson finally said, "Excellent!" which prompted the sommelier to fill my glass, and then Nelson's.

"Well, so far the service is great and the décor is impressive," I said, admiring the white linens, candles, and fresh flowers on every table. The lighting was low, and the gilded, throne-style chairs with cream brocade upholstery complimented the cream-colored walls, and matched the gilded, elongated mirrors perfectly.

As I looked around, I saw Nadia and Terrell tucked away in a private corner of the restaurant.

"Oh look, Nadia's here," I said to Nelson. "I'm going to go over and say hi."

"Tell her I said hello," he said, pulling my chair out for me.

"Will do," I agreed, silently praying that I wouldn't fall and break my neck on the slick, highly polished hardwood floor.

I approached Nadia and Terrell's table, and it was obvious that he was very smitten with her. They were holding hands and gazing into each other's eyes, when Terrell looked up and said to me quite rudely, "I'm not signing autographs, or posing for any pictures right now."

"She's not one of your damn groupies!" Nadia said, elbowing him in the side. "Terrell, this is my best friend, Tori. Tori, this is Terrell."

"Tori? Ah, my bad!" he said, offering a handshake. "Nadia's told me a lot about you."

"Likewise," I said, shaking his hand.

Steroid freak! Even if I were an autograph seeker, was all that necessary? I mean, he may be this tall, extremely fine, muscle-bound NFL star, but he ain't all that to be treating people so impolitely.

Terrell received a call on his cell phone and answered, "Hey, what's up, man?" loud enough for everyone in the whole restaurant to hear.

"Well," I said to Nadia, "what a coincidence."

"I know, huh? And you look good too, girl. Remind me to remind you to let me borrow those pumps. Fierce!" she said, with a finger snap.

"Now you know you can't squeeze those size elevens into these size eights."

"Watch me! You wouldn't believe how many model tricks I have up my sleeve," said Nadia. "So who are you here with?"

"Nelson," I said.

"Nah-who?" Nadia asked, teasingly.

"Stop playing, you know Nelson," I said. "And by the way, he said 'hello.' "

"Uh-huh." She gave me a suspicious look. "I thought you said you two weren't dating."

"We aren't! We're here to discuss *business*."

"Umph!" Nadia said with a laugh. "Well let me know how that *business* turns out, okay?"

Terrell ended his phone conversation and snuggled back up to Nadia.

"Well, let me get back to my table," I said, taking the hint. "Nadia, I'll talk to you later. And Terrell, it was nice to finally meet you."

"Same here," he said, with a trace of *Of course it was a pleasure for you to meet Me* in his voice.

What*ever*! If Nadia likes it, I love it.

When I got back to the table Nelson jumped up again to help me with my chair.

"I went ahead and ordered the appetizers," he told me. "I hope you don't mind."

"Are you kidding? I'm dining with a big-time food guy. You can order for me all night."

At that moment, a server brought what must have been the entire appetizer menu, naming each item as he set it on the table.

"Smoked salmon parfait with chive oil, empanadas with Kobe beef, portobello mushroom terrine, potato-and-basil-wrapped tuna roll, and this one is a trio of caviar, courtesy of the chef."

"And please give Chef Montague our thanks," Nelson told the server, and then ordered the five-course tasting menu for me, and one for himself. That's soup, salad, meat and fish courses, paired wines, plus two mini courses of dessert.

"Okay, this is a bit overwhelming," I said. "I have worked up a pretty good appetite, but there is no way I'm going to be able to eat so much food."

"You don't have to," he said with a wink. "But giving it your best shot is half the fun."

Indeed. I dug into the appetizers, which were so beautiful they looked like miniature works of art.

The food was beyond delicious.

I chewed slowly, savoring every morsel of every bite, noting that the flavors and textures of the food were so divine, it almost felt like I didn't deserve to be eating so well.

"This is the second time I've had to tell you this," shouted a male voice on the other side of the restaurant. "I want my steak well-done. Not red, with all this blood and shit dripping off of it!"

The noise level dropped a few notches as other diners halted their conversations to turn and gawk in Terrell and Nadia's direction.

"I'm not trying to catch no mad cow disease up in here!" Terrell ranted at the poor waiter, who bowed courteously while apologizing profusely.

"Apologize all you want," Terrell said. "But I'm gonna keep sending it back until you get it right. Comprende?"

The waiter scooped up Terrell's plate and ran off to the kitchen, close to tears.

I looked at Nadia, who appeared to be more angry than embarrassed, and if looks could kill Terrell would have detonated two minutes ago.

"What the hell are y'all looking at?" Terrell asked the diners who were staring at him.

Having had enough, Nadia threw her napkin down and stormed towards the exit. Terrell sprinted after her without bothering to pay the bill.

The second Nadia and Terrell left the restaurant, the dining room exploded into animated conversations.

Nelson and I looked at each other and shook our heads.

"And that, ladies and gentlemen," he said to me in a haughty British accent, "was another episode in Ghetto Theater."

"I'll bet that'll be front page news tomorrow."

"Speaking of news, I've got some good and bad news in regards to finding a caterer for you."

"Okay, let's hear it," I said.

"Well, you're absolutely right. Every chef in town is booked solid on that date, but the executive chef at the Mesa Grill said that he could squeeze you in on that date—"

"Yes!" I pumped my fist like Serena Williams.

"Don't get excited just yet," Nelson said. "The chef wants triple his normal fee, which is roughly ten-thousand dollars."

"Oh, well, that's definitely out!" I said. "I thought you said there was good news."

"Well, the good news is, I can cater the party for you."

I raised an eyebrow, and waited for the *Just kidding!* But it never came. The look on Nelson's face said that he was actually quite serious.

"No really, Nelson. What's the good news?"

"Ouch!" he said, clutching his heart and pretending to be hurt. "That *was* the good news."

"Nelson, if you don't stop playing . . ." I said, frustrated that he was failing to grasp the seriousness of the situation.

Nelson knows a lot about food, and from what I've eaten he isn't a bad cook himself. However! The expertise required to cater a party, *and* impress the guests with your food is a whole other level of cooking that I seriously doubt he's capable of reaching.

I mean really, those who cook, cook. And those who can't, write about it.

"Not to be mean, or anything," I said, "but you cooked me one great meal and all of a sudden you're Wolfgang Puck?"

"Oh, jokes!" he laughed, then reached across the table and patted my hand. "Seriously, Tori. I didn't always just *write* about food. I have spent some time working in the restaurant business, you know."

"Where was that?" I asked. "And slinging fries at Burger King when you were a teenager does not count."

Nelson gave me his whole résumé and biography, starting with the revelation that he is the only son of barbeque baron Oliver Tate.

I had no idea.

Nearly everyone in town knows the story of Oliver Tate, who came up from New Orleans in the early '60s, opened a small mom-and-pop BBQ joint, and turned it into a fine dining establishment that has been a legendary Kansas City institution for over thirty years.

Nelson grew up working in the family business and planned to make it his life's work, but Oliver would not allow it. Father told son that he had not slaved over hot pits for all those years, for him to come along and do the same. No way. Oliver expected his son to elevate the family name even higher, so Nelson chose law as his profession.

He served as a public defender for three years, hated it, and was too prideful to ask Oliver if he could come back into the family business. Nelson then enrolled in culinary school with the intention of one day opening his own eatery, where he would serve a fusion of Caribbean, Asian, and Latin foods.

So for my information, Nelson is a chef who just so happens to be working as a food writer for the time being. In the meantime, he views his job with the *Tribune* as a paid apprenticeship that allows him to be like that fly on the wall, taking notes, soaking it all in, and saving money towards the dream restaurant that he has already named "Utopia."

Hearing Nelson's story made me wonder what it is about practicing law that makes obviously intelligent people who went to school for eighteen years, get that degree, finally pass the bar, and then suddenly walk away from the profession to teach, open flower shops, write novels, and open restaurants.

"I meet more ex-lawyers than I can count," I said, just as dessert arrived at our table. "Why is that?"

"Well, for me it's because I went into it for the wrong reasons. The old man wanted to be proud of something other than serving the best ribs and barbeque sauce in town, and I wanted to be the source of that pride," Nelson responded. "But inevitably, the money and prestige are not enough to sustain you through the rough times when you are feeling lost, empty, and unfulfilled."

"Well, I commend you." I raised my wine glass in a toast. "It takes a lot of courage and conviction to just pick up and walk away from a career that you spent years building."

"Life is too short to spend your days doing something that

you loathe," said Nelson, clinking his glass against mine. "So have I convinced you that I'm capable of catering this party for you?"

"Listen," I said. "I am so convinced that I'm going to let you come up with the menu."

"Cool," Nelson grinned, looking excited by the challenge.

I am not afraid of storms, for I am learning how to sail my ship.
—Louisa May Alcott

WEDNESDAY

I'm starting to get the hang of this whole vacation thing. Not since I was a kid on summer vacation, have I woken up in the morning and wondered what I was going to do to fill my day. It's pretty fucking cool, actually.

I decided early into this sabbatical that whatever I was going to do with my days, it would be done with the television OFF!

Daytime TV is a wasteland that has the potential to deaden your soul. It also desensitizes and rots your mind. (Well, except for Oprah, *which I TiVo.)*

I had trouble adjusting to being idle at first, because growing up, Cedric and Diane Carter were of the belief that no one should be in bed past 7 a.m.

Even on weekends and during summer vacations, I was made to get up at the ass-crack of dawn to clean my room, dust everything in the house, wash dishes, clean out the refrigerator, the deep freezer, vacuum, fold the laundry, straighten the linen closet, and help tend to the vegetable garden.

To my parents, idleness was the devil's workshop, and nothing built character better than hard work, so if I still had energy left at the end of the day, then I hadn't worked hard enough, and they would double up on my workload the next day.

But, I have renounced my hardscrabble Negro upbringing, and am learning to embrace The Art of Doing Nothing, *which is a great book, by the way.*

I have even developed something of a routine.

Sleeping in until ten o'clock, and then going to work out down in the fitness room for an hour or so. After I'm done exercising, I come back upstairs and do one of my yoga DVDs, then take a long, leisurely bubble bath.

Lunch, lately, has been at swanky spots like Remington's and Le Froug. Sometimes it is with one or more of the girls, although yesterday, I had lunch with Nelson over in Westport, at a Japanese steakhouse he was reviewing.

After lunch, there are plenty of options. I may take in a movie, browse an art gallery, or spend the rest of the afternoon strolling in and out of posh stores in my neighborhood, pretending to be starring in my own fabulous version of Breakfast at Tiffany's.

Today though, the only thing I have scheduled is a dental checkup.

After that, I don't know what I'm going to get into.

Maybe afternoon tea service at The Fairmont, and then stop by UMKC Communiversity to sign up for salsa lessons.

Or maybe I'll go to a day spa for a facial and a massage.

TO-DO LIST:

1) Send Sophie a thank-you card and a bouquet of flowers—ASAP.

31

Mama called me at the crack of dawn this morning, and she was so hysterical that all I could understand was "Woody!"

"Okay, Mama, breathe," I said calmly. "Just take a couple of deep breaths."

I could hear the sounds of my mother inhaling and exhaling so sharply, that it sounded like she was having an asthma attack. The sounds finally dissipated after a minute, and I said, "Now, what exactly happened to Uncle Woody?"

"Well," Mama began, "you know Woody always did have trouble with his pressure, right?"

"Yeah . . ." I said, not liking where this was going.

"Well, come to find out that he stopped taking his medication because he felt like he didn't need it anymore."

"So is he alright?" I asked.

"No, baby," Mama said solemnly. "Your Uncle Woody had a blood pressure crisis and passed away last night."

"No!" I said, jumping straight up out of bed.

"Yeah, ain't that something?" Mama asked. "He and your Daddy were supposed to go fishing this morning and Cedric is the one who found Woody dead on his bedroom floor."

Uncle Woody and Daddy had been friends since childhood.

They came up from Shreveport, Louisiana, together and were brothers as far as they were concerned.

"Well," I said, "I know I was always on him about taking his medication, and he would always tell me he had just taken it."

"But he hadn't!" Mama screamed in frustration. "Why in the world do people do that? If the doctor says you need it, then obviously you do, so take your damn medication!"

"I know, I know," I said, trying my best to comfort her over the phone. "I'm just so sorry to hear that though, and I'm sure Daddy is devastated."

"Oh, he is. Cedric is so shook up right now, it's going to be a long while before he gets over this. If he ever does."

I just left from having Sunday dinner at my parents' house. It was horrible. Don't get me wrong, it wasn't the pot roast or homemade yeast rolls that were bad.

It was the somber mood. It was like—well, somebody had died. Mama couldn't stop crying, and Daddy was moping around the house drinking Scotch and listening to the blues.

The last couple of days have been a blur. It has been hard to stay focused on anything for more than two minutes at a time, because all I can think about is Uncle Woody dropping dead with no warning. One thing is for sure, death is not like what you see in the movies, with loved ones gathered around the deathbed saying their good-byes. In real life, death comes stealing so quickly that if there is time for closure and good-byes, then you should consider yourself lucky.

Just as we were all about to sit down and eat dinner, Uncle Woody's extended family showed up at the front door. They had made the trip from Shreveport and stayed just long enough to ask Daddy for the keys to Woody's house.

Never mind that Woody had not seen or heard from most of them in over twenty years. Uncle Woody had three ex-wives, but no children, so technically, these people were his next of kin, and they wanted their cut.

All hell broke loose.

"Well I'll be damned!" Daddy said when he saw the humongous U-Haul truck they had brought to take all of Woody's belongings back to Louisiana in. "Y'all are about the simplest, sorriest, sonofabitches I've ever seen in my life. The man's body ain't even cold yet, let alone buried, and here your monkey-asses are looking for whatever you can get!"

"Now you listen here, Cedric Carter," said the obvious ringleader, a short, morbidly obese woman, with a bad wig and a bum leg. "Woody was *our* brother, not yours! And you ain't got no right to keep us from what rightfully belong to us."

"Mayblean, I don't have a problem with you all getting whatever Woody may have left for you," Daddy said. "But y'all are damn sure gonna show some respect, and at least wait until the man has had a decent funeral!"

Daddy and the clan from Shreveport argued back and forth for several more minutes until Daddy went to the hall closet and pulled out his shotgun.

That was the end of that conversation.

32

"God doesn't close one door without opening another," Yvette told me after AT&T officially laid her off.

Ever the optimist, she sees the loss of her job as a sign that now is the time to go ahead and pursue her lifelong dream of being an R&B diva.

Clearly, Yvette has lost her livelihood, and her mind right along with it. Already, she is talking about vocal coaches, producers, studio time, and meeting with an architect to have her dream house built. Essentially, she's writing checks that her talent will not be able to cash.

"I'm telling you, Tori," Yvette said, "this time next year, I'm going be on top of the *Billboard* charts!"

"Studio time and music producers cost money," I said. "How do you plan to pay for all this?"

"I'm about to get a nice severance package from AT&T," she said. "And fifty-thousand dollars is more than most artists have when they first start out."

Okay, now I'm afraid. Very afraid.

Me, and everyone else who knows Yvette, have been telling her for years that what she hears when she sings is not what everybody else hears. Yet, she is still convinced that her vocal ability is right up there with Whitney and Mariah.

"Not to piss on your parade or anything, but I think you need to give this some more thought," I said as diplomatically as I could.

"I've thought about it, and prayed on it for years," Yvette said. "Now, are you going to come support me tonight at McGillicutty's, or not?"

I sighed.

Apparently, one of the local radio stations was running an open-mike contest, offering five-hundred dollars cash to the winner, and a subsequent showcase for record-industry executives.

Yeah, Yvette was dead wrong, but I would not be a good friend if I didn't support her efforts in whatever she wanted to do in life, whether she is right, wrong, talented, or absolutely horrendous.

So I said, "I'll be there, front row and center."

This should be interesting. Besides, after just losing my godfather/favorite uncle, I could use a good laugh.

Hours later, I walked into McGillicutty's Bar & Lounge, and took a seat in a plush lounge chair close to the stage, trying not to feel self-conscious about being by myself in a venue like this. Simone couldn't come support Yvette because she works as a youth counselor at the YWCA on Thursday nights, and Nadia has run off to New York to watch Terrell and the Kansas City Chiefs play against the New York Giants on Sunday.

I looked around, pleasantly surprised to find that the lounge wasn't the smoke-filled dive bar I expected it to be.

Located in a cavernous former warehouse in the River Market area, it was actually quite nice, with two floors, multiple bars, and a nice big stage.

My instincts told me that I was going to need something strong to get through this, so when the waitress came to take my drink order, I ordered a triple shot of Patrón, light on the ice, with plenty of limes.

At eight o'clock sharp, a short, brown-skinned sister with a huge smile walked out onstage. It was Julie Jones, the morning DJ from KPRS.

"Good evening, everybody!" Julie said. "Thank you all for joining us tonight in McGillicutty's search for Kansas City's next big star!"

There was a smattering of applause. The house lights dimmed, and first up was an old-school player with dark sunglasses and a shoulder-length perm.

He was rocking a Versace shirt, circa 1995, and what I call "the Eddie Murphy specials," which are tight, black leather pants that accentuate the male anatomy.

Old-School didn't sound half-bad singing Larry Graham's "One In A Million."

The crowd got into it, waving their hands and singing along, and you would have thought that he was the real Larry Graham. Especially the way the older women in the audience were screaming and swooning when he made eye contact with them.

After Old-School left the stage dripping in sweat, the music to "Crazy in Love" kicked in, and an overweight Beyoncé—wannabe hit the stage with an abundance of confidence and energy.

The girl may have been chubby, but she had Ms. Knowles's dance moves down pat. Sister-girl got to flipping that bad weave all over the place, and the audience was polite and encouraging at first. However, it turned into *Showtime at the Apollo* once the fake Beyoncé started this high-pitched, off-key shrieking that caused everybody to wince and cover their ears.

The hecklers were merciless. They start booing halfway through the song, and the poor girl was reduced to a pitiful, sobbing, off-key mess before she finally granted us mercy and ran off the stage.

Then it was Yvette's turn.

I clapped enthusiastically as she walked out on stage looking extremely confident in a yellow Hervé Léger dress and a white gardenia in her hair.

"Now this one is gonna be good," said a man sitting at the table behind me. "Everybody knows, big girls can *blow*!"

"How y'all doing tonight?" Yvette asked, sounding like Tina Turner.

"We're good!" I shouted, and waved to her.

"Alright, now . . ." Yvette waved back at me, and adjusted the microphone stand. "I'm going through something right now, y'all, so tonight I want to sing a song that has always inspired me, and helped get me through the hard times."

Yvette had barely begun singing "I Believe I Can Fly" when a drunken idiot near the back of the room shouted, "I believe you need to sit your ass down, and shut the hell up!"

"Hey," I shouted right back at him. "It's her first time, give her a break!"

"Is she a friend of yours?" asked the drunken idiot.

"Damn right, she's a friend of mine," I said, "so leave her alone and let her do her thing!"

"Well if you're such a good friend of hers, do us all a favor and let her know she SUCKS!"

"And she looks like Big Bird, too!" shouted another voice. And the audience just roared, laughing as if they were at a comedy show.

"Come on, girl!" I shouted to Yvette in support. "Sing that song!"

Yvette kept singing alright, but now she had the same panicked expression that she had at fifteen when she blanked out and forgot the drill-team routine at the homecoming pep rally. The entire school laughed at her, but she soldiered through it then, just as she was doing at that moment.

It seemed like it took an eternity, but Yvette finally finished the song, bowed graciously, and walked offstage with her head held high.

I whooped and clapped, pretending she was the best thing since Anita Baker.

"Ah, sit down!" a few people yelled my way, and I whooped and clapped even louder in response.

I felt so bad for Yvette that there was no way I was going to let her be a worse act than the fake-Beyoncé, so I ran up on stage, grabbed the microphone and start singing Gloria Gaynor's "I Will Survive," a cappella.

My singing voice is downright terrible, but I purposely made it even worse. Take the worst *American Idol* audition ever, and multiply that by a hundred and that was me. Bloody horrible, as Simon Cowell would say.

But I put so much feeling into the song that before long, people start clapping and singing along with me.

I didn't expect to receive a standing ovation, but I did.

"What's your name, girlfriend?" Julie Jones asked me.

I told her, and she said, "Tori Carter, ladies and gentlemen. Give it up!"

I took a bow, and for one brief, shining moment, I felt like a superstar.

There were ten contestants in all, and much to my surprise I came in fifth place.

The Old-School player took second, and the winner was a woman in her fifties who brought the house down with her rendition of Vesta's "Congratulations."

Old girl deserved to win because she tore that song up, but me coming in fifth place just goes to show how awful the others truly were.

Yvette came in eighth place, and she was so pissed off that she left the lounge without talking to me, or even saying good-bye.

33

Because he was a big man who was hard to find clothes for, Uncle Woody was buried in the same black pinstriped suit he always wore for every special occasion. The funeral was hard on everybody, but Daddy was especially distraught. He wept softly the entire time, and was so overcome with emotion that he was unable to eulogize Woody when it was his turn to do so.

A couple of days before the funeral, Daddy went ahead and let Uncle Woody's Louisiana relatives have all of his personal effects, and they came through and picked the place clean, as vultures tend to do. And guess what? Not one of them managed to make it to the funeral service.

The coolness of Uncle Woody's cheek brought tears to my eyes as I bent down to kiss him good-bye.

Not only was he Daddy's friend but he was also a friend to the entire family, giving of himself without a second thought. Uncle Woody loved his Johnny Walker Red, but he was never mean when he was drunk, as Daddy can sometimes be. He weighed over three-hundred pounds and was always breathing heavily, but he loved us kids so much, that he always took time out from the get-togethers to connect with us by tossing a ball around, throwing a Frisbee, and stuff like that.

The after-funeral repast was held at my parents' house, and

as soon as we walked through the door, Daddy poured himself a tall glass of Uncle Woody's favorite drink, which was Jack Daniel's with a splash of Coke.

With a houseful of company, Daddy took his drink and the plate of food that Mama had fixed him, and closed himself off in my old bedroom, which he had turned into a private study on the same day I had left for college.

"I sure hate to see him like that," I told Mama, helping myself to a slice of double fudge chocolate cake.

"If you think that's bad, you should see how he is when there's nobody here but us," she said, shaking her head sadly. "Baby, I know how you are, always wanting to do something special for people, but I really don't think your Daddy's going to be in the mood for a birthday party this year."

I chose not to tell my mother that plans for this party had been in the works for the past few months. In fact, I had already contracted with Donna Samuels, my favorite floral designer, to transform my condo into an elegant party atmosphere, and the only thing left to do was finalize the menu with Nelson, which I would do later on this week at the menu tasting.

So, I hated to do it, but for the first time since I was a teenager, I looked my mother in the eyes, and lied with a straight face.

"Believe me, I'm not planning a party for Daddy this year," I said, crossing my fingers behind my back. "I should be back to work by then, and I'll probably be busy that day anyway."

"Well good, because Cedric is just not going to be up to celebrating," Mama said, using a dish towel to wipe down the kitchen counter. "You keep that money you would have spent on a party and do something nice for yourself, for a change."

Little did she know that it was too late. The birthday boat had already set sail, and unlike Mama, I was sure that a party in Daddy's honor was exactly what he needed to help lift his spirits.

34

A few days after Uncle Woody's funeral, Nelson came over to my place around 7 p.m. with a notebook in hand, looking quite serious.

"You ready to see what I came up with?" he asked.

"Yeah," I said, leading the way to my kitchen table. "Let's see what you got."

I know I said I would let Nelson do his thing with the menu, but the control freak came out in me, and I had to have *some* input. We butted heads, going back and forth for nearly three hours, and this is the menu that Nelson and I finally decided to go with.

Starters

Crispy crab cakes with Old Bay remoulade

Arugula and walnut salad with berry vinaigrette

Main Course

Prime rib

Poached lobster in a white-wine sauce

White-cheddar mashed potatoes

Grilled asparagus

Oven-roasted tomatoes with fresh herbs

Dinner rolls

DESSERT

SEVEN-LAYER RED VELVET CAKE

MANGO-LIME TARTS

PRALINE BREAD PUDDING

It will be a sit-down dinner for fifty people, and we are going to have a dessert buffet. Simple yet tasteful, and not too far out of Daddy's comfort zone.

"So," I said to Nelson. "Now that the menu is out of the way, how much are you going to charge me to do the catering?"

"I'll tell you what—if your dad and his guests hate the food, then you don't have to pay me anything. If they love it, you owe me fifteen hundred."

"That's all?"

"That's it."

"And you're that confident in your skills?"

"Yes ma'am," he said with a cocky swagger. "Why wouldn't I be?"

"Well alright then!" I said, shaking his hand to seal the deal. "But I'm counting on you, Nelson. It's all on you, man!"

"Don't worry, Tori. I got you!"

I was hoping that those wouldn't be famous last words, when I got a phone call from Simone.

"Where are you?" Simone asked, with what sounded like a whole lot of commotion in the background.

"I'm just finishing up a menu consultation," I said.

"With that neighbor friend of yours?"

"Yes . . ." I said, looking at Nelson, who was looking at me. "Why, what's going on with you?"

"Hello! You said you were going to swing by and hang out with us tonight."

"Oh! I totally forgot," I said, slapping my forehead with my palm. "Alright, I'm on my way. You need me to bring anything?"

"Just your smiling face," Simone said. "Oh, and bring your friend, too. I think it's time I checked him out."

I hung up the phone, still looking at Nelson.

"What?" he asked, suspiciously.

"My girlfriend just invited the two of us to her place for a little kick back."

"Nadia, from upstairs?"

"No, her name is Simone," I said. "She's heard me speak of you on a couple of occasions, and she wants to meet you."

"Oh, I get it!" he smiled. "She wants to look me over to see if I'm worthy of her stamp of approval, right?"

"Get over yourself!" I laughed. "My friends' approval is only required when I'm dating someone, and since we aren't dating, just consider it a platonic invitation to hang out."

"Alright, I'm game. I'm always up for meeting new people."

Poetry nights at Simone and Rasheed's never fail to be interesting. There is always plenty of hummus and pita bread, fruit platters, vegetable trays, organic wine, ginger beer, and stimulating conversation to go around.

The smell of Nag Champa incense hung thick in the air as an eclectic group of creative types came together to share thoughts, ideas, and their respective arts. Among them were actors, writers, poets, visual artists, scholars, dancers, singers, musicians, and intellectuals.

When Nelson and I arrived at Simone and Rasheed's modest split-level bungalow, the lighting was so low that it took a few seconds for my eyes to adjust, and make out that Simone was standing beneath the massive black-and-white photograph of a stoic Billie Holiday that I had given her for her birthday a few years ago.

There were two-dozen or so people seated on the floor and wherever else they could find a spot to sit; all enraptured with one of Simone's signature poems. Rasheed strummed a soft melody on his acoustic guitar, while his woman delivered a dramatic performance piece with much sass and animation.

"I imagine myself in the depths of hell, trapped deep inside a miry pit. I look up, see a woman's outstretched hand, and take it. The woman is strong. She pulls me up and out of the pit with ease. She helps me to settle my feet on solid ground. I dust myself off and I look into the woman's face to thank her. I smile. This woman is not only strong; she is beautiful, radiant, and righteous. I smile because I recognize her. The woman is me."

Finger snaps, whoops, and lit lighters go up around the room.

"Alright, girl!" I applauded Simone as she came over to greet us. "Save yourself!"

"I'm so glad you made it," Simone said, giving me a hug.

"Me too," I said, kissing her on the cheek. "Simone Benson, this is my friend Nelson Tate. Nelson, this is my sister Simone."

Simone and Nelson hit it off instantly. They got to talking about everything from making your own turkey sausage to the benefits of juicing. The two of them were so far off into their own little world, that they didn't even notice when I left them to go mingle with some of the other guests.

"How's it going, Rasheed?" I asked, walking up on him having what looked to be an intimate conversation with a pretty, heavyset sister in a burnt-orange sundress.

"Hey Tori," Rasheed said, removing his hand from the small of Ms. Orange's back long enough to give me a hug. "What's up, girl?"

"Not much," I said, waiting to be formally introduced to the heifer he was so obviously flirting with. But Rasheed didn't make the effort. Instead, he allowed himself to be led away by another female admirer, who insisted that he serenade her with a rendition of "Cry" by Lyfe Jennings.

Rasheed's flirting doesn't mean anything, huh?

I just hope for Simone's sake that her trust in Rasheed hasn't been misplaced, because she is the last person in the world I want to experience the pain that I have been through.

"Hey, that girl in the orange dress, what's her name again?" I asked Simone as we assembled more veggie trays in the kitchen.

"Oh, Delilah? Yeah, she's cool. She's playing the lead in Rasheed's play."

"Well earlier tonight, I saw Rasheed giving Delilah the kind of backrub that should only be reserved for you," I said. "What's up with that?"

Simone laughed at me. "Tori, as long as you've known Rasheed, you should know by now that my man is just a harmless flirt. He doesn't mean anything by it."

"I'm just saying, speaking from experience, you might want to keep an eye on that."

"Well, I appreciate the concern, but I trust my man. And even though it turned out that you could not trust Roland, please don't come in here placing your negativity on my relationship, okay?"

Now I totally understand why some women hesitate to tell their girlfriends that their man may be up to no good. You always look like the villain, even though all you've done is express concern.

"Okay. You know what? My bad. Case closed," I said, chopping a celery stalk into one-inch pieces.

"Thank you!" Simone said, spooning hummus into a decorative bowl. "Now, tell me about you and Nelson."

I shrugged. "Not much to tell."

"I'm not buying that. He's here with you tonight, isn't he?"

"Just as a friend," I said. "Nothing more, nothing less."

"That's how it usually starts," Simone teased. "Rasheed and I were friends for about a year before we decided to cut out all the bullshit and become exclusive."

"Well, I wouldn't go placing any bets on this one," I said, chewing on a miniature carrot. "Nelson and I are just friends and I'm pretty sure it's going to stay that way."

"So what's keeping it from going any further?" Simone asked.

I relayed the story of Nelson screaming out Kara's name while we were having sex.

"Ooh!" Simone winced. "Now that could be a problem."

"I know, right? And how do you compete with a ghost?" I asked. "Especially one who is this perfect angel in his eyes. Seriously, if the woman had any flaws, it would have been something sappy like she loved him too much."

"Hmmm . . ." Simone said. "I wonder what Fatima would say about this situation?"

"Well this is one time I don't mind you discussing my business with her, because I would really like to know how to handle—" I stopped myself when Nelson walked into the kitchen.

"There you are," he said to me. "We're just about to start a Scrabble tournament—you play?"

"Do I play?" I asked, incredulous. "Simone, you better let him know who the reigning champion is around here."

"Tori's a beast when it comes to Scrabble," Simone told Nelson. "I'm telling you, the girl can kick some serious butt."

"Oh yeah?" Nelson said. "Well, I'm about to change all that."

"Yeah, we'll see about that," I said, letting Nelson lead me back into the living room, hoping he had not overheard enough to know that he had been the topic of discussion.

An hour later, I was systematically destroying the competition at Scrabble, while Nelson participated in a lively discussion on the state of Black America.

Everybody laughed until they cried when Nelson did a dead-on impersonation of Bill Cosby. "Stop calling each other niggas and learn how to read and write!" He rolled his eyes, did the Jell-O Pudding face, and continued, "Never mind my past indiscretions, and all the rumors you may have heard about me, y'all niggas need to get your shit together in a major way!"

"God bless Bill Cosby!" I said. "Somebody needed to stand up and say it."

My comment turned the heat up on the debate, and as Nelson valiantly defended my viewpoint, Simone nudged me and whispered, "I don't care what you say. I think we have ourselves a winner!"

Nelson and I left Simone's a little after midnight. He parked his Escalade in the parking garage of our building, and we walked over to the Cheesecake Factory where we had dessert out on the patio.

"Now this really reminds me of New Orleans," Nelson said, as a parade of horse-drawn carriages clip-clopped past the restaurant.

"It seems like you have a thing for New Orleans," I said, savoring my Godiva Chocolate cheesecake. "Have you been down there since Hurricane Katrina hit?"

"Oh yeah, no doubt. As a matter of fact, I had just gotten back from New Orleans that day we ran into each other at Home Depot. I spent two weeks down there helping my Aunt Edna get her restaurant up and running again."

"So how is it going down there?"

"Slow! I mean, it is ridiculous that most of those neighborhoods are still the same mess they were right after the storm first hit," he said with a bitter edge in his voice. "And those FEMA trailer parks—man! On the outside looking in, they look like hell on earth; I can only imagine what it's like to actually have to *live* in that type of environment."

"That's a damn shame." I shook my head. "It just seems to me that what's happening down there is criminal on so many levels."

"Yeah, you're right . . ." Nelson agreed, quickly wiping away a tear that had suddenly sprung to his eye. "I'm sorry," he said, clearing his throat. "It just makes me so mad to see all those kids living like—man, they just deserve so much better than that."

Nelson's anger about the plight of New Orleans was so palpable, and his passion so strong, that tears unexpectedly sprung to my eyes, as well.

I wrapped my arms around Nelson and rubbed his back with long, gentle strokes.

It is so refreshing to see a man passionate about something besides sports and sex. I felt Nelson's pain, though. The situation in New Orleans just goes to show that freedom ain't as free as we thought it was. If you have money in this country, then you have value. You matter when a natural disaster comes along. If you happen to be poor, then oh well! You're just ass out.

After a few minutes, Nelson was back to laughing and joking again.

We stopped by George Brett's Restaurant for a couple of drinks, and then went back to Nelson's place for a game of pool, followed by another kind of dessert.

35

The first thing I saw when I woke up this morning was a pair of hazel eyes peering down at me with grave concern. In my still-hazy state, it took a few seconds for me to process that the eyes belonged to Nelson, and that I was lying butt-naked in the middle of his bed.

"Good morning," he said, handing me an oversized Reggie Bush jersey to cover my nakedness. "It's nice to know that you're still in the land of the living."

I stretched and smiled, remembering last night's freaky escapades.

"You put it on me something fierce, but yeah, I'm still here," I said, pulling on the jersey. I noticed that Nelson was already showered and dressed. "What time is it, anyway?" I asked.

"A little after eleven o'clock. I was just about to feed you breakfast in bed, but since you're up—" He took my hand and pulled me up out of bed. "Come on, let's go eat."

I followed Nelson into the kitchen, where he had obviously spent half the morning whipping up a feast.

"Orange juice or coffee?" he asked.

"Orange juice is fine, thanks," I said, surprised and impressed by his thoughtfulness.

Nelson poured the juice and joined me at the table, where

we sat down to a breakfast of eggs Benedict, blueberry muffins, hash browns, and fresh strawberries.

After sampling the food, I gave Nelson an enthusiastic thumbs up, which he graciously accepted with a nod.

A gourmet cook and an expert lover all in one? I could definitely get used to this. But, I digress. After all, we are "just friends."

Nelson was staring at me intently.

"What?" I asked, helping myself to another muffin. "My table manners offending you, or something?"

"No," he said thoughtfully. "I was just wondering what your special friend thinks of all of this?"

"And what special friend would that be?" I asked.

"You know, the one you were so serious with that it made you deeply regret sleeping with me that first time."

Vincent.

"Oh," I shrugged, nonchalant. "It turns out that he wasn't so special, after all."

"So, does this mean we can do away with all this friendship stuff?" Nelson asked, and the question made my heart beat faster.

"You tell me," I said, playing it cool. "You were the one who insisted on all of that in the first place."

"Well, I've been doing a lot of thinking lately," Nelson said, while buttering his muffin. "And considering the chemistry between us and that we get along so great . . . I don't think it would be a bad idea to call ourselves dating. How about you?"

We smiled big at each other like two goofy teenagers.

"You like me?" I asked in a teasing voice.

"I like you a whole lot," he said in a suggestive manner. I was about to suggest what we could do with the strawberries when someone started pounding on Nelson's front door.

I continued to enjoy my breakfast while Nelson went and answered the door. A few minutes later, he walked back into the kitchen followed by a smartly dressed couple in their fifties. I was instantly self-conscious as they scrutinized me from head to toe: the morning-after sex glow, the Reggie Bush jersey and nothing else, the disheveled hair.

The couple raised their eyebrows at me, each other, and then Nelson.

"Well, who do we have here?" the man asked, his voice dripping with accusation.

Nelson had a sheepish look on his face, reminding me of the proverbial little boy caught with his hand in the cookie jar.

"Margaret and Frank, this is my neighbor, Tori Carter. Tori, meet my in-laws, Margaret and Frank Murphy."

Kara's parents? *Fuck.*

"It's a pleasure to meet the both of you." I smiled, extending a hand that neither one of them bothered to shake.

How's that for an awkward moment?

"Sorry to drop in unannounced," Margaret said, turning her attention to Nelson. "But Frank and I were on our way over to the cemetery and thought it would be nice if you could join us."

Nelson's face lit up as if he had just been invited on an all-inclusive trip to Jamaica. "Sure, why not?" he said.

All eyes were on me, and I took that as my cue to leave.

I told Nelson "Thanks for breakfast," nodded good-bye to the Murphys, and experienced a tremendous feeling of déjà vu as I gathered up my things and went home feeling like a discarded hooker.

36

Nelson, and the three culinary-school students he hired to assist him, invaded my kitchen at six o'clock this morning. I wiped the sleep out of my eyes and watched as they brought in dozens of plastic storage bins, filled with pounds and pounds of various ingredients.

Nelson immediately posted plans of action all over the place, which meticulously listed the menu, as well as the timing for preparing each dish.

"I prepared all the desserts and side dishes last night, and I'll keep them stored over at my place until an hour before the party," Nelson explained to me.

"That's fine," I replied, tight-lipped and nonchalant.

I really liked Nelson's preparedness, professionalism, and focus, and I would have told him so if I wasn't still mad at him.

It had been almost a week since we'd spoken, because clearly the incident with Kara's parents was a topic we both wanted to avoid.

"Now, I still have to prep all the lobster, and slow-cook the prime rib," Nelson said. "But everything is pretty much set except for the asparagus and salad, which we'll prepare during cocktail hour so they'll be crisp and fresh . . ."

While Nelson gave me a rundown on all he had yet to do,

I tuned him out and yawned as if I couldn't care less. After being dissed and dismissed so rudely in favor of a visit to the cemetery, I didn't have much to say to him.

I was all business as I showed Nelson and crew where to find whatever utensils they might need.

Once I was sure they were all set, I turned on my heel and was headed back to bed when I stubbed the shit out of my baby toe on one of the metal tables I had rented for the party. The pain was so intense that it blinded me for a few seconds, and a scream got caught in my throat.

Once I got over the initial shock, I released the scream from my throat and grabbed my toe, which only made it hurt worse.

"Are you okay?" Nelson asked, laughter all in his voice.

"I'm fine!" I said through gritted teeth, and then hobbled back to my bedroom.

The party was scheduled to start at seven this evening, but relatives and friends of the family started streaming into my condo as early as five o'clock.

The plan was for Junior and I to pretend to be taking our parents out to eat at the Hereford House.

Junior called me when they got downstairs in the parking lot, and I recited the lie that I was running late, and for them all to come on up because it was going to be awhile before I was ready to go.

Daddy must have figured it all out, because he walked in and wasn't the least bit surprised.

The rest of us were stunned, though.

There my father was, looking several years younger, and so spiffy that there were no traces of the country boy from Shreveport, Louisiana. Daddy was uncharacteristically GQ in a brand new Hugo Boss suit, and his hair all slicked back and wavy.

Seeing that he had shaved his trademark mustache brought

tears to my eyes because I have not seen my father's clean-shaven face since I was a little girl.

"What's gotten into Daddy?" I whispered to Mama as I hugged her. The pained expression on her face indicated to me that she was not really feeling her husband's new swagger.

The birthday boy wasn't shy about taking control of the festivities. "I'm glad you all could make it here to celebrate my birthday with me," Daddy announced to his guests. "This one is special to me because, as you all know, I lost my brother Woody a short time ago—"

"Big Wood!" Uncle Ray said. "Rest in peace, man."

"That's right!" Daddy said. "Woody's not here, but I am, and now I'm living for the both of us, so with that said—let's get down with the get down!"

And the party was on and popping.

Dinner was served on bone china rimmed with fourteen-karat gold, and the eating utensils were expensive sterling silver, which I saw Brent, one of the wayward cousins, sizing up and giving a nod of approval.

The culinary students had changed clothes and were now uniformed servers whose presentations were all synchronized as if they were serving royalty and heads of state, instead of us.

Cookie's parents, Uncle Nate and Aunt Rita, showed up well into dinner, reeking of gin and planting sloppy kisses on everybody, and even though the invitations clearly said Adults Only! Cookie boldly brought along her four bad-ass kids, who did what they always do, which was run around getting in the way, and getting on everybody's last nerve.

Everyone loved the food, even Daddy, which was a relief.

Even though we'd barely spoken all day, I had to give it to Nelson. He really came through for me. The taste and quality of his food surpassed my expectations a thousand times over.

After dinner, we all serenaded Daddy with the soulful version of "Happy Birthday," and then watched the first of two DVDs I had a videographer put together. Set to the Whispers classic "Just Gets Better with Time," Daddy's all-time favorite song, the DVD was a photo history of Daddy's life from the day he was born, up until now: snapshots from his childhood, wedding day, Army days, bad outfits from the '60s and '70s, and even in the hospital on the days his children were born.

When it was over, Daddy looked stunned but proud. "I haven't seen any of those pictures in over thirty years!"

"That was so beautiful," Mama said, and she had tears in her eyes, as did some other people.

Unimpressed, Aunt Vera sucked her teeth and cracked, "Still ugly after all these years!"

"Quick, somebody call Brother Edwards over here!" Daddy replied. "Maybe he can get this old goat to shut her big, fat mouth!"

The room lit up with laughter.

If you didn't know better, you would think that Daddy and Aunt Vera didn't get along, but they love joking and teasing each other. Usually, no harm is meant, and none is taken.

I put in the second DVD, which was like *This Is Your Life*, with Daddy's friends, co-workers, neighbors, and loved ones talking to the camera, giving shout-outs, well wishes, and telling funny stories about things my father had said and done over the years.

When the video was finished, Daddy stood in the middle of the room and said, "Everybody, give my daughter a round of applause for all the sweet and thoughtful things she does, not only for me, but for all of us."

As everyone clapped and cheered for me, I got choked up looking around at Mama, Junior, Aunt Vera, and all those other smiling faces. It was a special moment, because it was the first time that many of them had expressed any type of gratitude towards me.

Daddy hugged me with tears in his eyes and said, "I don't say this enough but I'm gonna start saying it every chance I get—I love you, baby girl. You mean the world to me."

And that right there, was worth the price of admission. I hate that it took Uncle Woody's death for my Dad to embrace life and express appreciation for his loved ones, but late is always better than never.

When it was time to cut the cake and open the gifts, my father was nowhere to be found. I went into the kitchen and there he was, having an in-depth discussion with Nelson on how he dry rubs and smokes his meat.

"I like to let it marinate in garlic and Italian dressing for a few days," Daddy explained. "When I'm ready to cook it, I put it in the oven for an hour just to tighten that skin and seal in the juices—*then* slow-cook it on the grill over wood smoke. See?"

"You're right, Mr. Carter," Nelson said. "That is a lot different from what my father does down at his restaurant."

"I know it!" Daddy replied. "And that special technique right there, is what makes Carter barbeque a heap better than Tate's barbeque."

I was so embarrassed. Nelson had this one-sided grin on his face like he was at some off-the-hook comedy show, and I wanted to punch him in the gut for patronizing my father.

"Daddy," I said. "Could you please come and cut your birthday cake before Cookie's kids do it for you?"

"Just a minute, Tori. I was just complimenting this young man on the food. Did you know that this here is Oliver Tate's son?"

"Yes, I did," I said, bothered that Nelson's cologne was permeating the entire kitchen, and that he was looking sexy as hell in a uniform that consisted of a white double-breasted chef's jacket, pressed black slacks, and a KC Royals baseball cap cocked just a little bit to the side.

"I have been getting some valuable advice from your father," Nelson said to me, and I'm not so sure he wasn't being facetious.

"Well, I used to be in the barbeque business myself," Daddy bragged. "Made a killing, hand over fist."

It is not a complete fabrication. My father has made a little extra change over the years by selling barbeque dinners to his co-workers down in the lunchroom at General Motors; but that's where it stops.

"That's it," I told Daddy, while cutting my eyes at Nelson. "No more fraternizing with the hired help."

I grabbed my father by the hand and walked him back into the living room, where he finally cut his birthday cake, and the festivities extended late into the night.

Aunt Rita and Uncle Nate were the last to leave because they both got so drunk, I had to call a cab to come pick them up. The husband and wife tag-team of alcohol consumption will probably wake up tomorrow afternoon wondering where their car is, but letting them get behind the wheel in their condition wasn't even an option.

With everyone finally gone, I went into the kitchen where Nelson was still cleaning up.

The dishwasher was running, and the culinary students had left hours ago. There wasn't much food left over, but what little there was, was neatly packed in plastic storage containers.

"You did an excellent job!" I said, handing Nelson a check for twenty-five hundred dollars.

"No, I can't take this." He handed the check back to me. "It's for a full thousand dollars more than we agreed to."

We went back and forth for several minutes with the whole *No, I can't take this*, and *Yes, you can. I insist*, before Nelson finally folded the check and tucked it into his back pocket.

I was just about to see him out, when he grabbed me around the waist and said, "I need to know what that funky attitude was all about today."

"You mean you really don't know?" I pouted.

"Why should I have to guess, Tori? If something I did, or failed to do, is bothering you, then you should be woman enough to come to me to talk it out."

"I didn't feel like talking about it at the time."

"So let's talk about it now."

"Well," I began. "It's just . . . Kara's parents made me feel like dirt that day they came over, and you didn't help the situation any by disregarding me and then running off to the cemetery with them."

"Look, I'm sorry if the Murphys weren't as warm and receptive towards you as they could have been, but it was Kara's birthday."

"And that gives them a license to be rude to someone they've never met?"

"Kara's folks are good people, Tori," he explained. "But they're just having a really tough time adjusting to losing their only daughter. Believe me, it wasn't anything personal against you."

"Well what about you just letting me walk out of your place looking stupid, as if you hadn't said, three minutes before, that we were officially dating?" I asked, and even as I was saying it, I felt silly.

I could tell that I was testing Nelson's patience because he took a deep breath and said, "It was an awkward situation for all of us, Tori. What did you expect me to say, 'It's too bad about your daughter, but by the way, meet my new girlfriend'?"

"That would have been acceptable," I said. "Anything to let them know that I am more than *just* your neighbor."

As soon as I said those words, I was aware that I sounded like a spoiled, self-centered brat.

Of course, it would have been highly insensitive if Nelson had made an announcement like that, and I probably would have lost some respect for him if he had.

Nelson tilted my chin up with his fingertips and looked me in the eye. "You still mad?" he asked.

"No," I replied, my heart fluttering as we kissed and made up.

37

The Monday following my father's birthday party, I received an interesting phone message.

"Sophie wants you to go ahead and take another two weeks of vacation; just to make sure that you're well enough to come back to work." That was the voice mail Erin left on my cell phone.

"Well enough?" I didn't like the sound of that. At all.

What am I? Unstable and deranged, now? I wanted answers, and since I repeatedly kept getting Sophie's voice mail, I decided to stop by Erin's apartment in North Kansas City, to get the lowdown on the happenings in the office.

Erin opened the door with flour in her hair, and explained that she was in the middle of cooking her first soul-food dinner. Roasted chicken, macaroni and cheese, and candied yams was the order Erin's new boyfriend, Lee, had placed for dinner.

I tried not to laugh at her too much, but it was hilarious because the poor thing didn't have a *clue* as to what the hell she was doing.

"So, how are things at work?" I asked Erin, adding more milk and butter to her overly sticky macaroni and cheese.

"Everything's going pretty well," she said, adding way too

much nutmeg to the yams. "Sophie is working on the Dawn McKinney sweet sixteen, and she also put me in charge of E-Money's album release party."

I reeled back, feeling like I had just been sucker punched by Mike Tyson. Sophie obviously had gone out of her way to convince Vincent and E-Money to give SWE another chance. Which does not look good on my track record.

"And I hope you don't mind," Erin said, "but I have temporarily set up shop in your office, just until you get back to work, of course."

My office? Oh, no she didn't!

Why do I always see these things in hindsight? Why couldn't I have figured out before now that Erin's aww-shucks-I'm-just-a-naïve-small-town-hick routine was just that. A routine.

"Good luck pulling off the E-Money event with just a ten-thousand-dollar budget," I snickered.

"Well actually, Hennessey has stepped in to sponsor the party and they've put up seventy-five thousand dollars towards the budget," Erin said with a condescending smile.

I suddenly felt as though I was onboard a sinking ship.

That's fifteen-thousand dollars in commission that slipped through my fingers, and right into the hands of a still-wet-behind-the-ears rookie who learned everything she knows about the business from me. In fact, Erin was a royal fuck-up the whole two years she interned for us. Just a nitwit to the Nth degree, and she only just recently got to the point where she didn't have to be micromanaged all day long.

I would have expected this disloyalty from anyone else in the office, but not Erin, my little protégée. I thought we were tight. Solid. She was to me, what I thought I was to Sophie.

"So you're heading up your first event," I smiled, even though I was seething inside. "Congratulations, Erin."

"Thank you!" she gushed. "I'm just so excited! And I don't know what I'm going to do with all that money; I've never had that much at one time before."

"Oh, I'm sure you'll figure it out," I said sweetly, while discreetly over-salting the chicken.

Choke on that, bitch.

Ironically, E-Money's rap song was playing on KPRS when I jumped in my Navigator after leaving Erin's apartment.

"Make ya mama and daddy proud, and POP dat boo-tee! POP dat boo-tee! POP dat boo-tee!"

"Pop Dat Boo-Tee" is the first single off E-Money's debut album and has been getting tons of airplay lately. The single is already platinum, and the album hasn't even come out yet. Just more salt in the wounds. But who knew? I sure as hell didn't. Because had I known, I would have taken that little ten-thousand dollars, bought a party-in-a-box, and called it a day.

Now Erin has a seventy-five thousand dollar budget to work with. If she does everything right, the party should be a smash and she will be on her way to blowing up, right along with E-Money.

In the immortal words of Whodini, "It was done so sweet it had to be a plan."

See, this is exactly why I don't like taking time off. Out of sight is out of mind, and your absence leaves the door wide open for someone else to step in and steal your shine. And apparently your fucking office too.

Tori out—Erin in. That's not so hard to conceive, especially in light of the fact that Erin is Sophie's niece.

Maybe I'm reading too much into the situation, but I'm going to get some answers, first thing tomorrow morning.

Since Sophie took away my electronic passkey on the day she sent me on "vacation," I had to use trickery in order to get upstairs to SWE's suite of offices.

"Jose!" I said, greeting the security guard stationed in the lobby. "Long time no see, buddy."

"Good to see you again, Ms. Carter," Jose said. "Are you enjoying your time off?"

"Oh, it was lovely," I said. "But now it's back to the grindstone."

Jose looked confused. "I was told you wouldn't be back for at least another two weeks."

"Well, that was the plan, but I talked to Sophie last night and we agreed it was best for me to cut my vacation short and come on back to work," I said.

Jose looked unsure. He was reaching for the phone to call upstairs for verification, when I slid a Krispy Kreme box across the reception desk.

"It's a full dozen," I smiled. "I know how you love the strawberry glazed."

Jose opened the box, and in his eyes, those doughnuts gleamed like polished diamonds. He handed me a passkey. "Thank you, Ms. Carter," he said, practically inhaling a doughnut. "Welcome back, and you have a nice day, now!"

I took the elevator up to the sixty-eighth floor, where I slid the electronic passkey across the black security box until the light turned green. The lock to the glass door clicked, and I was in. I made sure to show up halfway through the morning, which is usually around the time Sophie decides to make it to the office.

"Good morning!" I said enthusiastically to everyone who crossed my path. A few of my co-workers looked as astonished as they did my first day back after wedding-gate, but I did not stop for chitchat. I was on a mission.

Sophie's office was my goal, and once I reached the open door I saw Erin and Sophie quietly strategizing over an open file.

"Good morning, ladies," I said, stepping into the office. "Did you miss me?"

Erin smiled weakly, looking like a fat kid caught with a mouth full of pie.

Sophie played it cool, though. She reminded me of the Meryl Streep character in *The Devil Wears Prada.* "Tori, what a surprise," she murmured through those wafer-thin, nearly non-existent lips of hers.

"I'm sure it is," I said. "But I'm not going to stay long. I just came to have a quick face-to-face meeting with you, Sophie."

Sophie nodded to Erin to get lost, and Erin ran from the room without making eye contact with me.

So it's true. The disloyal, opportunistic heifer!

I closed the door behind Erin, and lasered in on Sophie.

There was no sense in pussyfooting around, so I immediately cut right to the chase. "Do you still plan to make me President of SWE when you retire?" I asked.

Sophie looked taken aback by the question, but her voice was calm and controlled.

"Glad you brought that up, Tori, because truthfully some things have changed in regards to the future of the business after I retire."

"And what would that be?" I asked.

"I have decided to keep SWE in the family."

"Really, now?" I asked. "So where does that leave me?"

"Tori," Sophie said, as if talking to a moron. "You helped build this company to what it is today, so of course you will always have a home and a career here."

"That still doesn't answer the question," I insisted.

"Will you be my successor? Unfortunately not," Sophie said. "But SWE can always use good coordinators, and that you definitely are."

Sophie's words were like a verbal slap in the face.

All these years of personal sacrifice and this is the thanks I get, a Blahnik heel right in the fucking back. Hell, I didn't even take sick days despite having the flu and temperatures of over 103 degrees, because that was how committed I was.

"So after all these years of telling me that I was your heir apparent, you suddenly decide to groom Erin for that position?" I asked.

"Well, she *is* family," Sophie said without a trace of emotion or loyalty towards me. "I didn't bring her here from Omaha for nothing."

"And just when were you planning to tell me all this?" I asked.

"Just as soon as you came back off of vacation," Sophie said blithely.

"I don't believe you. If I hadn't put two-and-two together, you would have waited until the very day you retired to give me the news," I said, amused at the precision with which Sophie had played me all these years. "What better way to keep a workhorse working than to dangle rewards and treats in front of it to keep it focused on the task at hand? In this case, it was *Work harder, Tori. It will all pay off in the long run. You're my heir apparent, you know!*"

"And I meant that at the time, but your recent screw-ups would have cost SWE in excess of two-hundred thousand dollars if I hadn't stepped in and cleaned up your mess. I don't play about my money, Tori. I told you that on day one."

Ooh! Didn't I say she was greedy?

I had a few lapses in judgment after going through a personal crisis, and this coldhearted woman turned on me like a rabid pit bull.

"You know, Sophie, I really wish you would have told me all this at our last meeting here in your office, because if you had, we wouldn't be having this conversation right now."

"So what are you saying, Tori?"

"Find yourself another workhorse, Sophie, because I quit!"

"So you're just going to take your ball and go home, all because you won't be the boss around here when I retire? Not exactly what I would call a team player," Sophie said in a condescending tone.

I opened my mouth to cuss her up one side and down the other, but I held back. We could sit here and play tit for tat all day long, and it still wouldn't change the bottom line, which is that Sophie will no longer be able to use and deceive me.

"Have a lovely fucking day" were the last words I said to Sophie as I left her office for the last time.

And that right there was my *Jerry Maguire* moment. While I cleaned out my office, I was so pumped up and proud of myself, thinking, *Yeah, I told that old bitch!*

It was only after I had walked back out into the light of day that I realized what I had done.

By the time the sun had set, I was in a complete panic.

Hysteria had taken over, because my prospects for a job equal to what I had were nil.

"What the hell am I gonna do now?" I wailed, as Nelson massaged my neck and shoulders. I had called him over to discuss my plight, because at that point he was the only person I trusted to give me a neutral assessment of the situation.

"You're going to do the only thing you can do," Nelson counseled, "which is pick up the pieces and move on."

Easier said than done.

I had picked up a newspaper on the way home, and perused the want ads right there in the 7-Eleven parking lot.

And guess what? Nobody is looking for an event planner.

Sophie pretty much has Kansas City locked down, anyway. Well, except for David O'Brien Designs, which is SWE's fiercest competitor. A male version of Sophie, David has shamelessly wooed away many quality employees right out from under us over the years.

In fact, the last time David stole an assistant of mine, I picked up the phone and cursed him out so thoroughly that I almost felt bad for him when I was done.

Almost.

So in light of the bad blood between us, there is no way I'm tucking my tail between my legs and asking David for a job. No way.

"I spent the best years of my life busting my ass for someone else, and I have absolutely nothing to show for it," I moaned, feeling a pity party coming on.

"That's not true, Tori," Nelson said. "You have a good reputation, and a wealth of creativity and experience."

"Whoopee!" I said sarcastically. "And that's going to pay a whole lot of bills, isn't it."

"It could if you would stop being so shortsighted and look at the bigger picture here."

"And what would that be?" I asked, wondering what picture he was looking at, because the one in front of me was pretty fucking bleak.

"Didn't you just say that you were practically running the show at SWE for the last couple of years, anyway?"

"Yeah . . ." I said feebly.

"Well, it seems obvious to me that if you want an opportunity you have to create one for yourself. Why don't you take a risk and start your own event-planning business?" He said it so simply, that I felt like a moron for not considering the possibility sooner.

I sucked it up, dried my tears, and gave Nelson a big kiss.

"What's that for?" he asked, surprised by my sudden change in attitude.

"For being you," I said. "And for helping me to see the bigger picture."

In order to succeed, at times you have to make something from nothing. —Ruth Mickleby-Land

THURSDAY

Of course! When you are the best at what you do, why not gamble on yourself and start your own business?

There is no one in this town, or in this world for that matter, who can do what I do as well as I do it. Since the start of my career, I have brought in millions of dollars in revenue for SWE, and now it is time for me to do the same for Tori Carter Creations. I chose the name for obvious reasons, and so that clients I have worked with in the past will know that I am now in business for myself.

I may not have the staff, resources, or beautiful office space that SWE has, but I do have a Rolodex full of client and vendor contact information, which besides a business plan, and a business license, is pretty much all I need to get started. My business will have to start off being a one-woman show operating out of my home office, but there is light at the end of the tunnel. It might be kind of faint right now, but where there is light . . .

TO-DO LIST

1) *Write up a Business Plan.*
2) *Go to City Hall and file documents for Business License and Sole Proprietorship.*
3) *Business cards.*
4) *Stock up on basic office supplies.*
5) *Update my portfolio.*
6) *Get color brochures printed up, listing the services I have to offer.*
7) *Have website built.*
8) *Go to bank and apply for a line of credit, and open a business checking account.*
9) *Hire an assistant.*

38

Within two weeks of leaving SWE, I am proud to say that Tori Carter Creations is now officially open for business!

The first thing I did after leaving the courthouse with my new business license was to pull out my Rolodex and start smiling and dialing. I informed all the vendors and clients who I've worked with in the past, that I am no longer working with SWE and am now in business for myself.

My goal is to make two hundred fifty calls every day until I get to the end of my list of eleven thousand contacts. In addition to the phone calls, I also plan to mail out letters to these people, which will include a brochure and my new business card.

So far, everyone I have contacted has wished me well, and promised they would call me when it comes time to put on their next event.

However, my luck turned around this afternoon when I contacted Sasha Daniels, an old friend of mine from college. Sasha happens to be the chairperson on the board of directors of the KC Jazz Coalition, and when I got in touch with her, she sounded both happy and relieved to hear from me.

"God is good!" Sasha said when I told her who was calling.

"It's time to start planning this year's fundraiser, and I was just about to go into panic mode when you called."

Sasha told me she called SWE looking for me a few days ago, and was told I had resigned with no advance notice or even an explanation.

I'm not at all surprised that Sophie would try to harm my reputation. She is an extremely shrewd businesswoman and I'm sure she already knows that I'm coming to give her a run for her money. Why not try to stomp out the competition before it has a chance to get started?

I assured Sasha that what she had been told about me was far from the truth.

"Oh, I figured that," she said. "After all, you were the best thing they had going over there at SWE, so of course they have to make it look as if it's you, and not them."

"Well, I definitely appreciate the vote of confidence," I said, with a sigh of relief.

"And just so you know, Tori, I'm on your side. You've been in charge of the fundraiser for the last several years, and I don't see any reason why that should change now. No one knows or understands our goals more than you do, and your concepts and ideas have helped to bring in millions of dollars for the coalition over the years, so, I'm afraid you're stuck with us for as long as you'll have us."

Yes!

The KC Jazz Coalition is all about the preservation of jazz music. The organization puts on an annual fundraiser, which benefits indigent musicians and provides scholarships for young up-and-coming jazz musicians.

I absolutely love working with them. They are all good people over there, and it is always rewarding to be a part of such a worthy cause.

Sasha and I set a time and date to sign contracts and further discuss details. I was so thrilled after hanging up the phone, that I did a couple of cartwheels across the living room floor.

I have my first client, now all I need is an assistant.

Someone who won't come in with the intention of learning the ropes on my time and my dime, and then run off to do their own thing as soon as they think they have a working knowledge of the business. I want an assistant who is trustworthy and loyal, yet capable of being creative and focused at the same time.

That's what I *want*. But realistically, I'm gonna have to settle for what I can get.

With the knowledge that most dynasties are built by keeping it in the family, I stopped by Junior's midtown apartment to offer him the opportunity of a lifetime.

Yeah, it's a risky decision and his middle name should be "fuck up," but I think that with the proper guidance, and assurance that he has a stake in something real, Junior will rise to the occasion.

Besides, he may be family, but I will fire his ass in a heartbeat if he doesn't perform up to my standards.

Junior's place always gives me the creeps. It's so filthy that I always have to shake myself off right outside his apartment door when I leave, in order to avoid taking some type of critter home with me.

"What's up, sis?" Junior said, letting me into his pigsty without an ounce of shame.

As usual, there were stacks of smelly, unwashed dishes in the sink, and it looked like the last time the kitchen floor was mopped or swept, was when I felt sorry enough for him to do it.

"What's up?" I asked, running a finger along the coffee table where there was a thick layer of dust. "Obviously not a cleaning routine."

"Ah, that's nothing," Junior said, grabbing a pile of clothes from off the couch and stuffing them into the hall closet. "Cop a squat."

"No thanks," I said. "I'll stand."

"So what did you want to talk to me about?"

"Are you still working down at Federal Express?"

"Nah, that gig didn't work out," he said. "But I'm in the middle of writing a book, though."

"And who's paying you to do that?" I asked.

"Nobody . . ." he stammered. "But it's a hip-hop crime novel, and it's gonna pay off one day. Trust me."

I rolled my eyes and shook my head.

Junior latches onto something new every six weeks. He goes from one pipe dream to another in an effort to avoid a real job in the real world.

First, he wanted to be a music producer.

Then there was Amway, eBay, distributing noni juice, and the clothing line that never got off the ground.

Now he wants to write hip-hop crime novels? Stop the madness.

"What do you even know about thugging it out on the streets?" I asked. "You've been sheltered and pampered your whole life."

"Shiiit . . . I've been through some thangs."

"Like what? Boy, you pissed the bed until you were nine, and you're way too lazy to hustle. So what is your source of inspiration?"

"Man," Junior said, sucking his teeth. "There you go, always shitting on my dreams. Why can't you be supportive for once?"

"Supportive, hmmm, let me see . . ." I said. "Like letting you live with me rent-free for months? Cosigning on a car you let get repossessed, bailing your ass out of jail, and kicking you out money like I'm your own personal ATM?"

"Anyway," Junior said, "what's really good? I know you didn't take time out of your day just to come over here and jump on my case again."

"No, actually I came over here to offer you a chance to pull your own weight in this world instead of living off the fat of the land, and preying on loved ones because you are too immature to grow up and finally stand on your own two feet," I said without taking a breath.

Junior sat looking at me as if I had just performed an amazing magic trick. "Damn!" he said. "You have been wanting to get that off your chest for a while, huh?"

"Look, Junior. I'm just a little bit stressed right now, okay? I'm starting up my own event-planning business, and I need your help."

"Say no more. What do you need me to do?" he asked.

"I want you to work as my assistant, which includes no slacking, or goofing around," I said. "This is serious business, with some serious money to be made, but you have to be on your toes at all times."

"Got you, sis," Junior acknowledged, looking serious. "When do I start?"

"Right now," I said, giving him a long list of errands to run.

"Now? I was just about to start a tournament on Madden!" he protested.

I was just about to rip into Junior, when he said, "Psych! I was just messing with you, Tori. Come on, let's get busy."

39

These past couple of months with Nelson have been so perfect, it almost makes me wonder if and when the other shoe is going to drop. The two of us have so much in common, it's crazy. For instance, Nelson and I are both art lovers, so we decided to spend this afternoon at the Museum of Art.

We had a great time browsing the exhibits, and just enjoying each other's company. Halfway through lunch at the Rozzelle Court Restaurant inside the museum, Nelson suddenly became quiet and disconnected.

"Nelson, what's wrong?" I asked, concerned that he may have been coming down with food poisoning, or something.

"Nothing." He shrugged, picking at his plate of pan-seared lime-garlic tuna fillet.

I dropped the subject and continued to enjoy my Cobb salad, but I noticed that Nelson kept glancing at something over my shoulder. I turned around, and seated right behind us was this woman with a wild bushel of curly brown hair, reminiscent of Kara's. The woman's back was turned, so I couldn't see her face, but she had the same complexion, mannerisms, and style of dress as Kara. Hell, if I didn't know better I would have thought it *was* Kara.

Then I understood why Nelson had become so sad and withdrawn. I didn't like it. But I understood.

I care for Nelson a great deal, but it was getting to the point where I was at my wits' end with this situation.

One day he is loving and sweet, the next day he's keeping me at arm's length. He wants to move forward, I can feel that. But for some reason he just will not give himself permission.

And that is why I decided it was time to pay Fatima a visit.

I needed to get information on how to effectively deal with Nelson being a still-grieving widower and all.

The relationship was progressing.

Nelson and I now had the keys to each other's condo, but I was troubled that Kara's voice was still on his answering machine, her toothbrush was still in the bathroom, and her BMW was still down in the parking garage in the same exact spot where she left it two years ago.

In fact, all of Kara's things were just as she left them. Her clothes and shoes were still in the closet, and even her underwear drawer was still intact.

The second I got home from the museum, I called Simone and asked her to set up an emergency meeting with Fatima for me. "Okay, I'll call her then call you right back," Simone said, sounding excited that I was finally going to get some "help."

A few minutes later, Simone called back and said, "Fatima normally doesn't work on Sundays, but since it's you, she's willing to make the exception."

Simone gave me Fatima's address and phone number too, just in case I got lost. There was no chance of that though, because I have a trusty GPS system I nicknamed Becky Sue, and she hasn't steered me wrong yet.

"Make ya mama and daddy proud and POP dat boo-tee! POP dat boo-tee! POP dat boo-tee!" was the first thing I heard when I turned on the ignition in my truck.

It seems like E-Money's career took off the second I refused to take him on as a client. Not only does he have a hit song tearing up the radio airwaves, but the video is also in heavy rotation on both BET and MTV. The album is expected to debut at number one on the *Billboard* charts.

Personally, I'm baffled by the success of "Pop Dat Bootee." Now, the beat is crazy. I love the beat. But the lyrics are so juvenile, any fourth grader could have written them.

Oh well.

I turned the radio off in order to concentrate on my driving. It took almost half an hour for Becky Sue's voice to lead me to Gardner, a new subdivision in a Kansas suburb. Nice area, but all the houses are identical, and just too damn close together for my liking.

I parked in the driveway, and by the time I made it to the front door, Fatima was there welcoming me with a smile, and outstretched arms.

"Fatima, nice to see you again," I said.

"My sister!" she said, hugging me as if I were truly a long lost relative.

A pretty and petite brown-skinned woman in her late thirties, Fatima has long, sandy-brown dreadlocks that were pulled back into a ponytail. She had on a turquoise and white muumuu, and bejeweled Indian sandals. Thankfully, she had bothered to get a pedicure this time.

Fatima led the way inside, and said, "Welcome to my humble abode."

Humble my ass! Apparently, life coaching pays very well these days. I walked inside to marble floors and extremely high ceilings. For some reason, I was expecting Fatima's home to resemble an African art museum, with kente cloth, masks, handwoven baskets, and statues everywhere, but there were only a few such items on display in her modern, tastefully decorated home.

I could smell the calming scent of lavender incense floating in the air.

Fatima took my hand and guided me out to a large sun porch, filled with what had to be every plant known to man, including several bonsai trees that were almost as tall as I am. Wind chimes tinkled somewhere in the distance, and there was a caged parrot in a far corner of the room whose favorite word was apparently "nirvana."

"Have a seat," Fatima said, offering a small floral sofa that was so comfortable when I sank down into it, that it automatically induced a state of serenity.

Fatima sat across from me in a chair that matched the sofa, and said, "So, I hear you're having man trouble."

Over jasmine-flavored green tea and banana-nut muffins, I told Fatima all about my dealings with Nelson, from day one up until right now.

"How do I compete with the memory of a dead woman still very much beloved by her grieving husband?" I asked. "Every time I turn around its 'Kara, Kara, Kara.' And I can't even tell you how sick I am of hearing that woman's name."

"Well that is your first mistake, right there," Fatima advised. "Stop looking at Kara as an enemy when in fact you owe her a debt of gratitude for helping to shape Nelson into the good man he is today. Now, she probably wasn't quite the saint he depicts her to be, but that's not your place to point that out. Be mature and secure within yourself, because at the end of the day, you are there in Nelson's bed—not Kara."

"And that's another thing," I said. "How can I tell how much of his passion during sex is him desiring me, versus him just using me as a stand-in for his deceased wife?"

"That's easy. You can tell by the way he treats you outside of the bedroom. Is he kind and thoughtful towards you? Does he still want you around even after you've made love?"

"Yes, to all of those questions. Nelson is respectful, thoughtful, attentive to my needs, incredibly sweet and eager to please."

"So there's your answer." Fatima nodded. "Now, it was definitely way too soon to have sex when you first did, but seeing as how he later approached you for a friendship means a lot. So apparently he does care for you, and the guilt he must be feeling because of his feelings for you could be complicating his grieving process even more."

"Yeah, I definitely think Nelson feels some guilt about being with someone other than Kara. I mean, they were college sweethearts, after all."

"Why is it that you feel threatened by the love he still has for Kara?" Fatima asked.

"I don't know if threatened is the right word, but I don't see how he can really move forward to the future while he's still clinging to the past."

I told Fatima about Kara's parents and how they seem to not want Nelson to move on. How they still throw birthday parties in their daughter's honor, and insist on getting together for a vigil on the anniversary of her death. In my opinion, the Murphys make Nelson feel guilty about the prospect of being happy with a woman other than Kara. They act as if he's cheating on their daughter, and disrespecting her memory in some way.

"It is natural," Fatima said. "The Murphys view Nelson's moving on as disrespectful because Kara will always be their daughter, and their loyalty is to her, first. Deep down they may be jealous that Nelson even has the option of moving on because he can get another wife. Unfortunately, the Murphys cannot get another daughter. Essentially what Kara's parents are doing is bullying Nelson into staying locked in a cycle of grief."

Oh! The light bulb went off in my head and not only did I finally understand the entire situation, but I also felt more sympathetic and compassionate towards the Murphys.

"Also," Fatima continued, "Kara is what linked them all together, and the parents may feel that if Nelson moves on to another happy relationship, he will forget about them and then they will lose him, too. Nelson needs to set boundaries. He also needs to stand up to them with the knowledge that he will probably never have their blessing when it comes to moving on."

"Should I tell him all of this?" I asked.

"I wouldn't. At this point, all you can do is wait patiently for him to discover these things on his own. Dating a widower is not hopeless, but you do need a certain level of patience and understanding," Fatima said with a smile. "In the meantime, though, if the situation is really uncomfortable and stagnant, then you have to put a time limit on how long you are willing to be there while he mourns his loss. Months? Weeks? Years? It's all up to you."

I left Fatima's house feeling enlightened, and glad to have finally given her a chance.

I like her. It turns out that she is not the scam artist I viewed her as, after all this time. She's comforting, and has a nurturing spirit about her. If I should have to go through a crisis that requires therapy, God forbid, I wouldn't hesitate to pay Fatima another visit.

As for Nelson, I'm willing to give him six more months.

If he doesn't have this whole Kara thing in check by then, I will seriously start considering moving on.

40

"Would you believe that bastard gave me chlamydia?" Simone raged, over chicken fingers and apple martinis at the Epicurean's happy hour.

Yvette, Nadia, and I all inhaled sharply.

Regardless of his flirting ways, Rasheed cheating on Simone and giving her a sex disease is news none of us ever thought we would hear.

"No!" I cried out, sorely disappointed. Aside from Will and Jada, and my parents, Simone and Rasheed were my role models when it comes to long lasting, loving relationships. The epitome of what a strong black couple looks like. Rasheed may have been a tad too touchy-feely at times, but the point is, he and Simone managed to hold it together for nine years. That's rare these days.

"Oh girl, yes!" Simone said. "I had this weird discharge, and was itching like crazy down there. So I went and had it checked out, right? Sure enough, Rasheed's been creeping around behind my back with some disease-infested skank."

"Ah man," Yvette said, almost in tears. "Rasheed was my boy! I never thought he would go out like that."

"Well, the proof is in the panties," Simone said. "Which is

exactly why I kicked his poetry-spouting, no-job-having ass out of my house."

"Do you know the heifer he's messing around with, or was it just some random chick?" Nadia asked.

"It was that sneaky, snaky bitch, Delilah," Simone said, turning to me. "You know that heavyset girl who's always at our poetry meetings wearing flowers in her afro?"

"The one who insists on boring everybody with those tired-ass poems?" I asked.

"That's the one!" said Simone. "And Tori, I really should have took you more seriously when you warned me she was trying to push up on Rasheed."

"See," I said. "It's always those fake, trying to act like they're your friend, heifers. Smiling in your face and all the while, steadily trying to steal your man right out from under you."

"Um, hmm," Yvette said. "And those are the same sluts who need their asses whooped because they *know* damn well that he has a woman at home."

"Well, it looks like everybody really does play the fool sometime," Nadia said.

"Church!" Yvette said, raising her martini glass in a toast. "Dirty bastards!"

Today, we all had big news.

Nadia is going ahead with the breast implants so Terrell can finally stop bugging her about it. And not surprisingly, the girls were all supportive and encouraging when I told them about the status of Tori Carter Creations, and that I am an inch closer to being completely in love with Nelson.

I have not seen much of Yvette since the open-mike night debacle, but apparently she's over it, and has since given up her dreams of superstardom.

Instead of fame, Yvette is focusing on her first semester of college, as well as her promising relationship with a white guy named Daniel who she said is a sweetie pie, and has this

Robert De Niro thing going on where he genuinely adores black women.

Good for her. Yvette deserves some happiness in the romance department, and I'm keeping my fingers crossed that Daniel will turn out to be husband number two.

41

I was right in the middle of cleaning my refrigerator, when Nelson called and asked me to come across the hall to his place. I had no idea what was going on, but I took off those yellow plastic gloves, powdered my face, and reported for duty as requested.

"What in the world is all this?" I asked, walking into Nelson's condo, which was in such disarray it looked like a cyclone had swept through it. Every cabinet and drawer was open. Heaps of clothing, boxes of shoes, and other miscellaneous items were piled high on the pool table and in the middle of the living room floor.

"I just wanted to let you know that I'm doing a little purging," Nelson said, coming out of the bedroom carrying a black, men's suit. "Stuff like this, I should have gotten rid of a long time ago."

"Why?" I asked, watching him toss the suit on the top of the heap.

"It's the suit that I wore to Kara's funeral," Nelson said, and I noticed that he looked drained. His eyes were red, and I couldn't tell if it was from exhaustion or from crying.

"Do you need some help?" I asked, giving him a hug.

"No, the Murphys are on their way over to get what they

want of Kara's stuff," he said. "And the Salvation Army is coming to pick up the rest of it."

What? This was huge. This was the pivotal moment Fatima assured me would come. Now that it was here, I felt like an intruder into an intensely personal and private matter.

He should be alone at a time like this.

"Look, um, I'm gonna go," I said.

"Thanks for understanding," Nelson said, kissing me on the forehead. "It's actually not as hard as I thought it would be, but it's still pretty rough."

"I'll be at home if you need me, okay?"

Nelson walked me to the door, and I was not at all pleased to see Kara's parents.

"Hello, son," Mr. Murphy said to Nelson. Once again, he and his wife looked right through me, as if I weren't even standing there.

Their rudeness was not lost on Nelson.

"Frank and Margaret, you've met Tori," Nelson reminded them.

"Ah, yes," Margaret said, looking down her nose at me. "The *neighbor*, right?"

"Well, actually she's more than a neighbor," Nelson said, his voice wavering just a tiny bit. "Tori and I are dating, and it's getting serious."

Say what?

I was just as surprised as Frank and Margaret to hear Nelson make that declaration.

There was so much tension, I knew the best thing to do was to quickly remove myself from the situation. Before I left though, I felt compelled to give the Murphys a piece of my mind.

"Listen, you two need to give Nelson a break. He loved your daughter dearly, and no one can take away what the two of them shared," I said. "But at the same time, he deserves another chance to love again. From what I knew of Kara, I think she would have wanted that for him."

"Don't you *dare* presume to speak for my daughter," Mrs. Murphy snapped, wagging a manicured finger in my face.

My first instinct was to snatch Margaret baldheaded, but she is a grieving mother, and for that, she deserves a degree of empathy and respect.

"Don't do this, Margaret," said Mr. Murphy, leading his wife away from me.

"Well, it was nice to see you both again!" I called out to the Murphys, who had walked past me and were looking over Kara's things.

Nelson gave me a grateful smile for maintaining my composure. "I think we should go out on the town to celebrate," he said. "How about you?"

"Alright," I smiled. "But take your time. I'm not going anywhere."

"The play was pretty good, don't you think?" I asked Nelson, as we claimed one of the private draped beds up on the rooftop terrace of East, a bar and restaurant popular for its unique fusion of Asian, Indian, and Middle Eastern cultures.

"Yeah, I was pleasantly surprised," he said. "Who knew that a play with just two men in it could be so interesting and entertaining?"

The two of us had just come from Crown Center, where we watched *Tuesdays with Morrie* at the Heartland Theatre. It was late afternoon when Kara's parents left Nelson's place with a bunch of her things, plus the keys to her BMW.

To celebrate our new couple status, Nelson and I started the evening with dinner at Stix Chinese Restaurant, and had come to East to cap off the night with cocktails and dessert.

A server approached our bed looking like she had come

straight out of *I Dream of Jeannie*. She wore a sheer bejeweled sarong, matching midriff-baring top, and gold thong sandals.

"Good evening, my name is Magda," she said. "Would you folks like hookah service tonight?"

"Yes," Nelson said. "And we'd also like a Pineapple Upside-Down Cake Martini for the lady, and I'll have a bottle of Budweiser Select."

I propped myself up on one of the bed's many large, fluffy pillows, and Nelson lay on his back with his head in my lap. I ran my fingers over the deep wave pattern in his hair, and looked up at the clear night sky, dotted with what looked to be a zillion stars.

A server walked by with a platter of Caribbean lobster tails, and the air around us was an intoxicating blend of anise, cinnamon, and sage.

Magda came back and set up the Moroccan hookah for us. After she left, I gently pulled on the mouthpiece, taking in coconut and strawberry flavored tobacco, made smooth by the water bubbling at the bottom of the pipe. Since I am not a smoker, all I needed were a couple of puffs and I was as relaxed and giddy as I needed to be in public.

Nelson took a few pulls, and then moved closer to me on the bed, rubbing his hands over the roundness of my behind.

"You have any big plans for this weekend?" he asked, kissing the base of my throat just the way I like it.

I am not usually the one for such extreme public displays of affection, but I didn't stop Nelson from doing what he was doing because none of the other couples on the terrace seemed to be paying us any mind.

"Nothing concrete yet," I said. "But wherever you are, that's where I want to be."

Nelson gave me that smile of his that lets me know that I have made him happy. "I have an assignment coming up and I want you to go with me on a road trip," he said.

"Okay, where are we going?"

"Not far, just a few hours away to a winery and a nearby bed-and-breakfast."

"Count me in," I said, unzipping Nelson's jeans, and sliding my hand into the flap of his Calvin Klein underwear.

"Damn, your hands are so soft . . ." he whispered, hooking his index finger around the crotch of my thong and skillfully pulling it off in one fell swoop.

I pulled the curtains closed around the bed, and laid back wondering just how many other bare asses had been on these very same cushions. Not a pleasant thought, but I went with the flow anyway because the mood was just too sexually charged not too.

42

St. Louis is a great city, but I haven't been there since my fifth grade class took a field trip to the arch. So I was beyond excited about going on a road trip with Nelson the next day.

The first thing I did when I got home from East, was to start packing.

As I selected the five or so outfits I planned to take, Junior showed up at my front door.

"Can you watch Trey for me tonight?" Junior asked when I opened my front door for him.

"*Hell no*!" flew out of my mouth before I could stop it. If there were such a thing as a demon child, I would definitely nominate Trey to be the poster boy.

Trey is three, going on thirty-three. He can rap, dance, and cuss like nobody's business, yet he still can't manage to get that whole potty training thing together. The last time I was graced with Trey's presence, he pulled down his pants, tore his diaper off, and took a shit right in the middle of my kitchen floor. On top of that, I still have some of his artwork on my walls, which he created with my brand new tube of M.A.C. lipstick.

"You still haven't repaid me for having to get my carpet cleaned after his last visit," I reminded Junior.

"Don't even worry about that, Tori. You know I got you."

"No, I don't know that," I said.

"Look, I'ma pay you back as soon as I get my income tax check," he said, hitting me with his usual delay tactic.

I sighed. It would have been much easier to stick to my guns if Trey weren't asleep on Junior's shoulder, looking so sweet and angelic.

Besides, it was not as if I had much else to do, anyway.

Nelson was working to meet a deadline before we leave tomorrow morning on our road trip, and the only plans I had were doing laundry, packing a suitcase, and reorganizing the shoes in my closet.

"Well, I am impressed with how hard you've been working for me lately, so I guess I can help you out," I said. "Has Trey eaten already?"

"Yeah, he just had some Burger King," Junior said.

"Just make sure you're back by seven tomorrow morning, Junior, because Nelson and I are leaving for St. Louis at eight o'clock."

"I'll be back way before that," Junior said, laying Trey on the couch and handing me his Transformers backpack.

Trey woke up the second Junior walked out the door.

I was sitting next to him on the couch, and my heart melted when he curled up in my lap, and gave me a big kiss.

"Tay sank you," he said, looking up at me with those big brown eyes.

Trey currently has his C's and S's mixed up with his T's so what he actually meant was "Say thank you."

"Sank me Auntie Cori. Sank me!"

"Thank you for the kiss, Trey."

"You welcome," he smiled, and then wiped his snotty nose with the back of his hand.

It was a beautiful Hallmark moment, and I was so thrilled that Trey had obviously learned something from one of the books I had bought him for his birthday.

However, the memory of that moment was shattered fifteen minutes later when Trey suddenly frowned at me and shouted:

"Gimme a tookie!"

Now, as I have said before, Tori loves the kids. But that precocious smart-mouth stuff that everybody thinks is so cute nowadays does not work with Tori. I don't mind kids, so long as they mind me.

"Gimme a tookie!" Trey demanded again, this time with the attitude of a grown-ass man.

I'm old school when it comes to dealing with kids, but I don't subscribe to the Bernie Mac philosophy of hitting kids in the stomach or the throat, so I tried a little tenderness instead.

"Gimme" is not a nice way to ask someone for what you want," I said sternly. "Say, 'May I have a cookie, *please*?' "

"Nay I hab a tookie, *peas*?" he repeated, barely above a whisper.

The diction was still far from perfect, but I could not help but smile at his sincere effort. I set Trey up at the kitchen table with a glass of chocolate milk and two Mrs. Fields chocolate chip cookies.

"Sank you," he said, and then accidentally spilled his glass of chocolate milk on my freshly waxed hardwood floor.

No good deed goes unpunished. The next morning, seven o'clock came and went with no word from Junior, forcing Nelson to have to leave for St. Louis without me.

Livid is not even a strong enough word for the way I felt about being taken advantage of by my brother yet again—just when I thought he was on the road to getting his shit together.

And the worst part of it was, I was literally stuck with Trey. I couldn't get in touch with his mother, Ashley, and my parents were on day four of the ten-day Caribbean cruise I had given Daddy for his birthday. Cookie, Aunt Vera, and everyone else I attempted to drop Trey off with, just flat out said "No!" which is what I should have done in the first place.

I was so upset with Junior that I was in tears when Nelson had come over to get me so that we could head out on the road trip.

"Oh Tori, don't cry," Nelson said, pulling me into a comforting hug. "This is not a big deal, okay?"

"But I was looking forward to spending that time with you," I sobbed.

"I know, but listen, this is what we're going to do," he said. "As soon as I get back, we are going to sit down and plan a trip to New York. We'll take an eating tour of the city, check out *The Color Purple* on Broadway—the whole nine. All right?"

I nodded and blew my nose, because a trip to New York is one helluva consolation prize.

It wasn't until way late in the evening that Junior finally came to pick up his child.

"Ah Tori, I'm sorry. My cell phone went dead—"

"Stop! I don't even want to hear it," I said.

I handed Trey's Transformers backpack to Junior, gave my nephew hugs and kisses, and had not one word for Junior as I closed the door behind his unreliable ass.

I had been cooped up in the house with a three-year-old for a full twenty-four hours, and I definitely needed to get out and socialize with some grown folks.

It was just going to be me and the newly single Simone hitting the town tonight, because Yvette was all caught up in her new relationship with Daniel, and Nadia flew to Miami last Tuesday to get her boobs done at a steep discount rate.

I had just gotten out of the shower, still dripping wet, when I heard knocking at my front door. I threw on my terry cloth bathrobe and ran to answer the door for who I assumed was Simone. Instead, I was face-to-face with Roland.

"Daddy's home!" he said, his breath reeking of alcohol. "And it looks like I'm just in time."

I suddenly felt dirty and in need of another shower, as his eyes roamed lustfully all over my body.

"Just what the hell are you doing here?" I asked, tying the belt to my robe even tighter.

Roland stooped down in my face and said, "We need to talk," then walked in without being invited.

"Okay, first of all, your breath *stinks*," I said. "And second, you left me at the altar in favor of your baby mama, who you were masquerading as your "friend" for all these years. What else do we need to discuss?"

"I fucked up," he belched. "I want you back, Tori."

I burst out laughing, because that was like the funniest shit I had heard in a long time. "You want me back?"

"Yes! I must have been temporarily insane when I made the decision to leave you for that ho-ass Veronica," Roland slurred. "I want you back, baby. So bad that it hurts."

"And you know what, Roland? People in hell want air conditioning, but it ain't happening, baby. So bounce!"

"Naw, this is my home, too," he said, making himself comfortable on the couch. "This is where my heart really is. I can't leave here. Not again."

"Oh, the hell you say! You're getting your ass up out of here, right now!"

"Nope, can't do it . . ." he said in a low, sleepy voice.

There was another knock at the door. This time it was Simone. "You ain't hardly ready," she said, looking me up and down.

"I know, I got interrupted," I said. "Girl, you have to come see what the cat done drug back up in here."

"Oh no, this Negro didn't!" Simone said when she saw Roland, who was now passed out on the couch, snoring.

"Girl, that's what I said. He showed up here a few minutes ago, drunk out of his mind."

"Phew!" Simone said, covering her nose. "What the hell has he been drinking? Gasoline?"

"He must have been drinking some liquid crack if he thinks I'm getting back together with him."

"Un-unh!" said Simone.

"Ain't that one helluva nerve?" I asked. "Now please help me get his stanking ass up, and out of my house."

I slapped Roland hard across the face a few times, and even tried to rouse him by throwing cold water in his face. None of it worked. That fool was passed out so cold, it was almost like he was dead.

"Call Junior," Simone suggested. "He's big and strong enough to get him out of here."

"No, they can't be within fifty feet of each other because of the restraining order," I said.

"Well, go on and get dressed," Simone said. "You can spend the night at my place, and with any luck, Roland's ass will be sober and gone in the morning when you get back."

43

I walked back into my condo the next morning and was relieved to see that Roland was no longer on my couch. However, it felt like I was in a bad dream when I heard cheerful whistling coming from my bathroom. I was debating whether to investigate or go running and screaming from my condo, when Roland opened the bathroom door and stepped out into the living room. He was butt-naked, with his sausage swinging every which-a-way.

"Why are you still here?" I asked through clenched teeth.

"Waiting for you, my love," he said, trying to hug me.

"Get out!" I said, spinning out of his grasp. "You have about two minutes before I call the police."

"Now why is all that necessary?" Roland asked. "After everything we've been through together, and this is how you treat me?"

"Hah! That's fucking rich. Look, this might be hard for your ego to take, Roland, but I got over you months ago. So whatever happened between you and Veronica, I suggest you go work it out because you have nothing coming over here. I got a new man now. A *real* man."

"Oh, so that's what's up with all the condoms and sex toys in the nightstand?"

"Yep!" I said. "And he's hitting it better than it's been hit in *years*."

"Wow, Tori!" he said with a look of disgust. "You're just all out there, huh? First my man Gary sees you at Pierpont's with some old crazy dude, and now you're screwing the neighbor?"

How in the hell did he know about Nelson and me? I put my poker face on and held my cards close to my chest. "And what neighbor is that?" I asked. "There are quite a few single guys in this building."

Roland looked taken aback. "Damn!" he said. "Just how many of the neighbors are you kicking it with?"

"All of them!" I said. "Now will you please get the hell out of my face?"

"You know, I got sentimental last night and felt bad about how I did you," he said. "And in that state of mind, I really thought I wanted to re-declare my love for you, but now—"

"Oh, shut the fuck up!" I exploded. "Please do not flatter yourself into thinking you have the power to make that decision, because I wouldn't take you back if Bill Gates paid me to do it."

"Okay . . . Okay . . ." Roland said. "Just answer one question for me, and I'll go. Is Nelson from across the hall supposed to be your man?"

"What gives you that idea?" I asked.

"Because he came over this morning, and we had a little man-to-man talk."

"I don't believe you," I said, starting to see red.

"Go ask him. He said he cut some trip short and wanted to let you know he was back."

"And what else did you two talk about?" I asked, trying to sound nonchalant.

"You, me, and he." He sang the melody to the Mtume classic, and then laughed. "Remember that song?"

"Fuck you, and that song," I said bitterly. "What did you say to Nelson?"

"That's between me and him, but let's just say that if he was your man, I don't think he is anymore."

I felt a rage coming on. With my blood boiling, I grabbed my trusty baseball bat out of the hall closet and started swinging at Roland. His butt-naked behind ran wildly around the condo trying to avoid being hit. I managed to whack him across the shoulder with the bat, and he started screaming like a terrified little bitch.

"Cut that shit out, Tori!" he shrieked. "Have you lost your fucking mind? You could seriously hurt me with that thing."

"And that's exactly my intention," I said, throwing Roland's clothes and shoes out in the hallway.

"You're fucking crazy!" were the last words he said to me as I forced him out the front door by bat point, wishing it were a gun instead.

"And don't you dare bring your black ass around here anymore!" I yelled at Roland through the door.

I watched through the peephole as the man I used to love scrambled to get dressed, all the while mumbling that I was a psycho bitch.

When I was sure Roland was gone, I ran across the hall and pounded on Nelson's door for about ten minutes straight. I just wanted to see him. Just needed to talk to him so badly that I didn't care what it must have looked like to the neighbors, who were, one-by one, opening their doors to see what all the ruckus was about. Ignoring their snickers and pitying looks, I kept pounding on that door for I don't know how long. And I knew damn well he was in there, because I used the key he had given me and the safety chain was against the door.

After about forty-five minutes, Nelson finally opened the door. He stood in the doorway with his arms crossed, and did not invite me in.

"What's up?" he asked, his tone dry and disinterested.

"I've been trying to get in touch with you, that's what's up. Didn't you get any of my messages?"

He shrugged. "I haven't even checked my machine."

"That's a lame, boldfaced lie and you know it."

"Either way, what difference does it make?"

"Nelson, don't do this. I know that on the outside looking in, it looks pretty bad. But Roland being over at my place is actually a lot more innocent than it looks."

"Is it really?" he asked. "A man you were with for years answers your door with nothing but a towel wrapped around his waist and you call that innocent?"

"Nothing sexual happened between us, Nelson. I didn't even spend the night there—"

"So how did he get in?"

"I assumed it was Simone, and I opened the door without checking to make sure," I explained.

"So that means you let him in, right?"

"Technically speaking, yes I did. But I was trying to get him to leave the second he walked through the door."

Nelson sighed. "Regardless of what you obviously think, I'm not stupid. Plus what am I supposed to believe when that man tells me you two still love each other, and are working on getting back together?"

"You're supposed to believe me," I said softly.

"I want to, Tori, but I just can't," he said sadly. "If I were a little less intelligent then I probably would believe your story, but frankly, it sounds like a bunch of bullshit to me."

"So what are you saying, Nelson?" I asked, but I already knew the answer.

"I think we need to chill, and give each other some space."

"Fine," I said, my voice trembling. "If you want to talk to me, then you know my number and you definitely know where I live."

Nelson nodded, and stepped back inside his condo. I quickly turned my back to him, refusing to give him the opportunity to close the door in my face. Or to see the tears that were streaming down my face.

He who finds diamonds must grapple in the mud and mire because diamonds are not found in polished stones. They are made.
—Henry B. Wilson

SUNDAY

I can't believe this is happening. Not only did Roland ruin our relationship, but he also came back and ruined the budding relationship I had with Nelson—a relationship that I was truly starting to treasure.

Bastard.

Simone was right. I didn't have any business out there dating so soon after breaking up with Roland in the first place. The second relationship in less than a year to go down in flames, and the common denominator is me.

This time, I really am moving. There is no way I can stay around here, now. Too much tension to have to deal with every day.

44

"I can't believe you're gonna let some man run you up out of here," Yvette said, while helping me pack. "We've had some good damn times in this condo."

We were in the living room, carefully wrapping my African statues and other fragile decorations in newspaper, while waiting for the moving company to show up.

Simone was working, as usual, and Nadia was still in Miami, so it was just the two of us.

"It's my own fault," I said. "Like Simone said, I let my hormones overrule common sense, and this is the end result of it."

Yvette sighed and said, "Yeah, well, I guess you gotta do what you gotta do."

"That's the same thing my parents told me. But at the same time, they're happy I'm staying over there because they wanted to keep the house in the family, anyway."

"If my money wasn't so funny, I would buy this place myself," Yvette said, looking around.

Ten days after my big breakup with Nelson, and my condo is officially on the market. The realtor at Remax said that the building is located in one of the most desirable areas of the city, and he assured me that it would sell within sixty days.

That's fine and dandy. But I don't want to stay in this building two more weeks, let alone two months.

Just the other day, I passed Nelson in the lobby on my way to the parking garage, and I might as well have been invisible. He didn't speak or acknowledge me in any way. What are we, in junior high school? He can't at least be civil about this whole thing?

I know Roland answering the door to my condo as if he still lived there looked bad, but Nelson's refusal to hear me out leads me to believe that he is using this situation as an easy out. Clearly, the two of us getting together was just too much for the poor guy and this is a convenient excuse for him to push me away, crawl back in his shell, and go back to being the lonely widower.

While waiting for my condo to sell, I am staying at Uncle Woody's old house, which he left to my father in his will.

Several hours later, Yvette rode with me as I drove over to my new place with the moving company van following behind us. Junior was already at the house, and was Chief Operating Officer of moving. His duties were to make sure that the movers placed the furniture where I had specified, and that the boxes marked "kitchen" were actually put in the kitchen, and so forth.

It took less than fifteen minutes to get from my old place to the new one, located in the historic Brookside area. The two-story limestone house has an old-fashioned charm. It has four large, airy bedrooms with oversized windows, two-and-a-half bathrooms, French doors, a formal dining room, and antique oak floors. The backyard is a secluded one-and-a-half-acre lot populated with towering walnut and apple trees, and even a huge vegetable garden with its own automatic watering system.

It's one of those neighborhoods where the kids are all grown up, and have left behind their elderly parents.

I haven't met all of the neighbors yet, but I have known Mrs. Clarkson, who lives next door, for years. She is a kind, bible-toting, God-fearing woman who lives alone with her two perpetually barking Chihuahuas.

I had barely pulled into the driveway before Yvette shouted, "Who the hell is that?" practically breaking her neck to get a good look at Larry, my other next-door neighbor, who was pulling into his driveway at the same time. Larry is a fine, bald brother the color of Hershey's Special Dark chocolate. He waved at us as he got out of his car, and headed inside.

"I don't know much about him except that his name is Larry, and he's a forty-two-year-old bachelor who bought his property at auction a year and a half ago," I said. "And he is also off limits to you."

"Why are you cock-blocking?"

"Because I moved over here to get away from drama," I said. "And if you two get involved and it doesn't work out, I'll be stuck in the middle of that shit, and I'm not having it."

"Not necessarily . . ." Yvette pouted.

"Forget about it, Yvette. Besides, you have Daniel, remember?" I said, reminding her of the white guy she met at Club Heifers a few months ago, and has been dating ever since.

"Yeah, but it's always good to have a spare around, just in case."

"Now there you go with the next best thing syndrome," I said, shaking my head in dismay. "Daniel is a good man who adores you, helps pay your bills, *and* has added your ass as an additional card holder on his American Express card. You would be crazy to mess that up for some knucklehead who probably doesn't have anything to offer except a big dick, and a smile."

"Girl, I'm just joking around. I may have a weakness for dark chocolate, but Dan is the man! I'm telling you, if things keep going like they've been going, I see us getting married."

"For real? It's that serious?"

"It's *that* serious," Yvette said emphatically. "And that myth about white men being less endowed? Not true . . ."

I looked over at Yvette, and we shared a good, long laugh before getting out of my Navigator, and getting down to the business of moving me in to start my new life.

45

I had just left from meeting with the KC Jazz Coalition's board of directors, when I got a call from Nadia saying that she had returned from Miami.

"Why the hell did you have to go and move?" she asked, as if I had moved just to upset her.

"You know why," I said.

"Well, can you come over to my place as soon as possible?" she asked. "I really need to talk to you."

I headed over to Regency Park Place, wondering what was so important that Nadia couldn't talk to me about it over the phone. When I got to the building, I parked in the visitors parking area, surprised that though I had moved less than two weeks ago, it no longer felt like home.

Before taking the elevator up to Nadia's floor, I stopped and checked my mailbox, which was full despite the fact that I had gone to the post office last week and filled out a change of address form.

The mail consisted of my Bank of America Visa bill, a new *Essence Magazine*, and a letter of acknowledgment from a vendor to whom I had sent an information package regarding Tori Carter Creations.

Moving hasn't affected by new business at all. I had to backtrack and have business cards and stationery printed up again, but that's about it.

I knocked on Nadia's door, and when she opened it I was surprised at what I saw. Nadia looked pale and drawn. She was dressed way down, in jeans and a thin aqua T-shirt, that accentuated her noticeably larger boobs. Her makeup was minimal, and her hair was gathered into a ponytail, which was very uncharacteristic of her.

"You traveled looking like this?" I asked, having a seat on her French provincial sofa. "Something is definitely wrong."

"I'm pregnant," she blurted out, appearing to be on the verge of tears.

"What!"

"I told Terrell and his exact words were, 'So, what do you want me to do about it?' Then the pissy bastard hung up on me! I don't need him. He can't fuck worth a damn anyway."

"Are you sure?" I asked.

"Yeah girl," she said. "I told you, them steroids got him all fucked up. Calling him a minute man would be giving him too much praise."

"No, I mean are you sure you're really pregnant?"

Nadia looked as if I just sucker-punched her with a right hook. "Well, let's see: I haven't had a period in almost three months, and I took two First Response pregnancy tests which were both positive. So yes, I really am pregnant." Then she started to cry.

"Don't do that," I said. "Everything is going to be alright."

"I can't believe you're second-guessing me," she sobbed. "The one person in this world I thought I could turn to . . ."

"Girl, you know I'm here for you," I said, pulling her into a comforting hug. "Sorry to offend you, but I just had to ask because I know how we women sometimes play those fake pregnancy games in hopes of keeping a man."

"Well this ain't 1995 and this ain't a game," Nadia said. "My main concern right now is finding out whose baby this is."

"Nadia! I thought you said it was Terrell's."

"No, I said I told Terrell I was pregnant. He knows all about Byron, and those are the only two candidates, so it's not like I'm gonna have to keep going on the Maury Povich show, or anything."

Nadia started crying even harder, which frustrated me because I couldn't think of a thing to say that would be comforting, so I decided to try a little humor.

"Nadia, can I ask you a question?"

"What?" she sniffed, then blew her nose.

"Are you gonna be able to breastfeed with those things?" I asked.

Nadia looked down at her newly acquired boobs. She stared back and forth from the left one to the right for a minute, and then laughed until she cried some more.

I don't care how much a man may consider himself a failure, I believe in him, for he can change the thing that is wrong in his life anytime he is prepared and ready to do it. —*Preston Bradley*

FRIDAY

It's showtime.

After tons of hard work and laying the groundwork, the annual fundraiser for the KC Jazz Coalition is happening tonight. I have so much riding on the line that it's scary. My reputation, pride, and the future of TCC all rest on the success or failure of this one event.

The client is the KC Jazz Coalition, and the venue is the Kansas City Jazz Museum. The tickets are 150 dollars, which will get you access to an open bar, and all the gourmet food you can eat from various specialty food stations around the event site.

I also have an all-star lineup of living jazz legends scheduled to perform tonight. I'm talking about living legends like Ida

Macbeth, Wynton Marsalis, Chuck Mangione, Angela Hagenbach, and Bobby Watson.

What I am most proud of, and what will probably bring in the most money, is the Casino room, which we are setting up with roulette, craps, blackjack, and poker tables. Guests will also be given door prizes, goodie bags, and the chance to bid on memorabilia such as Charlie Parker's saxophone, and Dizzy Gillespie's trumpet.

Besides Junior, I cannot afford to put anyone else on the payroll right now, so for this event I am the florist, set designer, lighting technician, and whatever else that needs to be done.

Thankfully, I was able to secure sponsors for every aspect of the event, and we have an army of volunteers who will be helping us out. Still, I expect an uphill battle, because volunteers are more likely to end up spectators at the event, rather than actually working hard.

So, in the wee hours of the morning, Junior and I prayed together, and then headed down to the historic 18th & Vine jazz district to set up shop. There is so much that has to be done that it will literally be a race against the clock.

46

Two hours into the event and I could not have been more pleased. The weather was perfect, and crowd turnout was better than expected.

The guests all seemed to be having a grand time, and Sasha had already pulled me aside to say that she and the rest of the board of directors were happy with the job I've done.

Wynton Marsalis was onstage performing, and I was inwardly congratulating myself on a job well done when I saw Simone and Fatima coming towards me, *holding hands*. I inhaled so sharply that air got caught in my windpipe, and I started to choke.

"You alright, Tori?" Simone asked, not looking the least bit uncomfortable to be *lovingly* holding the hand of another woman.

"Simone, Fatima," I said, trying to recover. "What are you two up to?"

"Just out enjoying this beautiful event that you put together," said Fatima. "Bravo, sister!"

"Thank you." I smiled, even though I felt nauseous. "Simone, can I talk to you for a quick sec?"

"Sure—" Simone said, probably getting whiplash from how fast I pulled her away from Fatima for a private conversation.

"Okay, I know you look up to her and everything, but damn!" I said. "Is this who's been rocking your world since you broke up with Rasheed?"

Simone nodded yes, and grinned. "I can't even begin to tell you how happy she makes me." She gushed like a twelve-year-old.

I was in shock. I had so many questions, like: when, where, how, and most of all *why?*

"So is Fatima like, your woman now or what?" I asked, confused about how these things work. "Have you completely switched over to women, or is this something you're doing just to see how well you like it?"

"Sorry if this makes you uncomfortable, Tori, but I refuse to put labels on it," Simone answered. "Just know that Fatima and I care a great deal for each other, and it is an honest, healthy relationship."

Well alrighty then! You think you know somebody for thirteen years, and they turn out to be an undercover carpet muncher. Don't get me wrong; I am far from being homophobic. It's just that seeing the longtime sister-friend I *thought* I knew so well, all huggy-kissy with the woman who is supposed to be her mentor, is—it's weird, it's wrong, and it's just nasty, okay?

I didn't have much else to say to either one of them after that.

"Well, if you two will excuse me, I have to go get the silent auction started," I said. "Enjoy the rest of your evening."

The evening was winding down, when I saw Mr. Nelson Tate in my peripheral vision. He was standing by the gourmet dessert station talking to a statuesque model-type with a short, chic bob, and cheekbones to die for. She was gorgeous, and I was jealous as hell because the two of them looked quite comfortable and familiar with each other, just like all the other happy couples milling around the venue.

I still cared for Nelson. It had been almost three months

since we'd spoken, and part of me felt I should go talk to him to see where his head was at.

However, the Carter pride reared its stubborn head and reminded me that I left the ball in his court.

So fuck him.

Nelson and I briefly made eye contact, but as soon as we did, I turned on my heel and walked in the opposite direction.

Overall, the fundraiser was a huge success.

More that 5,000 guests attended, and over $750,000 was raised for the Jazz Coalition.

Cha-ching!

After tearing down the event space and overseeing the cleanup, Junior and I unwound with a couple of cocktails at Chuck & Taylor's, a bar near the Jazz Museum.

"You did good, kid," I told Junior as the two of us settled in at a small table. "But what did you think?"

"It was cool," he said. "I actually liked it so much that it really didn't even feel like work—well, except for cleaning up."

"Well that's part of it, and that's why you get the big bucks," I said, handing him a check for two-thousand dollars.

Junior's eyes lit up like a kid on Christmas morning. "Ah yeah, this is it right here!" Junior said. "Me and you are gonna be business partners for life."

"Slow your roll," I said. "Maybe one day I'll make you a partner, but this was just your first event, Junior. You still have a lot of growing to do in this business."

"I know. And I'm gonna make you proud of me, too," he said, sincerely. "Watch and see."

"I got faith in you, baby boy," I said, clinking my glass of Long Island iced tea against his bottle of Corona.

"I ran into Nelson tonight," said Junior. "Did you see him?"

"Yeah, I saw him . . ." I shrugged as if I couldn't care less.

"So what's up with you two? Y'all cool?"

It felt weird at first, but I opened up and had my first real heart-to-heart talk with Junior.

I told him all about my relationship with Nelson. Well, not *everything!* Then how Roland came along and messed it all up. Junior seemed to be truly sympathetic, and I realized that he can be a good listener when he wants to be.

With Tori Carter Creations' first successful event under my belt, it was nearly two in the morning when I finally made it home. The first thing I did was chain the door, bolt the deadlock, and set the alarm on the home security system.

Paranoia runs high when you are alone at night. Especially when you're relatively new to a neighborhood, where as far as you know, Freddie Krueger could be living next door.

And since most violent crimes occur between ten at night and five in the morning, creaking floorboards and the other noises a house makes when it "settles" for the night, are amplified a thousand times, and are automatically converted into some sinister reason to get up out of bed and investigate—with a butcher knife and baseball bat in hand.

That is exactly the type of paranoia I was feeling when I heard knocking noises, and it was well past what Mama calls "visiting hours."

Then I reminded myself that it was probably just Uncle Woody's ghost haunting the house.

At least once a day since I moved in here, I get the eerie sensation that I am not alone.

You know that feeling you get that someone has just walked into the room and is standing over your shoulder? That happens a lot. And even though Woody was a kind, friendly person, I still haven't slept in the master bedroom where he died. You never know what might piss off a ghost. Instead, I have been camping out in the living room at night, enjoying my new cushy chaise lounge that feels like one big ol' pillow.

I heard the knocking noise again, and that time I went to the front window, pulled the white lace curtain back and saw Nelson standing on the front porch.

How in the hell did he find out where I live?

"Can I come in?" he asked when he saw me looking out the window.

I let the curtain fall without answering. I wasn't sure if I wanted to be bothered with his ass. After all, his mistrust and wrong assumptions were the reason why we broke up in the first place.

I mulled it over a minute or two, and finally decided to open the door. "Yes, may I help you?" I asked, as if he were some strange door-to-door salesman.

"Hey Tori," he said, looking as spiffy as always, in Seven jeans, a white Claudio St. James shirt, and YSL shoes. "Can I come in and talk to you for a minute?"

"About what?" I asked tersely.

"About us."

"I wasn't aware that there was such a thing."

"I expected you to give me a hard time," Nelson said. "But just hear me out, okay?"

"I'm listening . . ." I said, crossing my arms.

"Well, I had a long talk with your brother tonight, and after he explained everything to me, I just wanted to come over here and apologize for not taking your word in that situation that happened with Roland."

My heart leapt for joy. It was the first favor Junior had done for me in his life. I never would have thought the day would come when my baby brother would come through for me in such a big way.

I was happy to see Nelson. Still, I didn't want to let him off the hook that easy. He needed to suffer a little more in order to fully appreciate my forgiveness. "Apology not accepted," I said, stepping back to close the door in his face.

"Tori wait!" Nelson said in such a heartfelt way that it made me pause.

"What is it?" I asked.

"You're really not gonna make this easy for me, are you?" he asked, almost pleading.

"And why should I listen to you, Nelson? After everything you unnecessarily put me through?"

"Because I see things differently now. My mistake was allowing people to make me feel like I was betraying Kara by being happy with you," he said. "It just seemed easier to walk away than to have to deal with all those conflicting emotions."

Nelson's honesty and sincerity touched my heart. I recalled Fatima's take on the situation and softened towards him. Just a little bit.

"I know you'll always have Kara in your heart to a certain extent, Nelson, but it is possible to have more than one love story, you know."

"I know that now, and that's why I'm here. I have so much love for you, Tori," he said. "I want us to stop all this back and forth, where we're on one day and off the next. I want us to be exclusive."

"What about Miss Thing I saw you with at the fundraiser tonight?"

"Now there you go with the assumptions," Nelson chuckled. "You didn't notice the family resemblance? In fact, if you had bothered to look closer you would have seen that I was with a whole group of family members." To prove it, Nelson pulled out a wallet-sized family portrait.

"Oh," was all I could say when I saw Miss Thing standing next to Oliver, and a woman I presumed to be Nelson's mother.

"Peace offering?" he asked, holding up a takeout bag from Capital Grille.

"It depends on what you have there."

"It's all probably ice cold by now, but I have some lobster rolls, caviar, and I also brought a couple of mango-lime tarts that I made myself."

Okay, that did it. I moved aside and allowed Nelson to step into the foyer. He immediately pulled me to him, and we hugged for what seemed like forever.

47

Two Years Later

There wasn't a dry eye in the house when the good Reverend announced, "By the power invested in me, I now pronounce you man and wife!"

The wedding was beautiful from start to finish.

Of course, I'm just a teeny bit biased because I planned the whole thing, but it turned out to be a fantasy come true, just like I had envisioned it would be.

Yvette was a beautiful, blushing bride. Then again, it was the middle of July and 110 degrees inside the church, but she was a blushing bride nevertheless.

"Say cheese!" the photographer said, as the wedding party posed for pictures on the steps of Greater Missionary Baptist Church.

Nadia, Simone, Alicia and I all served as bridesmaids, though none of us were crazy about the yellow taffeta dresses with the wide satin sashes that Yvette insisted we wear.

But at least Yvette looked beautiful, in a silk, champagne-colored Vera Wang gown.

I like Daniel for Yvette. Not only does he have a warm, kind heart but he also mellows her out, and treats her like she is the queen of his dreams; the one that he has been waiting for all his life.

As for Nelson and me, well, we have been together a little over two years now, and while we are growing closer by the day and enjoying each other to the fullest, neither one of us feels compelled to rush to the altar.

However, with the way things are going between Simone and Fatima, there just may be another wedding on the horizon.

It only took me a month or so to apologize to the both of them for the cold shoulder I had given them the night they came out as a couple. True, it was a shock to my system, but it did not warrant being so close-minded and unsupportive. I had been avoiding Simone partly because I didn't know how to be around her since she turned lesbian, which is stupid because as it turns out, she is still the same sweet, free spirit I met during my first week of college.

Simone and I have seen each other through some of the best and worst times in our lives, and no matter what, she will always be my friend. I don't care who she's sleeping with.

"Is it just me, or is this dress itchy as hell?" Simone asked, after the picture-taking was over.

"It's not just you," Nadia and I said at the same time, and laughed.

Yvette said, "I'm so sick of hearing you all complain about those dresses, I don't know what to do!"

"Anyway, congratulations, girl," I said, giving Yvette a hug. "You did it!"

"Thank you!" she squealed, grinning from ear to ear.

"Yeah, looks like all those how-to-get-a-man manuals paid off for you, girlfriend!" Nadia said, taking her son from Alicia, who had been holding him.

Nadia and Terrell weren't together anymore, but they did share a beautiful eighteen-month-old son.

We were all worried about how good of a mother Nadia would be since she wasn't exactly what you would call the maternal type. Plus, she was ambivalent about her pregnancy all the way up to the moment she gave birth to Quinn, but now she is so in love with that little boy, you can hardly peel her away from him for any real length of time.

I have to give it to Nadia. She doesn't date or party the way she used to, and her newfound maturity proves that there is no better way to grow than to be forced to think of someone besides yourself.

48

Tori Carter Creations grossed 1.7 million dollars last year. Not bad, but this year I'm pushing for at least three million.

Junior has a lot to do with the fact that TCC is thriving. Yeah, the boy's gonna be alright, after all. He now has the same energy and enthusiasm for event planning that he had for playing basketball, and is so committed to his career, he hasn't called in sick on me one time. On some mornings, Junior even beats me getting to the spacious office that I lease in Midtown.

In the event-planning industry, business is always slow in January, so I decided to close the shop for a week, and take a much-needed vacation. I didn't have any specific plans and had not even given leaving town a thought, until Nelson said, "Let's go to Hawaii."

We were at my house, cleaning up the kitchen after having just finished my infamous spaghetti dinner.

Now, you know me. I normally ask the five W's before making decisions, but all it took to convince me was one look outside where it was thirty-two degrees, and snow was falling from the sky.

"Hawaii, here we come!" I said, breaking out into a happy dance.

Nelson got on the phone and started making the arrangements, and I got busy packing.

The whole airport experience was a nightmare.

The crowds, the confusion, extra-tight airport security, and the ick factor of having to stand barefoot on the same filthy carpet that thousands of other barefooted people have stood on.

However, all was forgotten the moment we touched down in Maui. Hawaii is so tranquil and serene, it forces you to slow down, sit quietly somewhere, and just appreciate your surroundings.

And that is exactly what we did.

Besides shopping and attending a luau, Nelson and I didn't see much of the island for the first two days.

What can I say? Hotel sex is the best!

Besides, we were going to be there for five more days, so there was plenty of time to get around to taking a helicopter ride around the island, snorkeling, and all that other good stuff.

Earlier this evening, Nelson and I were snuggled together on the veranda of our suite at the Wailea Beach Resort, watching the sunset. The gentle breeze coming off the ocean was warm, and carried with it the glorious smell of the tropics. To me, it felt like romance was literally floating through the air.

At that moment, Nelson laid his head on my shoulder and casually said, "Let's get married today."

"We can't do that!"

"And why not?"

"Because there are some things you don't just jump up and do at the spur of the moment. And getting married is one of them."

"And yet, people elope all the time."

"Well that's not my style," I said. "When I tie the knot, I want to be surrounded by family and friends at an extravagant ceremony, followed by a lavish reception."

"I know that you're all about the bling, Tori, but how many ostentatious, high-priced weddings have you been to, and after a few years, the couples aren't even together anymore?"

"Several," I had to admit.

"And that right there should tell you that it's the love and dedication that is most important." Nelson cupped my face in his hands. "It's not about the cake, the dress, the flowers, or any of that other stuff. Everything we need to make this happen is already here—and that's me and you."

He definitely had a point. Nelson waited patiently while I mulled it over for a few minutes. My mind was saying, *You deserve to have that big, beautiful, fantasy wedding that you were robbed of.* But my heart was saying, *Why not marry this man today?* I have come to love Nelson with every fiber of my being, and I trust him with my life. Not only is he my lover; he's my best friend, mentor, and number one cheerleader. Besides, how can you not want to marry a man who brings you coffee in bed every morning, along with turkey bacon, a fruit cup, and a whole-grain muffin with whipped honey butter that he has made himself?

After reminding myself of all the reasons I didn't want to be without Nelson, my apprehension dissolved into certainty. The only problem was that I had packed a couple of nice sundresses, but nothing near good enough to get married in.

"What am I going to wear?" I asked Nelson.

He smiled, taking that as a yes.

"I'll see if the concierge can help us out." He dashed into our suite to make a phone call.

I stayed outside on the terrace, continuing to watch the sun set into the Pacific Ocean, thinking that Mama and Daddy were going to kill me for not sharing my wedding day with them.